Five interesting things about Suzanne Macpherson:

1. When I was ten I wanted to be a girl detective when I grew up, like Emma Peel in *The Avengers*. I went sneaking around in my black stretch pants and black turtleneck in the dark, scaring my parents and the chickens quite often.

2. I think I had a past life in England in the twenties and thirties.

3. I love old movies so much I consider Myrna Loy and Cary Grant my best pals. New movies like *Cold Comfort Farm* will do in a pinch.

4. I have a china collection that has gotten completely out of hand. I've collected ever since I was sixteen and went nutty over Booth's Real Old Willow. But my girlfriend and I always say 'she who dies with the most china wins' so I guess I'm not done yet, having recently fallen in love with Royal Doulton Provence Noir, and besides, she has more than I do, so off to the shops we go!

5. I have three sons and a daughter and her first word was 'shopping.'

By Suzanne Macpherson

The Forever Summer
She Woke up Married
Hysterical Blondeness
Risky Business
Talk of the Town
Switched, Bothered and Bewildered
In the Mood

Talk of the Town

Suzanne Macpherson

little
black
dress

Published by arrangement with AVON BOOKS
An imprint of HARPERCOLLINS PUBLISHERS, USA

The right of Suzanne Macpherson to be identified as the Author of
the Work has been asserted by her in accordance with the
Copyright, Designs and Patents Act 1988.

First published in 2003 by
AVON BOOKS
An imprint of HARPERCOLLINS PUBLISHERS, USA

First published in Great Britain in paperback in 2009 by
LITTLE BLACK DRESS
An imprint of HEADLINE PUBLISHING GROUP

A LITTLE BLACK DRESS paperback

1

Cataloguing in Publication Data is available from the British Library

ISBN 978 0 7553 4330 0

Typeset in Transit511BT by Avon DataSet Ltd,
Bidford-on-Avon, Warwickshire

Printed and bound in Great Britain by Clays Ltd, St Ives plc

Headline's policy is to use papers that are natural, renewable and
recyclable products and made from wood grown in sustainable forests.
The logging and manufacturing processes are expected to conform to the
environmental regulations of the country of origin.

HEADLINE PUBLISHING GROUP
An Hachette UK Company
338 Euston Road
London NW1 3BH

www.littleblackdressbooks.com
www.headline.co.uk
www.hachette.co.uk

This book is dedicated to
Kimberly Fisk, Pipper Watkins,
and Tracy Rysavy.
'Hot Damn' all around, girls!

Acknowledgments

To Mrs. Fisk for the brilliant title she bestowed upon my first book; Stef Ann Holm for kindly sharing her L.A. insight; Janice Stayton for her never-ending support; Debbie Macomber for some amazing nail polish colors; and to my dream team – Lucia Macro and Karen Solem.

October

So much for the honeymoon.

Kelly Atwood bent down and pressed her fingertips against her husband's neck to see if he was still alive. His pulse thumped against her touch. How about that, she thought. Raymond takes a lickin' and keeps on tickin'. Even though she was mad enough to have done him in, it was a relief that she hadn't.

Out cold. Kelly had never knocked anyone out cold before. For that matter, she'd never hit anyone at all. Raymond's slow-motion descent backward onto the glass coffee table and the thousands of little shattered safety glass cubes glittering around him had a cartoon-like quality. His head had made the most amazing thud. She was almost as stunned as he was. Almost.

She rubbed her cheek where Raymond had slapped her. Her return punch had been a purely spontaneous act of self-defense. She'd do it again in a heartbeat.

Raymond clearly hadn't expected her to throw a left

hook. He'd probably forgotten she was left-handed, which was funny, because he was a stickler for details. Something she'd found rather endearing a few hours ago when she'd married him.

That was before she'd found the little *detail* of a large bag of cocaine in the lining of his suitcase, all packed for their Jamaican honeymoon, and confronted him. Leave it to her to feel around the bottom of a bag for more shoe room.

Kelly noticed her one-carat marquise wedding ring had made quite a dent in Raymond's nose, which was still bleeding. Echhh. She twisted the ring off her finger and flung it on his chest. Jerk!

The ring clattered to the floor. She felt hot anger rise inside her. She had trusted Raymond. He was the one who made her feel so secure. Oh, yeah, mature, hardworking Raymond.

Once Ray's hand had made contact with her cheek, Kelly had known the truth. She'd been taken in by a truly talented con man. The other truth was that thirty seconds was too long to stay with any man that laid a hand on her.

A faint moaning sound came out of Raymond and startled her into action. He'd probably be mighty upset when he came to. She'd better get out of here – and fast.

Kelly ran into the bedroom, grabbed the car keys, half the wad of traveler's checks, and her six cashmere sweaters. Like hell she was leaving her cashmere sweaters. She dumped out some of the tropical beach clothes and stuffed the sweaters into her honeymoon suitcase.

From the living room she heard another moan. This time it had more life in it. Panic hit her like a 7.3 L.A. earthquake. She snatched up her best Italian boots, her suitcase, her purse, and bolted for the front door. No time to think now, just *run*!

Kelly ran down the hall, took one turn, and plowed right into a short, round, dark-suited man. She and the man went sprawling, her suitcase popped open, and its contents flew in every direction.

She mumbled an apology from the floor, untangled herself, and started gathering up her sweaters. The man growled like a dog, got up, and flung her purple and black satin Frederick's of Hollywood honeymoon bustier off his face.

'Let me help you there, ma'am,' came another voice. A man stepped out of the shadows. He was tall and thin but looked very muscular. Great, she thought, Laurel and Hardy. Instead of lending her a hand, Laurel picked up the suitcase, emptied it again, and ripped out the side pockets with his big muscles.

'Hey, you moron!' Kelly shrieked. She clutched her purse close to her. No one was taking her money. Ignoring her, Laurel chucked her belongings on the carpet and stalked away, followed closely by Hardy.

'Thanks a bunch, guys!' Kelly yelled again. Stuffing things back into the bag, she sat down hard on the top to get the clasp closed, then dragged everything with her the six feet to the elevator. Hitting the button with a stray high-heel shoe, she threw the rest of her loose clothes and the suitcase in when the doors opened.

This day was getting worse by the minute. As the doors whooshed shut, she whacked the parking-level button, took a deep breath in, and let out a long, searing, cleansing scream.

That felt better. Sort of. At least she was safe in here. It would take Ray at least twenty minutes to get his brain back in gear, and Laurel and Hardy were headed in the other direction looking for their next hall mug victim, no doubt.

Staring at her dark reflection in the bronze glass elevator walls, she began to laugh – a sort of hysterical, *I've-lost-my-mind* laugh – at the comical picture she was seeing. Most of her abundantly caked-on makeup was streaked on her cheeks. Her short, modern, off-white leather and lace wedding gown was completely disheveled, and a ripped veil hung sideways on her jet-black dyed hair. Yep, she looked about as attractive as a psychotic crow.

To top it off, here she was on the run. Just like when she was a kid. She'd run away so many times, fed up with her mother's terminally bad taste in men. Fed up with the drinking and drugs that finally ended up killing her mom.

Her suitcase had been permanently packed under her bed since she was about twelve. She'd slept in train stations and fast-food rest rooms, and learned how to beg strangers for money.

Kelly closed her eyes and felt the pain of memories

ache in her chest. She'd gone back to her mom, or been returned, a dozen times. Then, finally, when she was barely old enough to make it on her own, she'd run away from her mom's San Francisco hippie flophouse, all the way to L.A. She was just sixteen. She'd worked hard, clawed her way through life, and finally found a way to make decent money.

Then Raymond had come along and given her life an upgrade: elegant apartment, nice car, and beautiful clothes. Even though he was her boss, she'd felt like a partner in their swanky European designer showroom. The clothes were beautiful, she was proud of the line, and she'd worked hard to make it a success.

She'd let all that blind her to the fact she'd been stupid enough to end up with someone just as screwed up as her mom. Raymond just did a better job of hiding it under his tailored Italian suits and the touch of gray at his temples. At this point she wondered if that gray was real. Well, that was all over now.

Another wave of sick emotion struck her. She bit her bottom lip hard. She'd be damned if she'd give Raymond her tears. Kelly stared down at her leather lace-up bridal boots; like old-fashioned 1880s shoes. She'd loved them this morning at ten when she'd gotten married.

Maybe she could dye them. She dyed everything. She was the dye queen. Her hair had gone from blonde to red to black. She couldn't even remember her natural color. Hell, she'd dyed bedspreads and sewed them into clothing when she was living in the back room of a tattoo parlor at seventeen – a very creative runaway.

So, yes, she was running again. But she sure had a good reason at the moment. Even so, when was she ever going to stop? She wasn't a teenager anymore. She was twenty-eight. She needed to change this pattern.

'How profound, I have a pattern,' she snapped, tired of her own psychobabble. It was the best theory she'd gotten out of the twenty books she'd read on the subject of growing up the child of an alcoholic, but sometimes you had to stop reading and start living. All those books don't mean a thing unless you apply the knowledge to real life. 'This is the last run, Kelly, old girl,' she said out loud to the elevator walls.

Where to run was the real question of the moment. She sighed and pressed her hand against her own reflection in the mirrored panel. Where could she go that would let her stop running forever?

The door opened on the parking garage level to reveal a slick yuppie couple. They stared at her. She could just imagine what they thought: *'Skip, there seems to be a Bride from Hell in that elevator. Yes, Muffy, it's shocking.'* The couple moved to take the next elevator over, whispering to each other.

'Just having a bad hair day,' Kelly explained loudly. She used her foot to shove her suitcase between the doors so she could finish picking up her things. Over and over the automatic doors whapped against the bag. It made kind of a nice rhythm.

She gathered her belongings, took four steps out of the elevator, ditched her veil in a trash can, and headed toward Raymond's precious black BMW, pulling the keys out of her purse as she walked. Raymond wouldn't even think to head after her here, at least for a while. He would never believe she'd have the nerve to go for the Beemer.

The parking garage was lit with mercury vapor lights that made everything look eerie. Her high heels clicked and echoed in the emptiness. Kelly punched the key alarm off, unlocked the car, and popped the trunk.

There in the trunk was Raymond's neat and tidy black attaché. He was so organized, already packed. There was no time to waste rummaging through it now. He could find it and the car later. She pushed it aside and loaded her things in the compartment, then shut the lid.

Kelly slid into the soft black leather seat, shut the car door with a snap, and flicked the locks. The dark tinted windows would hide her for a few minutes.

From the side pocket of her purse she pulled the wad of traveler's checks she'd taken from his dresser. Three, four, nine, *ten* of them at a thousand dollars each, and a few smaller ones. That was about nine thousand more than she figured she'd grabbed. Raymond must have been planning to do some purchasing in Jamaica.

She fingered the wad for a few minutes and counted the checks again. She knew the money had come from their savings. For two years they'd been putting quite a bit into a mutual fund, supposedly with the idea of buying a house.

When she divorced Raymond, she would ask for a

settlement, since her income had been combined with his to cover the household expenses for the last two years. So this was a good start. An early withdrawal. Enough money to start her life in a new direction.

She decided to call this money 'damages.' Which reminded her she should stop at the bank and clean out half of whatever was left in their account. Altogether, if he had taken out, say, twenty thousand, and she was holding half of that, she probably had another three thousand due her.

Maybe she would put the money down on a small house somewhere in a town where no one knew her. The kind of town where women still quilted and sang in the church choir. She had a pretty good soprano voice. When she started singing her favorite carol, 'It Came Upon a Midnight Clear,' her voice croaked. No warm-up.

A woman passed by the car and looked at her through the dark window, startling Kelly. Better move it. She twisted the key to start the BMW and watched with relief as the gas gauge needle registered a full tank. She'd have to get rid of this car quick. *It's one thing to knock Raymond out, but mess with his car, and you are roadkill.*

Of course, he liked to conveniently forget that the car was half hers, or at least a quarter. She'd contributed a big chunk to the down payment. That was enough to justify its use for a few days. She looked nervously behind her for the first time in five minutes.

Kelly popped the parking brake, pushed the transmission into drive, and moved her ass. The chain-link gate rose as she zipped the parking card through the scanner. One left turn and she was out of the building, with the freeway only ten blocks away. She hit every red light in the history of Los Angeles before she finally found the on-ramp.

She cranked the fine car through its paces, into fifth gear, then opened up a path down the Hollywood freeway. Twenty minutes and she'd hit Interstate 5. In a split-second decision she picked north. The traffic was merciful to her this afternoon.

In her rearview mirror the boxy buildings of L.A. rose sharply behind her. Unclenching her fingers from the steering wheel, she punched the CD button and leaned back against the black leather seat. Patsy Cline was singing 'Crazy,' and that was just *sooo* true.

North was a good direction. She'd lived in Seattle with her mom for a while, in a formerly grand old house where they had rented a room. She had happy memories of exploring the crannies of that house and reading a library copy of *Little Women* curled up on a faded red velvet window seat. Her mom sure as hell wasn't Marmee, but that book gave her a vision into another way that life could be: a life where people actually took care of each other. God, she'd been sad to leave that old house. She'd even managed to make a couple friends in school for the nine months they stayed.

A glimmer of a memory was carrying her north.

The ride was sweet and smooth and dotted with Dairy Queens from L.A. to Oregon. It's amazing how much highway you can cover driving like a bat-out-of-hell with a radar detector. When she finally got too tired she parked at a rest stop and slept in the car. Good thing her cashmere throw was still in the back seat from their last evening out.

A few hours later she shivered awake, startled by a car door slamming next to her. A pair of old women were letting their poodles out for a pee. There's nothing quite like that cramped-up, coffee-deprived, life-has-gone-really-whacked-and-that's-why-I'm-sleeping-in-a-car feeling. Kelly uncurled herself out of the car and stretched. The air was cool and scented with a mixture of evergreen and pine.

She was supposed to be in Jamaica having breakfast on the hotel terrace with her new husband right about now.

The ladies with the poodles came back to their white Cadillac and gave her some pretty odd stares. Maybe she'd be a little less conspicuous if she changed out of the bridal duds. She probably looked like a hooker with the strapless lace-up bustier bit and its matching skirt. Not to mention the satin bustle and bow.

Raymond had picked out this dress for her. It was Italian and considered very *chi-chi* back in L.A.

But not at a rest stop in Oregon at, what, six in the morning? Boy, those ladies were up early on a Sunday.

In the rest stop bathroom she stripped off the leather wedding dress and climbed into a comfortable black spandex skirt, high-heel boots, and her favorite black cashmere sweater, then zipped up her black leather jacket to stay warm. She was Cat Woman now. Raymond would never catch her.

She giggled at her own joke. Life was looking up. Her suitcase even held all of her stray clothes once she repacked. The wedding dress could stay in the trunk of her car forever.

Kelly absently toyed with Raymond's black briefcase. It had a combination lock, but knowing his ego, it was probably his own birthday – 3-31-67 – a good year for Ford Mustangs, but not for men.

She was right. The locks snapped open and Kelly took a big gasp as she raised the lid. Neat little rows of fifty-dollar bills – the funny ones with the big head off center – were lined up in the case. They looked fake. She slipped one out of its band and held it up to the light. There was the authentic watermark, and the paper felt right, so they must be real, or perhaps really good fakes.

A minivan full of high school athletes, no doubt headed for a very early match, pulled up beside her, so she closed the briefcase, shut the trunk, and climbed back in the car. This would take some thinking.

Raymond must have been up to more than she'd figured. Those two extremely rude thugs in the hallway clearly were not Avon calling. Kelly spent the rest of her drive putting the puzzle pieces of Raymond's behavior together and deciding what to do with the money. Drug money, after all.

So all the time she and Ray were showing beautiful high-end clothes to buyers from all over the West Coast,

Ray was doing some high-end drug dealing on his own? No one would believe she wasn't involved, and that *really* pissed her off. It was like flushing the years she'd spent building a good life and good reputation right down the crapper.

Why marry her? Just for a trip to Jamaica? A cover-up honeymoon? That didn't seem likely.

A few days ago Ray seemed like the top man in the garment business in their corner of L.A. They'd been together for four years, lived together for two of those. He appeared stable, organized. His life seemed so well ordered. Just what she'd been looking for most of her life.

Because of all that, she'd finally let her stainless-steel-coated guard down and consented to marry him.

What had she missed? It made the hair on her arms chill up to think he'd been deceiving her so well for so long.

She made Seattle in record time. There was nothing like a high-performance car and a nearly empty highway to get you out of town fast. *Really* fast.

Kelly left the car parked under the viaduct by the waterfront. Somewhere on her drive she'd decided to take a Greyhound from Seattle, headed farther north, and leave the driving to them.

The BMW would eventually make its way back to Raymond, she was sure of that. But she wouldn't. She was sure of that, too. And just to be sure, Kelly decided to take his briefcase with her. Then she could say goodbye and get a proper start, somewhere else.

When the city bus to the convention center and Greyhound station stopped, she jumped in and never looked back. Goodbye to Raymond's car, goodbye to Raymond; sometimes you just had to say goodbye.

In twenty minutes the bus driver announced the Greyhound station stop. Kelly bumped her way down the steps with her suitcase and Raymond's briefcase in tow.

There was a West Bank two blocks back that looked open. She got all the way into the lobby before a rush of fear came over her.

Three things hit her all at once. One, she was holding a briefcase full of cash. Two, if she took out the remaining three thousand dollars from their account, Raymond would know where she was, instantly. He'd trace the withdrawal much faster than the towed car would show up. Three, she was holding a briefcase full of cash. Kelly pretended to search in her purse as if she'd forgotten something and made a graceful exit out of the thick glass doors of the bank.

She steadied herself outside. There was a Bartell's Drugstore on the same block. When panic hits, buy a new lipstick.

Kelly hooked a basket across her suitcase handle and rolled her way through the store. She picked out a veritable tote bag full of Miss Clairol strip it – fix it – put-it-back-in hair products. God knows how long it would be until she found a good hairstylist.

She added a pile of necessities: Bobby's Orange

Buick lipstick, matching nail polish. Man, where do they get these names? She picked up three Nuts Over Chocolate Luna bars and all the other stuff women need. More chocolate.

The Greyhound bus station had a Starbucks coffee stand. Only in Seattle, she thought with a smile. It was the best coffee she'd ever tasted: Kenya, double-shot, no-foam, lighten-me-up and spin-it-on-my-head, or something like that.

She let the wondrous stuff bring her alive. Maybe food would help, too. She added a bagel with cream cheese . . . to go.

Kelly bought a ticket to Vancouver, Canada, figuring she would find somewhere between here and there to stop and gather her wits, or continue on north into Canada to *wherever*. Good thing she had her passport all packed and ready to run.

Greyhound bus, transportation of the really strange.

And strange indeed was the old woman who sat down next to Kelly on the bus.

'Midnight Madness – L'Oréal Number Twenty-four.' The old woman pointed a bony finger at Kelly's black hair, then plopped into the seat beside her.

'My God, you're right,' Kelly replied, truly stunned.

'I'm the best there is, honey. Hi, I'm Myrtle Crabtree. Mind if I keep ya company?' Myrtle Crabtree had on a turquoise sweater with large reflective sequins knitted into it, matching earrings, and silver lamé leggings. Her should-be-white hair was dyed very bright red. 'Titian

Red. Miss Clairol, with a touch of ash blonde to take out the brassiness,' she told Kelly after about three minutes.

If Myrtle was trying to tone down the brassiness, it wasn't working.

'I just hopped down for a beautician's convention in Seattle. Aromatherapy! That's the new wave,' Myrtle declared with hand gestures worthy of an orchestra conductor. 'We knew that back in the sixties, incense and all that,' Myrtle continued. 'Now they just fancy it up and charge three times as much.'

Kelly let herself relax against the comfortable bus seat. 'Where're you from, Myrtle?'

Myrtle settled in and took out a knitting project nine miles long with six different shades of wool. Mostly in the garish hues.

'Paradise, the sweetest little place in the world. I have a beauty shop just off the main drag. Had it since 1952. I can tell you everything about every man, woman, and child in that town. They all tell old Myrtle everything. Help me with this yarn, dear.' Myrtle took Kelly's hands and positioned them, then started winding lime green yarn in a loop from one to the other.

'Tell me all about it, Myrtle.'

The miles drifted away as the old woman spun tales of Paradise better than any Garrison Keillor Lake Woebegon episode. Myrtle did indeed seem to know everything about everybody.

Paradise, a place just like Kelly had imagined ever since she was a child growing up in shabby apartments with her mother and the man of the season.

Paradise, like the town in *Little Women* where the neighbors bring you hot baked rolls when you're feeling bad.

Paradise, Washington, USA. Yep, land of white farmhouses, and clotheslines with sheets flapping in the wind; a town where everyone mows their lawn on Saturday morning.

She'd driven by these towns before, wondering what it was like for the women in those houses. Were they happy living there? Making pot roast on Sunday? Doing the wash?

She'd wanted to be one of them for as long as she could remember.

Kelly's favorite pastime was imagining the perfect town. Her tiredness blended with her daydreams and Myrtle's voice, hypnotizing her. She huddled with Myrtle, telling tales and bonding in that way women do. It always amazed Kelly how two women would end up telling each other every intimate detail of their lives in two hours.

Finally Myrtle helped her make the plan to stay and try out Paradise . . . what a name!

By the time Myrtle started packing up her knitting and said, 'This is it, Kelly girl,' Kelly felt like Myrtle and she were bosom buddies. Kelly knew Myrtle's colorful past, worthy of a redhead, and had told Myrtle almost everything about herself, too. Almost. She didn't mention the money.

They made a pact to keep each other's secrets, because for heaven's sakes, for the first hour of the trip

Myrtle thought she was talking to a complete stranger, not someone moving into town, and for heaven's sakes, Kelly didn't want anyone in Paradise to know she'd accidentally married a drug dealer.

'Here we go, honey, only another highway to go and we'll be there. You're going to love it. I'll take you to the Hen House – that's my salon. My pad is attached to the shop. You can sleep in my extra room while you get your bearings.' Myrtle hung on to Kelly's arm as they descended the bus stairs and kept right on chattering.

'I have a round bed I bought when Fred Hansen and I were having a flaming affair – before he married up back in '62. Fred was the only man in town with manicured nails. For that matter, he still is.' Myrtle snorted, and Kelly nearly collapsed in laughter. 'We sort of picked back up again after his wife passed on,' Myrtle explained.

They got off the bus near a sign that read EAST COUNTY ROAD PARADISE 37 MILES. The road cut a path east across fields of onions and alfalfa. Kelly stopped and sat down on her suitcase.

What a sight she must be: black L.A. clothes, short skirt, and pitch-black hair. But then Myrtle was quite a sight, too.

'Don't fret, the trucks all cut through here on their way to Canada to avoid the lines at the border. One will come along soon.' Myrtle parked her old 'camp' suitcase with stickers from every city imaginable next to Kelly's bag and plopped herself down.

'Maybe we should walk a ways and make some

headway,' Kelly said. She was suddenly impatient to get to her destination.

'I'm way too old for a stroll down the highway in these platforms.' Myrtle stuck her foot out and displayed a pair of strappy turquoise platform mules. 'Plus you sure as hell aren't going to make it far in them laced-up high-heeled bat boots, are you, now? That's one of my rules of life. Ya gotta have the right shoes for the occasion.'

Kelly stared at her boots. Now, that was something she hadn't thought of. *So true. You have to have the right shoes for the occasion.* Guess these weren't her thirty-seven-mile-walk shoes. She let out a laugh, which kind of echoed into country air. It was a nice feeling.

When was the last time she'd laughed with Raymond? In L.A. her life was not a laughing matter, now that she thought of it. Kelly wiggled her toes in her tight boots.

She felt a well of emotion ball up in her throat. It was the first time she'd let herself feel anything but anger since she'd left L.A.

She swallowed hard and stuffed it away. The world was full of men who pretended to be something else, then showed their true colors, and there you were, stuck. Unless you knocked them out, stole their money, and took their BMW for a long ride.

Actually it was half her money; California was a community property state. But that briefcase full of cash was another matter altogether.

'Don't beat yourself up for it, honey. Men are tricky devils.' Myrtle nudged her with a bony elbow.

'How'd you know what I was thinking about?' Kelly asked.

'I'm a woman. You had that look on your face. Eventually you'll need to get that outta your craw, ya know. A good long cry is nature's cure for a broken heart.'

'I'm not sure if it's a broken heart as much as pure pissed-offness, Myrtle. I feel used.'

'Didja love him?'

'No. I thought he'd give me stability.'

'Good. Then you'll get over him quick. Gotta clear your dance card for what the future holds.'

'I think my dancing days are over for a while. As a matter of fact, these boots are killing me.' Kelly bent over, unzipped her 'bat' boots, and slid them off. She rolled off her thigh-high stockings and curled her cramped toes up and down.

'Wowie, that's one amazing tattoo, sweetie,' Myrtle whistled.

'Believe it or not, I used to work in a tattoo parlor for about a year. I had artistic skills. I was about seventeen. The owner was a retired army sergeant and watched over me for a while. He did this. "Wild rose," he called it. I couldn't get the whole rose-covered cottage on me without compromising large portions of body expanse. So he gave me one climbing rose.'

'I like it. Suits you. Wild rose.'

The hot pavement felt great against her feet. 'Ahh, at least my feet are happy now,' Kelly said.

Myrtle stood up and stretched. Surprisingly, she

looked as flexible as a cat. A cat in a fish-scale sweater and silver lamé leggings.

'You are cute as a bug, honey.' Myrtle sat back down. 'You'll have the men around here howlin' at the moon.'

'I'd rather be burned at the stake than get involved with anyone right now, Myrtle.'

'Honey, I know just the man that will have you burnin' faster than you think,' Myrtle said with a sly smile. 'As a matter of fact, it must be fate that brought you here to Paradise. I feel it in my bones. We'll do the tarot cards when we get home.'

Home. Kelly liked the sound of that.

Half an hour later, a semi truck Myrtle had flagged down let them off right smack in the middle of Mayberry, USA. Main Street. It really was Main Street! Colorful fall maple trees lined both sides of the road. There was Miller's Hardware, Van Decker's Ice-Cream Parlor, Esther's Fabrics, and Cora's Café. From where she stood she could even see a movie theater marquee with **DORIS DAY ROCK HUDSON PILLOW TALK** in large black letters.

Kelly stood on the clean sidewalk and gawked like a country hick come to New York City for the first time, only in reverse. There should be a sign that read WELCOME TO THE TWILIGHT ZONE.

S am Grayson scanned through the 'Woman Seeks
Man' ads in the *Seattle Weekly*, a yellow highlighter
poised for action.

SWF, 27, HWP, Seeks SWM HWP no STD's for
possible commitment. Must be open to interesting
combination sex and leather.

Possible commitment to what, the nuthouse? Maybe
he was going about this the wrong way. Maybe he
should write his own. He set his highlighter down and
took up his best black pen and a legal pad:

Regular Guy, 32, 6′2″ HWP, seeks regular girl to settle
down and have some kids. No drugs, no bugs, *no trouble*!

Well, that was sixty-eight dollars' worth. He should
have done this in Philly. Maybe then he wouldn't have
ended up engaged to Chelsea.

No, that wasn't fair. Chelsea had looked and acted
perfectly normal when he met her. Okay, a little wild, a
little bipolar, but that passed for fun at first, like a roller
coaster ride. Trouble is, roller coasters lose their thrill
after too many trips and just make you dizzy and sick
and boy do you want to get off the ride.

Sam drew geometric cubes on the side of his paper. Chelsea had some great qualities. But her party never ended. Maybe if he hadn't been so immersed in his law career, he would have seen her heading for a fall.

He sure didn't blame her for breaking up with him. He wanted to settle down, she didn't. He was ready to go to work. It was her last year at the University of Pennsylvania, and she was out to party. That was never so clear as when Chelsea got herself arrested for driving under the influence. Then Chelsea's party came to an abrupt stop.

Sam still couldn't believe he'd ended up being the public defender assigned to Chelsea's case when Chelsea's society parents wrote her off and left her with no funds for legal counsel. He'd thought he could have gotten her off on a first offense with probation and treatment, but up popped her prior conviction. How he hated surprises like that.

He would never forget the look on her face as she heard the stiff sentence. There wasn't much he could have done. They were in the hands of a no-nonsense judge, she had caused an accident, and hey, she obviously needed a wake-up call. Even so, there is nothing quite like seeing your former fiancée hand-cuffed and taken out of the courtroom. The backward glance she had given him – he would have to live with that forever.

It bothered him that he hadn't seen Chelsea's growing problem with alcohol. If he'd only known about her past, he would have kept an eye on her or encouraged her to get help. But then again, they had already broken up when he got the call to defend her.

Sam stood and paced the length of his office to the large window. He could see the whole of town from his sixth-floor viewpoint. At seven stories, the building that housed the law firm of Grayson and Grayson was the tallest building in town.

He was happy with the decision he'd made to come back home. Sure, it was partly because of what had happened with Chelsea, but it was also because of his growing distaste for big-city law and big-city life. He wanted to shake off the past and focus on his future in Paradise. He wanted to contribute to the community in a big way.

Paradise was like swimming a perfect, easy lap. Just smooth water. Even his legal cases were easy: wills and estate planning, with an occasional property dispute that seemed to resolve quickly with his guidance. All that was missing from his life was a wife. That should be easy, too, but it wasn't turning out that way, and that was driving him nuts.

That empty place in him burned bright. He wanted a marriage like his parents' marriage. His youngest sister had gotten married last year, and at all the family functions it pained him to watch the happiness marriage was bringing both his sisters and his parents. That wasn't fair, and he hated the feeling. Plus everyone had that tone – that look in their eyes. Who can we get for Sam? Damn, that was annoying.

Sam was determined to create a life for himself here

in Paradise. This community had given him a great deal. He was here to give something back. In Paradise his actions would have a positive impact. He liked that idea. And part of that life should include a wife and family.

Sam thought about his parents, off on another one of their art tours. Every trip they made was like a second honeymoon. He saw the love between them still alive and well even after all these years. There was a special glimmer when they looked into each other's eyes. Sometimes his dad would take his mom's hand in a spontaneous gesture of affection and press it to his lips in a gallant kiss. He'd be so lucky to find a woman to share that kind of enduring love with. Maybe he was asking too much in this day and age.

Of course, there was Lynnette Stivers, his old high school girlfriend. Everyone had expected him to take back up with her. She *seemed* perfect. So perfect it made his teeth hurt. Sam knew she'd had her sights set on him coming back to her.

During his first days back in town she'd shown up at the office with a picnic lunch and helped him unpack his legal books. That was quite the picnic. Perfect fried chicken, red potato salad, cold hand-squeezed lemonade, red-checked tablecloth.

He didn't notice till too late that *he* was dessert. He smiled to himself. She'd sure made a lunge at him. It's damn hard to pull a woman off you if she's got her mind set on it.

He'd done a pretty good job of it, though. Gave her

the old let's-be-friends speech and helped her back into her perfectly pressed oxford button-up blouse. Amazing the way that thing didn't wrinkle when she'd practically ripped it off.

Lynnette, with her ponytail pulled so tight it squeaked. Sam actually wished he could fall for her. Even in high school during their senior year and at the prom he remembered wishing he felt something more for her.

He'd changed since high school, since law school and doing time as a public defender in Philadelphia. Now he knew that whatever Lynnette appeared to be, it left him empty on his end. And that wasn't what he wanted in a marriage.

Thank God he'd never slept with her in high school. At least he'd had the sense that if he really didn't love her, he shouldn't have sex with her, a rare moment of clarity for an eighteen-year-old.

He reached for the binoculars on his file cabinet and focused on Paradise High School. It still gave him a great feeling. He'd spent the best years of his life so far in that building.

There was a big banner across the front of the building that read: HOMECOMING OCTOBER 4, 2003.

Lynnette should get a clue. Tom Blackwell would marry her in a heartbeat. He'd been in love with her since their junior year. As it was, if Sam so much as raised an eyebrow in her direction, she'd be cooking him dinner every night and darning his socks. Scary.

So he would keep his eyebrows very still around her.

Seemed like everyone in Paradise knew he wanted to get married, and they'd made it their business to get involved. It was a hobby for the whole damn town.

He moved his view to Main Street. There was Mrs. Williamson headed into Esther's Fabrics. She had her own key just in case she needed quilting supplies on a Sunday. That was trust for you. You'd never see that in a big city.

She'd set him up with her niece, Ada. One-eyebrow Ada. Not that her appearance would bother him if they'd had any sort of spark of commonality.

But Ada was focused on becoming a country music star and told him up front she was headed for Nashville, if he'd like to come along.

There was Mr. Miller sweeping up in front of his hardware store, even on a Sunday afternoon when he was closed. Red Miller was going to wear out the sidewalk someday, Sam swore. Red had submitted his wife's cousin Charlene for blind date number ten. Charlene was four years Sam's senior. Charlene wanted a rancher and was quite dismayed to learn Sam had no plans to take up cattle.

Paradise seemed to be short on age-appropriate women – at least any that he felt drawn to. Most of the girls he'd gone to high school with had either left or gotten married. Except for Lynnette, and he'd nipped that one in the bud.

Sam adjusted his binoculars and caught sight of Myrtle Crabtree as she jumped out of the cab of a semi. What the heck was that crazy old broad up to now? Her suitcase was handed out. She must have gone to one of her conventions.

He had to look twice to believe his eyes as a pair of incredibly shapely legs stuck themselves out of the truck door with no shoes on them, followed by an extremely short black skirt.

Sam leaned against the window and refocused. What was that? Some sort of vine or snake design started at the ankle and went up . . . up.

The rest of the emerging woman was just as well proportioned, in a tight black sweater and cropped black leather jacket. The whole package was topped off with a shock of spiked black hair and . . . a nose ring. Damn.

Sam took a long, hard look. Heat rushed around his body. He felt beads of sweat on his forehead.

The semi drove off with a honk. Myrtle waved. Nose Ring parked herself on the sidewalk and slipped into a pair of long black boots that zipped up the side and laced up the front. It took her quite a while. His binoculars steamed up. Damn!

He moved away from the window, set down the binoculars, and sat with a thud at his desk. Sam put both hands on the sides of his head and encouraged the blood to seek his brain again instead of his other parts.

Why did he go for the ones with trouble written all over them? It must be the same thing as being a lifeguard. He must be compelled to save people.

Not this time. When Myrtle called, as she undoubtedly would, he'd just tell her thanks, but no thanks, and to let the rest of the good folks of Paradise know all blind dates were off. Sam was going to do this wife-hunt on his own.

He shook himself like a dog to snap out of whatever had possessed him.

Sam took up his black fountain pen again. He'd come downstairs from his apartment to his office for a reason on this Sunday afternoon. He wrote, *no tattoos, no pierced anything*, on his ad draft.

The afternoon sun was making Kelly sweat in her black leather jacket and warm sweater. They'd walked quite a few blocks to get here. She peeled off her coat as they stood on the steps waiting for Myrtle to unlock the Hen House door. The shades of the shop were drawn and a CLOSED sign hung inside the door.

'We're always closed Sunday and Monday,' Myrtle said as she whipped out her many keys and opened the glass-paneled door. Inside, it was dark and stuffy. She flipped on a few lights and a ceiling fan. The air started clearing right away. They dragged their suitcases in the door.

The Hen House had an extraordinary amount of Halloween decorations up, Kelly thought. She jumped, startled at a witch dummy with its black and gray hair in curlers, sitting under a dryer.

A stuffed black cat with glowing orange glass eyes perched menacingly on the counter. Kelly touched it and let out a gasp. It was real. Well, formerly.

'Mavis Peterson's cat. She had it stuffed. She lets me borrow it every year. Name's Fluffy. Scariest damn cat

I'd ever seen in real life. I figure it's his destiny to be a Halloween icon.'

'You take this Halloween thing pretty seriously, Myrtle. It's only the first week in October,' Kelly said. 'Are you a witch?'

'Depends on who you talk to. Some people said I put a spell on Fred Hansen to make him fall in love with me. But on a general day-to-day basis I'm just a wise-ass old woman.' Myrtle ripped open a plastic bag and refilled a bowl of Halloween candy corn and little candy pumpkins. She offered one to Kelly, who waved a no-thanks, then popped one in her own mouth.

'Okay, sweet cakes, your new digs are right through that door over there.' Myrtle talked with a candy pumpkin in her mouth, then gave up and pointed. She led the way through the door into her adjoining house. Her multiple keys tinkled as she walked. Kelly noticed a Power Puff Girl swinging from the key ring.

Myrtle's kitchen was pink and black. The tile work checkerboarded around the countertops and comple-mented the yard flamingos standing among the potted ferns in the corner. She had a black and white vinyl and chrome luncheonette diner ensemble straight from the *Happy Days* set.

'Park it there at the table, Kelly. I'll make us some lunch. I had one of my girls pick up some eats. I'm always hungry when I get back from conventions.'

'Wow, this is great stuff.'

'Had it since 1955. I was about your age, as I recall. My

first husband, Eddie Crabtree, and I bought it together.'

'You kept his name?'

'He was my favorite husband. After the third one died, I went back to Eddie's name.'

'You outlived three husbands?'

'Men are fragile creatures. Also they smoked cigarettes and ate bacon back in those days.' Myrtle opened the door of the rounded white Frigidaire and rummaged, then reappeared with her arms full.

'You said on the bus you had no children, right?'

'Female problems. In my day there weren't no cure for those things. Thought about adopting with Eddie, but he died pretty early on.' Myrtle plopped some containers on the counter.

'Oh, Myrtle, I'm sorry.'

'I'll see him again. He'll pick me up in his red and white '57 Chevy at the Pearly Gates. He loved that car.'

Kelly saw that Myrtle got a far-off look in her eyes, then turned back to fix lunch.

Suddenly Kelly's current problems felt insignificant in the face of a woman widowed three times.

'Here, let me help with that.' Kelly got up and went over to Myrtle's side.

After ice-cold Nesbitt's orange soda and macaroni salad Myrtle said came from Cora's, a local restaurant, Myrtle gave Kelly the tour of Chez Crabtree. The rest of the house was equally eclectic and fifties-driven.

Kelly grabbed her bags and headed upstairs, led by Myrtle, to the guest room. It was done up Hawaiian style. Myrtle flipped on the hula-girl bedside lamp so

Kelly could see the tropical palm wallpaper in shades of turquoise and blue. The round bed, as Kelly could have predicted, was covered with a wild floral-patterned bedspread.

Myrtle flopped herself on the bed and patted the mattress. 'Damn hard to get these sheets. I have three sets a gal in town handmade for me.' She jumped up and smoothed out the coverlet. 'Okay, then, here's the house rules. If ya got a guy up here, hang yer brassiere on the doorknob. I'll do the same on my door. That's a sign for one of us to get to the movies for a few hours. Got it?' Myrtle winked.

'Yes, ma'am. Myrtle, you're a wild woman.' Kelly swung her suitcase up on the bed and left Raymond's briefcase on the floor. She'd have to find that case a hiding place. 'When are we going to see the town?' Kelly yawned as she spoke.

'Seems to me you missed a whole lot of sleep drivin' from L.A. How 'bout you have a rest? I'll wake you up for supper, and we'll see the whole dang town tomorrow. We'll have a regular Monday mornin' outing.'

Kelly's brain was fuzzing out. She yawned again and stripped off her leather jacket. Myrtle backed out the bedroom door, waving. Kelly gave Raymond's case a shove with her foot, sliding it under the bed.

She slowly took all her clothes off, pushed her suitcase onto the floor, and fell into the smooth pink sheets of Myrtle's round bed. As she drifted off, she thought she heard Hawaiian music from somewhere in the distance.

Heaven. She was in . . . Paradise.

*

Kelly opened her eyes to morning sun outlining the edges of a pull-down shade like a solar eclipse. Myrtle hadn't called her for dinner, that was for sure. She surveyed her surroundings slowly. This wasn't the paradise she'd imagined waking up in this morning. That had more to do with white sand beaches. Of course, she also could have been waking up in a Jamaican jail with her charming husband. She sucked air in through her nose and tried to breathe out the ball of anger in her chest. She was furious with Raymond.

Pitching the covers off, she planted her feet on the furry white carpet. *To hell with it.* She'd just be angry. Kelly grabbed up her suitcase, smacked it down on the bed, and unzipped it. What angry little thing could she put on?

She'd go for her James Dean look. Black jeans and a white T-shirt plus her black leather cropped jacket. But the boots were out. She dug for a pair of black sandals that were walkable.

There was a beautiful blue-painted dressing table on one side of the room, between the two sun-edged windows. She sat down in front of the mirror and ran her fingers through the shock of black hair on her head. That just made the spikes stand up in a more vertical direction.

Kelly clutched her folded clothes in front of her naked body and gazed into the mirror. Where had all the hard edges come from? She was thin. Maybe too thin. Her bones seemed more angular than she remembered.

'Honey, are you awake? I heard creaking floorboards.' Myrtle's voice came softly from the other side of the door.

'I'm awake, but I'm naked as a jaybird,' Kelly answered. She didn't move from her perch on the vanity's upholstered bench seat. Funny how she felt so much trust toward a woman she'd only met yesterday.

Myrtle snickered. 'There's clean towels for ya in the upstairs bath. Oh, and a robe on the hook in the closet in there. You get scrubbed up, I'll make us some breakfast.'

Kelly heard Myrtle clomp down the stairs.

She took one more look into the mirror and got up to grab the robe. A shower would help. Even the thought of it gave her a more orderly feeling.

She took a moment and pulled up the covers on the round bed, smoothed it flat, and plumped the pillows around. In the small closet she found a Hawaiian cotton robe on a hook. Pulling it around her, she headed for the bathroom, grabbing up her clothes as she went out the door.

She hadn't noticed some of the more quirky details of the bathroom yesterday during the tour. The walls were papered in a photo enlargement of a beautiful Hawaiian beach. The claw-footed tub had a bright blue and green shower enclosure with 3-D fish swimming all over it. The soaps were all shaped like seashells, and the bathroom mirror was framed in pretty pink and white shells. There was a mermaid on the hand towel.

It all made her smile. She was forgetting to be angry. She'd have to work into it again.

Kelly took a long, hot shower. The power of hot water and soap to set you right was awesome. She washed her hair in Myrtle's Green Apple shampoo. When she was all rinsed off, she toweled dry and dressed in her James Dean clothes.

The thick, white, sleeveless T-shirt felt comforting for some reason. Clothes were like that for her. Probably because there'd been little else to comfort her most of her life. Better a cotton shirt than drugs, anyhow.

Bacon. She smelled bacon. Wow.

Downstairs Myrtle had scrambled eggs, toast, orange juice, and real – not from a turkey – bacon all ready for her.

'Mmmm, I love you, Myrtle. Will you marry me?' Kelly pulled up a chair and pulled the aroma of her breakfast up into her head. She was starved.

'Nope, my marrying days are over. I'm retired.'

'Then let's just shack up.'

'You got that right. Two wild women. We'll just rename the place "Love Shack."' Myrtle served her own plate up, turned off the stove, and sat across from Kelly. 'Ready for the grand tour of Paradise?'

'Just let me get some bacon under my belt, and I'll be ready for anything,' Kelly answered. She dove into her breakfast with gusto. Man, this was a huge improvement over the standard coffee and donut she'd been doing forever. Her body probably didn't know what to do with actual protein.

The ten o'clock air was October clear, like amber. Kelly and Myrtle walked down Jewel Street, two rows of older houses with green patch lawns.

Kelly took inventory of lawn ornaments. There were five gnomes of various extraction, one spinning daisy, and two pink flamingos. The flowerbeds were filled with petunias and snapdragons in the last blooms of fall. Chrysanthemums yellowed up most of the garden borders. The neighborhood must have all gone to the same sale on that one.

People waved from their porches as Kelly and Myrtle walked by. Kelly took care to check out the little houses close to town. There were several for sale. She hummed as they turned toward Main Street.

Paradise was in a time warp. They were in a 1950s Brigadoon. A town that undoubtedly only appeared every fifty years because of a curse put on it during a drag race by the loser's girlfriend. Peggy Sue got even.

'Purt'near the same as it was in 1952. Eerie, isn't it?' Myrtle pointed down the row of businesses.

'You ain't just kiddin', there, Myrtle,' Kelly answered.

Crossing the street, they passed Robert's Jewelers, Esther's Fabrics, and approached Miller's Hardware. Huge flowering baskets resplendent with fall color hung from the streetlamps.

A big man with gray hair, wearing overalls and a plaid flannel shirt, was out in front of Miller's sweeping the sidewalk. He smiled as they came near, handing out g'mornin's as he kept up the rhythm of his broom.

'Hey, Red. How's Betty?'

'She's up to her elbows in the church social, Myrtle. Thank the Lord it's this weekend. Then maybe I'll get a proper dinner again.'

'Red, honey, a little Lean Cuisine never killed anyone. I bet you're a whiz at the microwave.' Myrtle waved 'bye to Red as they passed.

Did they really have microwaves here? Kelly stopped and stared in the hardware store window. They had the coolest stuff she'd seen in years: Martha's green dishes at totally unhip low prices, a wood-sided Radio Flyer wagon full of gardening supplies, and pumpkins – lots of pumpkins. There was even a real eggbeater – a hand-crank spinner – sitting in a thick white crockery bowl.

She was going to stick out in this hick town like an alien from Mars. 'Who am I, Myrtle? What's my cover?'

'Hmm. That's a good one. I s'pose there is a chance that dumb-ass husband of yours might be on the search. How about you be some distant relative of mine? My brother-in-law's daughter was a wild hair. You could be her kid. Kelly Crabtree.'

'Wouldn't she have married and have some other name?'

'Naa, she's a free spirit, like me. But that's too easy, and too traceable. Let's just say you're my long-lost second cousin.' Myrtle caught her arm. 'C'mon, cousin.'

There she was again. In jeans. In person. Live. Going into Cora's. Where he was going. Steady, man, you're getting java and a muffin just like every day.

Oh, damn. She was extremely sexy. Wild black hair, tight jeans, black leather jacket. Her toenails were painted bright orange, and a silver toe ring glinted back at him.

'Hi, Sam. How are you this beautiful fall morning?' The face of Lynnette Stivers blotted out his view. She was her perfectly perky blonde self. Except that she was talking to him through gritted teeth.

'Just fine, Lynnette. Just catching a coffee break.' Translation: *Please move your perky ass and let me get my caffeine.* It occurred to Sam that since he came here almost every day at this time, it wasn't an accident bumping into Lynnette.

'Are you going to the church social Saturday? I'm baking up a dozen peach pies. You know, the ones with the pecans that you just love so much?'

'I've been commandeered by Dottie Williamson to transport potato salad. I'm sure I'll see you there,' Sam said as flatly as possible, keeping all hint of invitation or any ol' hint out of his voice. From the look on her face it didn't quite work as well as he'd wished.

'That'll be just fine, Sam. I'll save a space on my dance card for you.' Lynnette did smooth talk so well.

Translation: *I'm gonna get you hog-tied, Sam Grayson, one way or another*. Sam shuddered.

'I've got to get back to work. I'm sure we'll run into each other.' Sam wove and dodged and managed to get by her; red plaid pleated skirt, white blouse, and all.

And there he stood, smack in the middle between Lynnette and the Hot One. His head turned a couple times back and forth slowly.

'Usual, Sam?' Cora saved him.

'Yep. Coffee. Blueberry.' Cora knew that. He handed her his travel cup. She smirked at him.

'Sam Grayson, meet my second cousin, Kelly. Ain't she somethin'?' Myrtle gave the Hot One a small push in his direction.

Yeah, she was something, all right. Sam stuck out his hand. 'Hey, Kelly, I'm Sam.' *Oh, brilliant*.

Her hand came toward him slow and easy. Her eyes never left his. They were like cat's eyes: hazel green, pale, and huge. When their flesh came together it was like he'd touched her bare breast instead of her hand. Pure heat whip-cracked between them. Hurricane Kelly.

'Sam.'

Her voice was velvet. Smooth black velvet. Twenty-year-old Scotch velvet. He wanted to drink her.

Why did the universe torture him this way? What had he ever done to deserve this? He should be getting the big bone over Plaid Skirt Lynnette. She'd wash his underwear and cook peach frikkin' pie and keep his kids' noses wiped. She would.

This one would only break him. She'd run up his credit cards. She'd be incredible in bed and toy with his . . . affections. She was probably hiding out from the mob. She had tattoos. Right up her leg. And a toe ring.

'Sam.' It wasn't Velvet Voice. It was Cora handing him a paper bag and his travel mug full of coffee. He let go of Kelly's hand.

'Nice to meet you, Kelly, are you staying in town long?' Witty repartee. Translation: *Can I just take you to my place and get this out of my system right NOW?* Sam fumbled with his cup and bag. He dove into the hazel green cat's eyes again. What a swim.

'She'll be shacked up at my place if you'd like to pay a social call, Sammy.' Myrtle put her arm around the Kelly girl. Myrtle had on a bright orange jogging suit. They looked very Halloween together. Orange and black.

Sam felt two holes burning into the back of his neck. He turned. Lynnette had hands on hips and a quirky look about her. Time to get outta Dodge.

He nodded to Kelly and Myrtle and steeled himself as he bravely walked past Lynnette. She moved her elbow like a turnstile as he passed. Her eyes never left him, which took quite a head twist. No translation available.

Man, that was one good-looking small-town hunk. He was probably wearing the only suit in town. He probably *owned* the only suit in town. Kelly thumped down on a counter stool, shaken.

'Coffee, please.'

Myrtle joined her. 'Make it two, Cora,' she said.

Kelly watched him push the glass door open as he exited. The blonde chick in the red plaid started to follow him out, then changed her mind, turned, and stood by the pie case. Both Kelly and the blonde watched Sam's handsome figure go past the window outside.

'Would you like that to go, Kelly?' The lady behind the counter started laughing real hard. Myrtle did, too.

'Naa, we're gonna play hard to get on this one.' Myrtle slapped the counter and laughed the no-sound laugh.

'Listen . . . Cora' – Kelly had cocked her head and read the embroidered script sewn on the pink and white waitress uniform – 'and Myrtle. I'm not interested in Mr. Wonderful. I'm sure there's some nice local girl just up his alley.'

'That would be me, Miss . . . I didn't catch your name?'

Kelly hadn't noticed the blonde come her way.

'Kelly A-A-A-Applebee.' Oh, good one. She really was Myrtle's cousin now. Crabtree and Applebee. Sounded like a jam and jelly company.

'Just so we're clear on this, Miss Applebee, Sam and I have been dating since high school. Why, we even went to the senior prom together, if you get my drift.'

'And I should know this because why?' Kelly knew a controlling, crazy bitch when she saw one. She might be dumb on men, but women were clear as glass. She couldn't let this catfight go by.

Blondie bent forward toward Kelly. Kelly saw a crazy glint in those steel-blue eyes. Her words came out one at a time with great emphasis. '*Because-he's-mine.*'

Cora rattled a thick white cup and saucer onto the counter in front of Kelly. Kelly's eyes broke contact for a moment. The cup had thin green stripes around the top. 'Cream and sugar?' Cora's face was pink with suppressed glee.

Kelly moved her gaze back to Psycho-Blonde's face with a very big, very fake, smile. Her stare never wavered from those slightly too-close-together blue eyes. 'I'll have it all, please.'

'Run along, now, Lynnette, Cousin Kelly and I have some catchin' up to do.' Myrtle turned to her coffee and started pouring in sugar from the glass container with the chrome spout that Cora slid their way.

Kelly watched Lynnette turn about as white as her blouse. She straightened up stiffly, turned, and marched herself out the door with her ponytail swinging like the tail of a mad cat.

Kelly drank her coffee with some kind of weird satisfaction. It went down smooth and smug.

'Damn, that girl is nuts, Myrtle,' Kelly said.

'Yup,' Myrtle replied.

Cora leaned in close. Her hair was cornrowed on each side and probably dyed dark brown to hide the gray. No doubt some of Myrtle's handiwork. Her brown skin was still pretty and smooth. She must have been about sixty-five and was still beautiful, really beautiful. She reached across the counter and refilled Kelly's coffee.

That refill came with dirt on the side.

'When Sam got engaged to that girl in Philly, Lynnette climbed up on the high school water tower in her baby-doll pajamas and tried to scrub their initials off with Comet. Sheriff had to pull her down. Most excitement we'd had around here for a long time. Course, Sheriff Tom's been in love with her since they were juniors at Paradise High, y'know.' Cora put her free hand on her hip and smiled.

That was one big-ass, streaming video piece of gossip. Small towns were great that way. 'No shit? Oh, pardon me,' Kelly said.

'You are pardoned, dear,' Cora continued. 'Then she went after Sam like a bitch in heat when he got back in town a few months ago. We all figure he turned her down, 'cause she's been prowlin' around him ever since, but he acts like she's a case of the measles.'

'Who the hell is Sam, anyhow? Besides the best-looking man I've laid eyes on in ten years?' Kelly slurped up some coffee and dished with the gals. She reached for a donut off the plate Cora had left on the counter at some point. It was still warm.

Myrtle waved a spoon in among the three of them like a witch stirring her cauldron. 'He's the son of two of Paradise's best people. His father has had a law practice here for thirty years. Sam came back and joined the firm.'

So what the hell was a vital, handsome guy like Sam doing back in this stuck-water town? Inquiring Kelly wanted to know, but that'd be rude. It was their stuck-water town, too. She dipped her donut into the steamy coffee, which Cora seemed to refill magically without her even seeing. Man, the food in this town was good.

Myrtle answered Kelly's question before she had a chance to ask it. 'His fiancée in Philly, they broke up. Then she got into some kind of trouble and ended up in court, and he ended up defending her, but she went off to jail for a few months anyhow. I think he just got fed up with city ways and came back here to have a wife. Oh, a life, I mean.'

Myrtle's eyes kind of rolled around to Cora. She dabbed at her mouth with a napkin, hiding a grin that Kelly could see quite well. Cora straightened up, nodded meaningfully at Myrtle, and went on down the row filling coffee cups.

'You should hear that woman sing.' Myrtle changed the subject.

'I know what you're up to, Myrtle,' said Kelly. 'Let us not forget a few minor details. One, I'm still married. Two, I'm so not in the mood to be anyone's wife. Most likely if I'm attracted to a man, he's got some secret personality flaw that will rear its ugly head as soon as I say those two fateful words – *I do*. So I don't. Are we clear on that, Mrs. Crabtree?'

'Clear as mud, Miss *Applebee*. 'Nuther donut?'

'Don't mind if I do. Chocolate sprinkles, please.'

'So you're attracted to Sam?'

'Quit it, Myrtle.'

*

The smell of perm solution drifted up to Kelly's second-story bedroom and woke her. A decidedly unaromatherapy kind of thing. She was getting used to it by now. Just for fun she and Myrtle had draped tropical mosquito netting dotted with silk plumeria blossoms from the ceiling. Kelly pushed it aside, then scuffed her feet into a pair of rubber flip-flops.

She'd had a hell of a fun week. Myrtle was a shoo-in for mother replacement. Kelly's own mother had never done much of a job of it anyway, even when she was sober.

Myrtle said Kelly was the daughter she never had, and the cosmos sent her so Myrtle could finally pass down all her life secrets to someone.

All this week she'd luxuriated in the tub at night with lavender bath oil and a good book. Myrtle supplied her with every beautifying, smellifying product under the sun. It'd started to take the edge off her life, all that warm water and fragrance.

Kelly showered and shimmied into her new red three-quarter-sleeved crop top and its matching spandex skirt. Finger-combing her gelled-up hair into its usual crazy style, she caught a glimpse of herself in the dressing-table mirror. Still too thin, but damn, she looked good in red.

Kelly had a new job. In less than a week she'd gotten a job. Try doing that in L.A. Palmer's Emporium needed sales help. She suspected Myrtle pulled a few strings, but that was fine. New job, new town, she was almost . . . happy. She put on her red Carmen Miranda's

Hot Date lipstick. After this she wanted to get a job naming lipstick. And paint. She'd painted one wall of the beauty parlor Tickle Me Pink when she couldn't sleep one night earlier in the week.

Red sandals. Who'd have figured Yeackle's Shoes for red sandals this cute? She slipped them on and walked downstairs to the beauty shop to pour herself a cup of Myrtle's famous mud coffee. Every chair was packed. The big Saturday crowd.

'Mornin'.' She was even getting the town accent down.

'Mornin', Kelly girl. Hey, grab some of that apple cobbler there. Dottie Williamson baked a bunch for the church social tonight. That there is our personal supply.' Myrtle said all this with her mouth full of perm pins. She was unrolling Dottie's perky gray curls.

'Thanks, Dottie. Your apple cobbler smells divine. Isn't this about the third fattening thing you've brought in this week?' Kelly asked.

'Trying out recipes, you know.' Dottie smiled and pointed to a colorful baking dish full of delectable hot apple-and-cinnamon cobbler. 'You've all been my guinea pigs this week.'

'I'm not going to fit into my clothes if I keep this up.' Kelly got closer to the dish. Her mouth watered. 'On the other hand, I don't care.' She grabbed up a small plate off the stack and cut herself a big square.

She picked out her favorite cup, bought brand-new at Miller's Hardware; a Fiesta ware pink number. Kelly sat down at the little table on the far end of the shop that doubled as a sterilizing station and coffee break area.

'Honey, you look so much better than when you got here. You were so skinny you looked like one of them high-fashion, high-strung models from the big city,' Myrtle said.

Kelly hadn't even thought about L.A. in the last few days. Everyone seemed satisfied with the sketchy background she'd given them. No one seemed to be asking too many questions. She felt a darkness come over her as she thought about it.

There were a few details she needed to clean up. It helped that Myrtle had gotten her a new ID from some mysterious connection, and laundered all the traveler's checks into cash, which Kelly deposited in her new-name bank account at Paradise Savings and Loan.

That woman was amazing. She and Myrtle had done a lot of talking. About Raymond, about her life before Raymond, about this man *Sam* Myrtle said the cosmos had picked out for her.

Sam Grayson, the most eligible bachelor in town. Probably the only bachelor under forty-five, more like it. Kelly was curious, but, after all, she was still married and would have to do something about that – a concept that always confused her whenever she thought about it: how to get a divorce while living under an assumed name.

Then there was the briefcase full of money under her bed. Kelly had actually forgotten about it until this moment. She still wasn't sure what to do with the money except sleep on it – literally.

What she needed was a lawyer. Legal advice. Yep. *Oh, Mr. Grayson, I've got a couple hundred thousand dollars or so under my bed and don't know what to do about it. Can you give me some advice?*

She raised an eyebrow at her own absurd thinking and ate the last bite of apple cobbler with gusto.

'You better run along, hon, it's already eight-thirty. Mrs. Palmer will be wanting her scones,' Myrtle reminded her. Kelly got up, startled out of her thoughts. She put her dish under the table in the dishpan they kept for party cleanups. It seemed like every day was party day at Myrtle's.

Kelly grabbed her black leather jacket and draped it around her shoulders. She gave Myrtle's cheek a kiss as she passed by, pushed the screen door open, and stepped out on the stoop.

'Oh, sweetie, don't forget to go over to Dottie's house after work. You promised her help loadin' up for the social.'

'I remember. See you later, Mrs. Williamson,' Kelly called back through the screen door as it snapped shut behind her.

'Do you think this will work, Myrtle?' Dottie Williamson looked up into the huge round mirror at the reflection of Myrtle standing behind her with a comb.

'Them two just need a little help. They're like two ducks that keep swimmin' around the pond at the same time, goin' in circles. We just gotta get one of 'em to stop long enough for the other to run smack into 'em.'

Myrtle brandished her blue rattail comb dramatically over Dottie's head.

'Do you really think so?'

'Dottie, hon, I'd say you can start quiltin' up the weddin' quilt anytime. Them two is destined. It's in the stars.'

'Oh, Myrtle, that's sweet. Maybe I'll put stars on it.'

'You do that, Dottie. Stars.'

Myrtle put the finishing touches on Dottie's coiffure and reached for the hair spray. Something was afoot in Paradise. Them stars were off-kilter, and she wasn't sure exactly why. She'd do her cards later and see what came up. Nothin' a little female ingenuity couldn't overcome, of that she was sure.

Kelly knew the little daily task Mrs. Palmer had so politely asked her to take was for the sole purpose of throwing her in the path of the extremely good-looking Sam Grayson, who, she'd been carefully told, stopped at Cora's every morning for coffee and a bear claw, whatever that was, at exactly 8:45 a.m.

She hummed as she turned toward the main section of town. Three blocks down, she crossed the street and approached Red Miller, ready to hand out his usual g'mornin's. She'd gotten one every morning for three days now.

And there *he* was, rounding the corner headed straight toward her on his way to Cora's. He waved at her. She waved back, plowing smack into Mr. Miller, who steadied her, laughing a deep short laugh. Sam was really exceptionally handsome in his slate-gray suit, white shirt, and arty tie.

'Why don't you two just get it over with and talk?' Mr. Miller asked, continuing his sweeping.

Kelly realized what a total idiot she was being. She steeled herself and marched down the street, pushing Cora's steel and glass door open. Sam was standing at the counter with a newspaper and a white paper bag in his hands. Fabulous. Tall. Structural. She was being a very, very shallow girl. She tried to feel bad about it, but he was so yummy.

He turned to look at her when she entered.

'Hello.' Sam smiled at her.

'Hi.' That was it, huh? Date with destiny. She sat down and asked Renee, Cora's number one waitress, for Mrs. Palmer's scones, unable to face Mr. Destiny without her speaking ability.

Sam got his coffee and slowly walked by her, with a very odd look on his face. After he went through the door, she thumped her head on the counter facefirst. Renee set the bag of scones down beside her.

'Lost something?' Renee started to giggle.

'Yes, my mind, and stop that! I know what a fool I am already.' Kelly started to laugh, and so did about three other people close by. Renee set down a white to-go cup of coffee with a sugar packet on the lid.

'I already put cream in. It's on the house, honey. Invite me to the wedding, will you?'

'Sure, sure. Thanks, Renee.' Kelly made as graceful

an exit as possible, as the whole counter full of people said in unison, 'G'bye!'

Oh, brother. Group humiliation was always fun. The joke about the wedding – that was a good one. Particularly with the luck she had as a bride. Oh, yes. Which reminded her, she was definitely going to have to call someone and see about divorcing Raymond. He'd probably already drawn up a divorce and just didn't know where to send the papers. If she were even going to think about this Sam character, she'd have to deal with that first.

If Sam could just figure out what it was about Miss Kelly Applebee that drove him crazy, he could ignore her and live a normal life. This Kelly girl just seemed to derail him from his steady track. Part of him had danger signals going off like emergency bells inside his head. The rest of him wanted to grab her up on his horse and ride bareback together into the sunset, find a field and . . . caution be damned.

Okay, just because she appeared to be trouble didn't mean she was. Appearances could be deceiving. Maybe underneath that wild hair and that tight red skirt and those luscious . . . oh, *shit*, he was screwed.

PALMER'S EMPORIUM was painted in black letters on the plate-glass windows of the double storefront. Kelly pushed the swinging door open and stepped inside.

Several people were already hard at work, and the fans were running to keep the temperature cool. She shivered in the breeze, pulling her coat around her. The last swallow of the coffee warmed her up.

After Mrs. Palmer discovered her vast retail merchandising skills Kelly had been put in charge of the women's and junior's clothing areas. Ah, yes, ten years in the L.A. fashion district can teach you a lot about clothes. Of course she'd been a little vague about her actual experience, but the fact that she was living with Myrtle seemed to fling most doors wide open around her.

In the three days she'd worked here she'd learned enough about the Palmers to fill a spiral notebook. Paradise was alive with the sound of gossip.

Kelly walked past rows of children's fall jumpers and rompers. Palmer's was a family business. Will Palmer, the youngest son, ran the advertising and promotion for the store. His holiday displays were a big attraction.

Even people from nearby towns would take a special trip by to see the windows.

He was about thirty-one, and his wife Ginny worked in the store. She was the same age as Kelly, fun, even though they were as different as dog breeds. Ginny had two kids and wore calico skirts.

The oldest Palmer son, Robert, acted as assistant manager. He had an obvious, but gentlemanly, interest in Kelly.

Kelly stashed her handbag and jacket in the back room and checked her reflection in the mirror. She got out her red lipstick to do a little repair, setting the scones on the shelf.

She, on the other hand, had no interest in Robert, who was a total dork and around forty, and . . . bird-watched.

She had no interest in *any* man, for that matter. She wanted to spend some time getting to know herself, getting her life in order, and starting over.

Myrtle kept hinting about Sam and her fate and all that. She just didn't feel it. Dottie Williamson and Myrtle had been spending much of their spare time plotting, which seemed contrary to the cosmic design Myrtle claimed it was all supposed to fall under.

At the same time, the store had seen an amazing increase in bachelor business in the last three days, according to Ginny, with several grease monkey types coming in wearing their best Western snap shirts, accidentally finding themselves in women's lingerie and practically running out of the store.

Kelly was suspicious that someone was sending a stream of men her way. Probably Mrs. Palmer. Or Myrtle, or even Dottie. Everyone in town had a hand firmly on the rudder of the good ship *Destiny*, didn't they?

Myrtle had been right about one thing, though. Sam Grayson was a notch above the crowd, for sure. There was something about a man so good-looking he left you completely speechless.

She puckered up her lips in the mirror to even out the lipstick. A few calm nights and clean air had done a great deal for her complexion ... and her disposition. Normally she might actually be pissed about all this meddling in her life. Somehow now it felt wonderful. Seriously wonderful.

She popped a piece of Chiclets gum in her mouth for her chew-with-the-rhythm-of-the-mark-downs ritual. Wow, could you even buy this gum in the real world anymore?

Once again she decided Paradise was a time-warp town – stuck in 1955. She took one extra piece on that thought and headed out. Seven rounder racks waited for her *20% off* stickers. Preholiday sale.

Kelly settled into the routine of straightening stock, folding T-shirts, and re-sorting the round racks for mark down. It was a quiet morning.

Then *he* walked in. Kelly stopped dead in her tracks. Was he here to follow up on her incredibly stupid hello? My, he was actually tall, dark, and handsome ... how cliché – she smiled to herself – but true. Yes, that slate-gray suit was filled out with a very amazing body, too. She could see muscles outlined under the fine wool jacket.

Kelly knew her suits, too, and his wasn't from Palmer's men's department. Armani, most likely.

Well, to hell with that, she thought, and stuck a sizer on the rack. Size twelve.

Money ain't everything; it buys lots of trouble if you let it. Take rich Raymond, for instance. Take that pesky bag-o'-money under her bed.

But that suit sure did hang well off Mr. T.D. & H. She started up her sorting again, ignoring him. Maybe he was shopping.

He smiled directly at her. She smiled back. He continued walking closer to her. His eyes were like a dark blue night sky. Her breath caught, and the gum went with it. She swallowed her gum. Badly. It stuck somewhere in her throat.

Through tears of distress she saw Sam's compelling blue eyes widen in surprise, then change to alarm. The gum wad was lodged somewhere near her vocal cords, and all she could do was wave her arms wildly and turn purple.

With the speed and agility of a quarterback, Sam dodged display cases and straight-armed a rounder that stood between them.

'Are you choking?'

She tried to say no, but she wasn't so sure.

One large hand took her shoulder and whirled her around. Fisting both hands beneath her breastbone, he squeezed her tightly to his tall frame and tugged upward. He jerked her off her feet with his quick move. Her gum flew out of her mouth, across the room, and stuck on a display of a half body in swimwear, somewhere around the navel area.

Kelly started to laugh in the middle of coughing her last cough. They shifted around and Sam offered his handkerchief. It was white linen with a G embroidered on it. He still had one arm around her. Their closeness would have been exciting if she weren't trying to get a breath in. Actually, it was exciting anyway.

'Thank you,' she squeaked out. What a sight she must be. She slowly regained her composure. God, he smelled good. Her ribs hurt. She rubbed them.

'Sorry about that. I hope I didn't hurt you,' he said, extending his hand. 'Are you okay?'

'I am.' Her voice still squeaked. She wiped at the tears streaming down her face, then handed him his makeup-stained handkerchief. He took her whole ice-cold hand in his instead of the handkerchief. He had strong, warm hands, and kept hold of hers for a long time. She looked up into his eyes. He smiled at her again, a devastatingly *nice* smile.

Oh . . . my . . . God. Suddenly Kelly wanted a social life again. Actually, Kelly wanted Mr. Tall, Dark, and Handsome to take her in the back room and kiss the red sandals right off her feet, very hard and very deep. She sort of melted into his handshake.

'Are you sure you're all right? Can I get you anything?' he said, and released her hand at last.

Yeah, he could get her a big, passionate kiss right now – to go, please. If he only knew what she was thinking. She realized her face must be seven shades of scarlet. An improvement over purple, though.

'We met in Cora's, remember?' he asked.

Did she remember? Damn straight she did. She looked in his eyes and caught just a hint of amusement.

'I don't usually have this effect on women.'

'Don't get yourself too built up, there, Mr. Grayson, I often choke my way through the day.' These words kind of blurted out. She immediately wanted to choke on them instead of the wad of gum.

What was she, *nuts*? 'But thanks for the bruised ribs.' Things were getting worse, she was definitely nuts, but he was provoking her, really he was. He looked even more amused, and there was an effort on his part not to laugh out loud at her, she could see this clearly.

'I'm sorry about that. How about I make it up to you by buying lunch? Is today acceptable?'

Is right this second acceptable? Instead she said, 'That would be nice. My break is at twelve-thirty.' Well, she wasn't completely nuts.

'Twelve-thirty it is.' He extended his hand, and they touched again. 'I have a meeting scheduled with Mrs. Palmer. Is she in yet?'

Eleanor Palmer breezed into the store just in time to catch them red-handed. And Kelly, red-faced.

'Sam, you handsome devil, I see you've met the prettiest girl in town. Now what will I do for a boy-friend?' Mrs. Palmer's silk chiffon scarf puffed around her in the breeze from the fan. She was a slim and fashionable woman, still very attractive.

'Kelly had a startling effect on me, Mrs. P.'

'I forgive you, and Mr. Palmer will be relieved, I'm sure.' Mrs. Palmer wound her arm through Sam's. 'Come upstairs to my office and have some tea and scones. It was very kind of you to meet me here on a Saturday. I think better in my own space these days. Kelly, dear, you might want to freshen up a bit, then bring up my scones, will you?' Mrs. Palmer winked at Kelly, then ushered Sam toward the office stairs.

Kelly suspected a conspiracy – Myrtle, Dottie, and Mrs. P. were definitely up to something. It was no accident Sam had come to the store. After a moment of thought, Kelly decided she was willing to play along. After a few minor things were cleared up. Like her being married. Maybe Mr. Grayson was just the person to help her with it all.

'Sam.' She corrected herself out loud. She still had his handkerchief. She put it to her nose and inhaled. His clean, bar-of-soap kind of scent lingered around her.

'I think he prefers it to Henry, his given name.' Ginny Palmer came up beside her, grinning her cat-ate-canary grin. 'Sam is what folks have called him since he was a child. Yikes, hon, you look . . . er . . . here – better take a look.' Ginny pointed to the back room and followed Kelly, chatting on the way.

'Hope you didn't scare him away,' Ginny said with a laugh. 'Henry Samuel Grayson Jr., attorney at law, is the best catch in town. He and his father practice together.

Sam went away to law school back East, then surprised us all by coming home to Paradise a year ago. He's a nice lawyer, and that's a rare thing.'

Here it comes, Kelly thought. Gossip, Paradise style.

Kelly looked in the mirror and shrieked. Her hair was flying sideways from being flipped over by Sam's Heimlich maneuver; her lipstick was smeared down to her chin; her eyes were red and teary. Her mascara? She was definitely having a Tammy Faye moment. She started some quick repairs.

'You say he asked you to lunch?' Ginny asked with a smirk on her face.

'Shut *up*! This is not amusing.' Kelly laughed. 'Well, it is, but please take these scones upstairs while I fix myself, and then come back and help me find that gum ball I projectiled onto a bikini body, okay? Take pity on the horridly embarrassed new girl.'

'Not a problem. I kind of like you, red dress and all. Even if you are way skinnier than me.' Ginny grabbed the bag of scones and headed out. 'At least you can stun him as he exits the building. Make up for it.'

Kelly heard giggles all down the main aisle as Ginny went to the stairs.

She was starting to get a feeling about Sam. He was a great guy. Too great. He was just too damn nice for her. She was a mess, and her smeared lipstick was the least of it. She'd lived a rough life. She wasn't soft and easy like Ginny. She was complicated and hard-edged and . . . married. Besides all that some horrible thugs were probably looking for their briefcase full of money by now.

Shoot, that was a new thought, and it chilled her down to the bone. Whatever Raymond had planned for that money had undoubtedly gone very badly, and he'd send them her way.

But who would look for her *here*? If they found the car, they could only track her as far as Seattle. She could be anywhere. She hadn't used her credit cards, and no one was looking for a Kelly Applebee. Maybe she was safe. But one thing was for sure; she needed some legal advice.

She squiggled her skirt down a little and tidied up her top, which was twisted sideways.

Ginny came back to warn her that they were almost done upstairs. They both went out on the sales floor and acted . . . normal.

Lawyer descending a staircase, Kelly thought as she watched Sam out of the corner of her eye. This time she was ready for him. She lifted up her chin and looked his way, smiled, then wiggled her finger at him to come to her. He got *very* close.

'Miss . . . I don't think I got your last name?' Sam asked.

'Applebee. But you can call me Kelly. I mean, you saved my life. I think that's first name stuff, don't you, Sam?' She hated lying about her name to such a very nice guy. He'd probably never told a lie in his life. Well, maybe. He was a lawyer, after all.

'My pleasure, Kelly.'

'I wonder if you'd mind if I turned our lunch hour

into a business meeting? I have a legal matter I need to discuss.'

'I wouldn't mind, but Mrs. Palmer told me you were free for a few hours today, so let's go ahead and eat before we get down to it, shall we?'

Kelly held on to a forest-green, size sixteen ladies polar fleece jacket to keep from falling over. The closer he got, the more she wanted to *get down to it*, all right. 'Oh, she did, did she? Well, she's the boss. Lunch it is, then we can walk to your office?'

'That would be fine.' Sam scratched his chin for a minute and stared at her with a smile. 'I'll see you in a few hours.'

'Great,' Kelly answered. There was a huge, empty pause in the conversation. Okay, let's move it along here, she thought. She couldn't take the long pauses. Sam seemed to get the hint and started toward the door.

'By the way . . .' Sam said to her as he backed out the door.

'Yes?'

'You clean up great.' He smiled his dazzling smile and strode out.

He may be nice, but he's got a streak of something in there, Kelly thought to herself. A gleam in his eye she didn't quite trust.

Kelly and Ginny spent the next two hours shifting stock and sharing tidbits about Sam Grayson's life. Ginny and Will Palmer had gone to high school with him. Sam was a swimmer back then and had set some state records. That was a new one.

Then the engagement story again: engaged to a girl after law school in Philadelphia, broke it off for some unknown reason. Kelly actually knew more about that one than Ginny did. Amazing.

Everyone was delighted to have him back home. He had taken the job as fill-in prosecuting attorney while Dave Newsom was on vacation for the summer, but was back to regular family law now: estate planning, property stuff, and the occasional divorce.

'Who ever gets a divorce around here?' Kelly asked.

'No one I know in the last ten years. Well, that's about it about Sam. Thirty-two, single, rich, and mmmmmm,' said Ginny.

'Rich doesn't matter. Money can get you troubles.'

'Get a grip, Kelly. Poverty can get you troubles, too.'

'True. I just mean it's his heart that matters.' Kelly frowned. And maybe some guys' hearts are too nice to break, she added to herself.

'Well, it looks like you get the privilege of exploring that area. Here he comes.'

'He's early!' Kelly bolted into the back room, grabbed her purse and coat, and came out casually.

'Did I scare you again?' Sam asked.

'Not at all, I just went for my things. Shall we?'

'Have her back by midnight,' Ginny said sternly.

'I'll be a perfect gentleman.' Sam smiled his bright, white, Robert Redford smile and escorted Kelly out of the store.

'You already *are* the perfect gentleman,' sighed Ginny to herself as they left.

*

Sam and Kelly sat across from each other on white wrought-iron chairs. The red-and-white-striped cushions blended in nicely with her clingy red outfit, but that was all that blended. Sitting in Van Decker's Ice-Cream Parlor with a spiky-haired, tattooed lady just didn't happen here in Happyville USA.

Sam knew that because he had been going to Van Decker's since he was a kid. He used to order licorice ice cream to make his mother crazy. Old man Van Decker – the original patriarch of the clan – used to keep it in stock, special, just for him.

So what was he doing bringing Wild Thing here? For some reason he wanted to see if this woman knew her way around a hot fudge sundae.

A buzz of whispers surrounded them, a swarm of gossiping locals. When there was not much going in town, a lunch like this could make the local papers.

It was probably good they didn't know what he was really thinking about the Lady in Red. Right now it had something to do with the fact her nipples were hard from the cold.

This Kelly thing just didn't fit in with the wife hunt thing. Kelly Applebee clearly wasn't the marrying kind. She was the other kind. His eyes slid down to her slightly exposed navel. There was a tiny gold ring in it with a glittering diamond attached. He almost dropped his menu.

Dinky Van Decker, the unmarried twenty-year-old daughter, came to take their order. She winked at Sam about five times while she scribbled.

Kelly ordered a salad and a root beer float. Sam thought that was a very interesting combination. An attempt at healthy eating, countered by some pleasure. He decided to go for a cheeseburger and make it a classic blast-from-the-past meal. Cheeseburger, Pepsi, fries, just like high school.

Dinky winked a few more times, grabbed their menus, and left. He really loved knowing everyone deep down. It was strange that coming back to Paradise was such a great experience for him. He'd been so focused on getting out of town after graduation. Now his entire focus was Paradise, and doing his part to keep good things happening here. Every community needed people willing to give back if it was going to stay a great place to live. He really was a hometown boy deep down.

Hell, even a hometown boy needs an occasional distraction. And Kelly Applebee was one hell of a distraction.

The silence was drawing out. She pulled at her skirt and showed less leg. Didn't matter, there was plenty of leg to go around. Sam put his hand up to his temple. What was he, just starved for sex? Any man worth his salt would get to know a woman before he let himself get this hot over her, wouldn't he?

'What brought you to Paradise?' he asked her,

'A bus.'

He leaned back and looked at her hard. She wasn't going to make this easy. Maybe she was just nervous. Okay, he decided, let's take another tack.

'It's a great little town, I'd be glad to show you around.'

'Myrtle gave me the grand tour.'

Sam gave up the chitchat and took her in while she nervously sipped her water. Her long tan legs took up a great deal of the package. Boy, he was definitely a leg man. Then there was the twining rose vine running up her right one. Ankle to . . . wherever. Wild rose.

As he shifted his gaze upward and found himself lusting after her shapely form, he felt another wave of guilt for being such a Neanderthal. He sat up and looked into her face.

It was a beautiful face, with some sadness around the edges. He was lonely for a woman with a soul inside her, and he thought he saw a glimmer of depth in her lovely hazel green eyes.

He sat back and took a deep breath. He felt extremely confused. Yes, he wanted to get married, but Kelly Applebee didn't fit the picture. Yes, he wanted to get laid, but he was an honorable sort, deep down.

Please, God, don't let me suffer in this dating hell forever. I've been a good man. Send me a sign, he prayed.

The waitress slid a luscious cheeseburger with perfectly crisp homemade fries in front of him and a great-looking salad in front of her. He took the perfection of his lunch as the sign. He was easy.

Between bites, Kelly carefully steered the conversation to avoid herself and learn more about him. Not much was really being said with words anyway. Their knees brushed under the table, and Kelly felt a wonderful warmth move up her leg. He was simply one burning, smoldering, sexy guy, and the best part was he didn't seem to know it. She reminded herself . . . several times . . . of her vow not to get involved in any relationship until she was free of Raymond.

Whatever. Being with Sam was so delicious, she savored every moment. That and the root beer float that arrived after she wolfed down the salad. It cooled her off a degree or two, so she started chatting again.

'Wow, this lunch is fabulous. Sometimes I feel like Paradise is a step back in time. I love that feeling.' She scooped up a big bite of vanilla ice cream off the top of the root beer and stuck the whole thing in her mouth at once. A dribble off the spoon ran down the corner of her mouth.

He watched her, unable to stop. A thin gold bracelet dangled from one of her slim wrists. It slid down her tan arm while she spooned in another bite. She finally reached for her napkin and dabbed her chin. Her nails were red, her lips were luscious, and the ice cream . . . he envied it.

Sam had lost his focus and not heard much of what she said somewhere after their knees had touched, except for her last words about liking Paradise.

What he did hear was the music of her voice. It was quite an extraordinary voice, sweet and low and sexy. And any girl who could eat like this – well, she had an earthy quality that he really went for. He reminded himself that he'd received a sign. What the hell, he might as well get to know her.

'Will you have dinner with me tonight, Kelly?' He took her spoon-free hand gently, and the buzz in the room stopped for just a moment, then went up a notch.

'Thanks for asking, but I promised Dottie Williamson I'd help her transfer food to the Presbyterian church after work.'

'Oh, wow, lowly Lutheran that I am, I've been assigned the same task. It slipped my mind in the ... heat of the moment,' Sam said. *Thank you Dottie Williamson and your potato salad*, he added silently. He wanted more time with her, right away.

Kelly's spoon remained poised in midair for a minute, and she looked at him funny. 'Well, isn't that a coincidence? I want to warn you, though –' Kelly lowered her voice and looked around. ' – people will talk.'

'I think they already are. Shall we go somewhere more private? We can discuss that legal matter without it ending up in the *Paradise Pioneer*.' He signaled for Dinky to bring the check.

'Shall we go Dutch?' Kelly asked. She didn't want to owe handsome anything.

'The hint of Italian in me would rather treat you, if you don't mind. Don't forget this is the rib bruise apology lunch. Besides, I'll overcharge you for the legal advice and recoup in no time.'

Man, he was smooth. 'Well, thank you again.'

Sam paid the bill with cash and the wacky winking waitress kept up her eye-batting. Kelly figured the girl must have a tic. Actually, the whole *town* must have a tic. He held her coat for her like a genuine gentleman. She slipped into it. At least he didn't button her up. They walked out with all eyes upon them.

'My goodness, are you a famous celebrity in this town?' Kelly looked behind them.

'I've been out of commission as far as dating goes since my return. It's a shock for them to see me with a woman. There's probably a bet out since the last time. How many months will it take Sam Grayson to date again? Whoever picked six months will be buying a round at Town Tavern tonight.'

'There's a tavern here? And Town Tavern is the actual name?' Kelly watched Sam smile a confirmation. Unbelievable. 'And this lunch qualified as a date?' she continued.

'I'd say the criterion was for me to appear in public with a gorgeous woman. You definitely filled the bill. Plus don't forget I took your hand in public. That was probably worth another twenty bucks. Bonus bucks.'

'I'm happy to oblige. I'm thrilled to be a bonus buck kind of girl.' Kelly felt an edge in her voice. She had the feeling Mr. Grayson was categorizing her in some very interesting slot.

Plus she was also getting very nervous about telling Sam Grayson her problems.

5

They went four blocks north to the neatly landscaped Grayson Building. Her red sandals were starting to pinch. Wrong shoes for the occasion, and somehow this occasion was starting to feel like a trip to the principal's office in junior high.

The Grayson Building was placed in a parklike area of Japanese maple trees and expanses of lawn, along with a bank and medical center. The building had a very modernistic, Frank Lloyd Wright feeling. Each floor had a terrace completely surrounding it, with plants dripping down the brick and stucco exterior.

It was different, yet blended in nicely with the rest of town. There was a modern angular bronze sculpture in the courtyard. The building was seven stories, by far the tallest building in town.

Sam pointed to the top row of windows. 'That's where I live. I took the top floor and converted it into an apartment. Our law offices are on six. The rest of the building has a few accountants and insurance agents.'

'What possessed your family to build such a modern structure in Paradise?' Kelly asked.

'I think Dad wanted to shake up the place a bit.'

'Paradise must look beautiful from up there.'

'It's very picturesque. Paradise was a wonderful place to grow up. I should be done pretty soon,' Sam said.

It took her a minute to get the joke, but she did. It was probably quite true. Most men took till at least thirty to grow up.

A surprising black marble lobby held another sculpture. It almost looked like a Henry Moore – a bronze of a woman with a child. Very modern and smooth.

'That's not what I think it is, is it?' she asked.

'My mother is an art collector.'

'Wow, she doesn't mess around, does she?'

'She's passionate. The office was built to house it. My dad and I just borrow it to practice law in.' Sam punched the elevator button.

'You're a very amusing fellow, you know?'

'Lawyers without a sense of humor are just not fun people.' He gestured to the opening elevator and held one side open for her.

They got in. He punched six and moved real, real close to her. She had a little flashback to her last elevator ride – in her wedding dress, running away from Raymond.

Sam smelled good. His warmth was pervasive. This was an improvement over her last elevator free fall.

The receptionist on six looked up at Sam, took Kelly in, and did a classic mouth drop.

'Faith, I'll be in with Miss Applebee for about an hour. Can you hold my calls, please?'

Faith snapped her jaw shut, then answered, 'You bet, Sam. I'll bring in some coffee.' She had on one of those purple sweatshirts with a white collar. It had puffy-paint chickadees on the front. Her desk was spread out with a very elaborate arts and crafts project that included a doll's head. Faith was clearly someone's grandmother.

'She's not your grandmother, is she?' Kelly asked, as they stepped into Sam's office.

'Unofficial. She bakes the best zucchini bread in the county, can dismantle a hard drive, reinstall the motherboard, type about five hundred words a minute, plus a bunch of other stuff. She's usually not here on a Saturday. Her husband George must be watching football, and she needed to escape, I'd guess.'

Sam sat down behind his desk. She perched herself on one of his client chairs. Brown leather. She batted at a huge office palm that reached its fronds out and tickled her cheek. She kept her coat on. She pulled at the hem of her skirt. She clutched her small red leather purse in her lap. Then she told herself to stop fidgeting.

Faith brought in two cups of coffee on a tray with sugar and cream, Kelly explained her usual – three lumps of sugar, black. Faith served both Sam and Kelly in fall leaf design mugs. It was so homespun. Homespun law, Paradise style. Faith exited, and Kelly sipped the coffee, then set it down on Sam's desk.

'Let me just change hats here from lunch date and rib crusher to legal eagle.' Sam opened a desk drawer, took out a green plaid golf cap, and placed it at a jaunty angle on his head.

Kelly started laughing. A thing she did when she was nervous. 'You are a total cornball, Grayson. You belong in a Jimmy Stewart movie.'

'Thanks. Now, what's the problem?' He handed her a Kleenex box. Her laughing tears were running down one cheek. Then he sat back with his mug and took a sip.

'I need a divorce.'

Coffee sprayed out of Sam's mouth. He coughed and reached for a napkin. His chair skidded backward and hit into one of the office palms, which fell on him. He fought it back into place.

Kelly jumped up. 'Geez, Sam, are you okay?'

'Fine.'

'Can I give you a Heimlich?'

'Maybe later.' He rose and grabbed the offending chair like it had betrayed him, then sat firmly down and faced her.

He straightened his golf cap. 'Where were we?'

'My divorce. It's a bit of a story.'

Married. She was married. He'd figured she'd been in an auto accident or had some other personal injury matter. He took out his damned yellow legal pad and smacked it on the desk. She jumped. He got a damned pen. He was an idiot.

'What state did you marry in?'

'California.'

'California?'

'Yes.'

He could feel beads of sweat form on his forehead. He smacked his hand against it and rubbed, then ran his fingers through his hair.

'You didn't hurt your head on that palm tree, did you?'

'Only wounded pride.' He took in a deep breath and tried to gather himself. There was a rock in the pit of his stomach. 'I can tell you the process. The divorce can be filed anywhere the court can get jurisdiction over both parties and their community assets, so where is the spouse?' He hated even saying the word.

'L.A.,' she answered.

'I do know someone down there. I'll do some research and see what I can find. You're not in a hurry, are you?' It was an odd question, and he wondered why he'd asked it.

'Not really.'

Okay, so she was married. She was getting a divorce. So what? He could pick up with her later, right? Divorced women were nothing new. She was taking a positive step. Right?

He took off his golf hat and stuck it back in the drawer with a slam. 'I'll need some information. Names, marriage date, assets, that sort of thing.'

A very long pause came from across his desk. Kelly shifted in her chair. In his experience this was not a good sign.

'The thing is, I'm not Kelly Applebee.'

The rock in his stomach rolled over. Here we go.

'My name is Kelly Atwood.'

'That's close.'

'I'm sorry I lied to you, but I have reason to believe my husband might try and track me down.'

Great. Crazed husband. Should he even ask? 'What makes you think that?' He went ahead, tapping his pen against his forehead, which was beginning to ache.

'I stole his car.'

Sam smacked the pen down and got up. 'Maybe you better tell me the whole story.' He paced the long side of the office.

'We got married.'

'How long ago?'

'About a week ago.'

'You're filing for divorce after, what, seven or eight days, and you stole his car?'

'I thought you were going to let me tell you the whole story.'

'Yes. Continue. Please.' He sat back down and stared at the car thief with the red dress, hot-red lips, stick-up hair, navel ring, and tattooed leg. This, he was thinking of dating. He might as well be in a B movie.

'We came home from the wedding and were getting ready to leave for Jamaica. I found cocaine in the lining of his suitcase. I confronted him about it, and he slapped me.'

'He slapped you?' Something in Sam got dark. He hated that kind of crap from a man. 'Had he ever done that before?'

'No. Quit interrupting.' She chewed at her lower lip,

which made it swell up, Sam noticed. 'Then I knocked him out,' she said.

Sam put his head in his hands and bowed over his desk. She went on.

'He must have forgotten I was left-handed, and I kind of surprised him. He fell against a coffee table and hit his head. I ran and got my stuff and when I heard him start to come to, I got out. I took his BMW. But it was partly mine. I helped pay for it.'

Sam lifted his head. 'You shared the car? Did you live with him? What's his name?'

'Raymond. Raymond Bianchi. Yes, we'd lived together for two years. We shared expenses, we worked together—'

'And you didn't know anything about his drug use?'

'No. He hid it well. Actually, I don't think he used as much as he probably sold.'

'He sold drugs.' Things just kept getting better. Car thief with red dress, hot-red lips, stick-up hair, navel ring, and tattooed leg married to L.A. drug dealer.

'As far as I know. We were only married three hours. Can't I get an annulment or something?'

Sam looked up into a pair of big, female, pale green eyes. Her lip was quivering, a small tear slid down her cheek. Why him?

'It looks like you may have some jointly held assets in California, so I'll have to check on California laws. It's another world down there. Co-habitating for two years adds another level to the mix. Exactly what line of work were you in? You and Raymond.' The rock in his gut jumped. What's it gonna be, escort service? Adult films?

'Fashion district. We repped high-end Italian and French designer clothing.'

'Repped?'

'Represented. Raymond owned a showroom, and I worked for him. Buyers from stores come and look at your goods and order for their stores. We were sort of unofficial partners. I handled things when he was out of town. That's about it.'

'Oh,' Sam said. Hell, it could have been worse. Way worse. Still, Sam felt like he'd been steamrollered. 'I'll make some calls and get back to you by the end of next week.'

She stood up and adjusted her skirt. 'I better get back to work.'

'Yes.' He stood as well. 'Can I walk you back?' He wanted to walk her back, but he wanted to think, too. Thinking clearly didn't take place within three feet of Kelly Apple . . . Atwood.

'No.'

'Okay.' He abruptly opened the office door. She went ahead of him. He walked her past Faith and out to the elevator. She pushed her own button.

'I guess I'll see you tonight?' she asked.

'What?'

'Dottie Williamson. Potato salad. Presbyterians.'

'Oh, yes, yes.'

She stepped into the elevator. Facing him, she stared right into him. The doors shut, and that was that.

*

Kelly cried. She had one Kleenex wadded up in her fist, and she put it over her mouth to catch her sobs.

Whatever the hell she was crying about, she didn't even know. So, Sam Grayson thought she was a criminal, and a slut, and a – who knows what? Who cares? She was here to give Paradise a go.

She liked the town. She liked the quirky people and the stuck-in-time feeling. Just because one person didn't fit into that picture, just because one man knew her real world – her before-this-world – it wasn't going to stop her from making a life in Paradise.

She'd just avoid him. The elevator opened. What the hell was this thing with elevators and her life?

She wiped her face with the shreds of Kleenex and started back toward town, down the wide sidewalks, down past the changing red maples turning rusty yellow.

When she passed Van Decker's her heart squeezed in her chest. 'Thank you for a lovely afternoon,' she said softly, to no one but herself.

What was she even thinking? Get a grip, Kelly. She was a married woman living under a fake name, with drug money stashed under her bed.

A guy like Sam probably had a girl in every county anyway.

Sam shifted the truck into second gear and rounded the corner of Pearl Street. Four o'clock. He'd had three hours to think through everything Kelly Atwood had told him.

After she'd left he'd sat with a legal pad and made a list. Pro and con. *Con* was long. She lied and she stole, though with some technicalities that could excuse both. She had huge problems. She made bad choices in men. She was married. She was tattooed. She was probably being pursued. She was undoubtedly going to blow out of town within the month, if not sooner. Paradise was just a hideout for her.

Pro was less specific, and very short. One, she had a sense of self-preservation and should be commended for leaving a terrible situation. Two, he'd really like to help her get the divorce. And three, she was delectable. Delicious. Desirable.

Damn.

He was going to cling to the long and negative *con* list with every last ounce of intelligence he had. He was going to make a wise choice this time, one that was not based on physical attraction. He might help her out of a jam, but that's the only thing he was going to help her out of.

He'd made a commitment to Mrs. Williamson. After that he could put in an hour at the social and graciously exit.

6

Sam drove up to the Williamsons' house in a cream-colored 1950s Chevy pickup truck. A peach of a vintage vehicle. Kelly was watching from behind the swagged sheer ruffled curtains of Dottie's living-room window, trying to act cool. Dottie Williamson was watching, too, but she wasn't even attempting coolness – she elbowed Kelly, and whistled, 'Now we're talking! What a hunk!'

'Dottie, I'm shocked!' Kelly laughed.

'Don't be, dear. I raised three teenage boys. I've seen it all.'

They both watched Sam stride up the walk. His casual clothes were quite a contrast to the lawyer suit, but the faded Levi's and soft white polo shirt still showed off his incredible physique. In fact, Kelly was rather in awe of this, and Dottie had to pull her away from the window before he got too close and saw them. He knocked. Dottie opened the door casually.

That gave Kelly a moment to remember that as stunning as Sam was, he wasn't for her.

'Why, hello, young man. You must be Kelly's new

friend.' Dottie stood at the door with her back to Kelly. Sam towered over her petite frame and blue-gray hair.

Great. Kelly's new friend. Like Dottie hadn't known Sam his whole life. This whole setup was crazy. She was going to have to have a talk with the local matrons and get them to back off. She needed to explain to them that the great Henry Samuel Grayson Jr. needed a straight-off-the-rack corporate girlfriend. How come he and Ponytail Blondie didn't hook up? Lynnette might be nuts, but she fit the part.

'Hello, Mrs. Williamson. Nice to see you again.' He brought a bouquet forward. 'These are for you.' He handed a bright bunch of cosmos, snapdragons, tiger lilies, and baby's breath to Dottie. Dottie looked at Kelly with that Paradise-wink look.

'Thank you, Sam. These are lovely. We'll take them to church for the table.' Dottie took two steps and toe-stretched a kiss on Sam's cheek. Kelly could swear she saw him blush.

'I'll just go put these in some water. You have lipstick on your face, son,' Dottie said.

There was awkwardness. Huge, zit-on-your-nose awkwardness.

Sam broke it. 'Ladies, let's get this show on the road.' He reached in his pocket, took out a blue bandana, and wiped the lipstick off his cheek.

'Right this way, kids,' Dottie took over. She directed the loading of foodstuffs, plus the addition of Sam's bouquet. Kelly was amazed at the amount of food Dottie had produced: three blackberry-blueberry pies, four huge bowls of potato salad, two big pots of baked beans, and two plates of fried chicken. Martha Stewart could just move on over. The Paradise women were her equals in every way.

'You ride with Sam, honey. My husband Walt will be here in a second to pick me up.'

Kelly was having second thoughts about having let Ginny stuff her into this countrified peasant blouse and a full gauzy red skirt – red with tiny flowers. It was the weirdest outfit she'd had on in her life, but it was working. The blouse had a habit of falling off one shoulder, so Ginny made her wear a strapless. It made her breasts seem more structured than normal. Funky. She slid into the bench seat next to Sam. He closed the passenger door and went around to his side.

The Chevy purred into action. The black and chrome dash gleamed with polish. The knobs had been re-chromed.

'Three on the tree, redone black leather, panoramic wrap on the rear window. 'Fifty-five?' she guessed.

''Fifty-six. Cameo.'

'Wow, that's rare.'

'Car buff?'

'I used to read *Vintage Car* magazine. One of my mom's more long-term boyfriends subscribed.' Kelly shut her mouth. She didn't want to tell Sam one more seedy, downtrodden thing from her past. She wanted to go to her first church social ever and pretend she was born here.

When they arrived at the church, they all pitched in

unloading. The reverend, Sam, and some of the other men were set to work putting up more chairs around the perimeter of the room.

The women organized the food buffet on long white linen-covered tables. Warm rolls, fruit salads. The seemingly endless offerings filled an entire side of the church hall.

Someone sat down at an old upright piano and started playing a familiar ragtime tune. Everyone's tasks took on a ragtime rhythm.

Kelly watched, amazed, as the event unfolded. The hum of conversations and greetings as people arrived took on its own music and got louder as more people came in.

The hall had a wall of French doors that opened to a lovely courtyard. Young people wandered outside with their plates of food.

Kelly wallflowered herself back behind the piano player and listened to people talk. She learned that Lydia Peterson, the church organist and sister of Mavis of the stuffed cat, was at the piano. Some of the choir members were singing. A few couples were dancing. Kids were eating big bowls of vanilla ice cream with chocolate or butterscotch sauce. Mothers were spooning bites into gleeful babies with gooey faces.

Kelly felt like crying again. She should be happy. This was exactly what she wanted. This was the Andy Hardy movie she'd been waiting for. But something was missing.

Ginny came up beside her with one of her kids draped over her shoulder, hollering.

'Scotty's having a time-out. Mind if we join you?'

'Not at all.' Kelly grabbed a cookie off the table and handed it to screaming Scotty. He shut up immediately, mouth full, and grinned at her over Ginny's shoulder.

Ginny turned and gave her a glare. 'Are you hiding back here?'

'Yes.'

'It's a social. That means you meet people. You're the new girl.'

'Thanks for the dress-up. I blend in better. Every third girl has the same outfit.'

'Happy to oblige. 'Course, only about two of them are your size. Now come and get a plate of food. Food is the door to acceptance in this town, in case you didn't notice.'

'Did you know I don't even know how to boil water? I'm a kitchen flunkout. I've eaten takeout food my entire life.'

'Time for a change. Try some of Dottie's chicken. She could teach you everything in a week. She would, too.'

'Myrtle is trying to fatten me up. It's fun.' Kelly was hungry. She grabbed a thick white church plate and started down the row. Where was Myrtle, anyhow? Kelly thought she was closing up early today.

There was a plate of biscuits still hot from the warming oven. Her mouth actually watered. The pile on her plate grew high.

Sam Grayson got in line behind her. His friendly voice, his friendly face. Why shouldn't she just have a good time with him? No harm in that.

*

'Damned amazing, isn't it?' So this was why Dottie Williamson had shoved him toward the food. Hell, at least he could be nice to Kelly. She was new here, and he'd watched her hide in the corner for twenty minutes until Ginny dragged her out. It was his civic duty.

'Yes. I've never seen this much food in my life.'

'I'm sitting with Will and Ginny outside. You're welcome to join us.' Polite. He was just being polite. Her blouse dropped off one shoulder. One bare, smooth shoulder, just inches away from him. Fortunately, his hands were full of plate and silverware.

Ginny and Will were seated under an old magnolia tree with the now-calm Scotty and his older sister Beth. Beth was picking up seed pods and lobbing them into her little brother's curly brown hair. Scotty kept brushing his hand up to figure out what was landing on him.

'Hey, Kelly,' Will said. A man of few words.

Sam had spread out a blanket next to Will and Ginny's and now positioned himself against the trunk of the tree, trying to balance a plate on his lap.

'Room for one more on the trunk here,' Sam said, trying to get his fork to stick into a piece of pineapple.

Kelly scrunched herself up next to him, rearranging her skirt to cover those great legs of her. Sam tried to focus on his sweet and sour pork.

Scotty started hollering again, his head full of pods. Beth tried to look innocent.

'We're going to the playground. C'mon, you two. Tell it to Dinky Van Decker. She's on playground duty.'

Ginny carried off the three-year-old, with the five-year-old in tow. Ginny whispered something to Will before she left.

'Thanks for this. I'm glad you asked me to the tree. I was being a wallflower,' Kelly said.

He gave up on his food for a minute, set the plate down. Like she could ever be a wallflower. She was truly a strikingly beautiful girl – even with that spiky hair. A brown leather belt with gold medallions cinched in her skirt waist and held that blouse up – sort of.

'Eating is the strangest thing to do in front of someone, don't you agree?' she went rambling on.

'Kelly, I find you extremely attractive, but . . . you . . . you're married.' His brain tried to sort things out. His body was winning, and his brain was most definitely losing.

She moved closer. A wonderful heat crept up his spine.

'Am I? Does a three-hour marriage I want out of count? If I hadn't married him for a few hours, I'd simply be free of a two-year relationship. Would you even think twice about it?'

'Probably not,' Sam answered. *Except for the rest of it*, he told himself silently. He searched his brain for the *con* list. It was in there somewhere. Fake name, stole the car— oh, there it was.

'And where is it written we can't just have a good time together? Does everything have to be so serious? How about we just enjoy the evening, then call it a night and move on to other people?'

'Makes perfect sense to me. Let's just have a good time,' Sam answered. It did. It made sense. He was so damned confused around her. It was the first thing that had made sense in two days.

'Good. Now I'm going to eat this hot biscuit before it cools off,' Kelly announced. She felt a huge sense of relief. Now she could just hang with friends and enjoy her church social moment.

She bit into the incredibly good biscuit and dropped a glob of raspberry jam onto her . . . boob.

Sam took his napkin and gently gathered the jam off her. Some got on his fingers, and he licked it off. Kelly swallowed what she had in her mouth before she choked on that, too.

'Beautiful church, isn't it? Great setting.' Sam said this as he wet another napkin with his ice water and wiped the rest of the raspberry jam off Kelly. Slow, long strokes.

Kelly was about to have an orgasm at the church potluck.

'Sam.'

He stared at her for a minute. She watched his brain kick in. He poised the napkin in midair, then set it down and grabbed up his plate. They ate in silence for a while.

'Ahem. Would you care to dance, Kelly?' Will Palmer stood in front of her. She hoped he hadn't witnessed too much of the boob moment, though how he could have avoided noticing, she didn't know.

What the hell, this might be a good moment for a break. 'Sure, Will.' Kelly got up, dusted herself off, and took Will's arm. She gave a backward glance at Sam. He was looking mighty surprised.

Will took her hand and led her inside the hall onto the dance floor. Lydia, the organist, had been joined by two very old men, one on a bass fiddle, one with a violin. Wait, it was Red Miller on the bass. The trio was playing 'Let Me Call You Sweetheart.' Four members of the choir sang in barbershop-style harmony.

Ginny's husband guided her into a swaying waltz to match the 1890s tune. He was a pretty good dancer. No talk, just dance. He spun her around. She laughed from a part of herself she probably hadn't felt since she was a little child.

The piece finished, Will gave a bow, partners traded, and she found herself with Reverend Evans, who did a lively foxtrot, whatever that was. Across the room, she saw Sam dancing with little Bethie Palmer, her black patent-leather shoes on top of Sam's brown leather loafers as he guided her through some high-spirited steps.

Kelly felt her heart ache. It wasn't a bad ache. It was a good one. She looked all around the room at the residents of Paradise.

Myrtle had made an entrance at some point and was being danced around the room by a very distinguished-looking older man. She gave Kelly a wave. They looked like Fred and Ginger doing some pretty fancy steps.

Myrtle looked stunning in a bright green two-piece knit suit. Kelly wondered if it was from Myrtle's past. It looked very fifties and made her red hair stand out even more. She also wore about a two-inch stack of beads, must be crystal, all catching the light. Myrtle was really something.

As they changed partners for the second time she was paired with Red Miller's cousin Carl, who grinned the whole time as they did a sort of modified swing dance.

She caught a glimpse of yellow – the girl from the coffee shop, Lynnette, had on a yellow shirt-dress. Ponytail Lynnette. Sam had ended up dancing with her, and looked trapped.

The song ended. Some quick moves on the part of some familiar faces, like Dottie and Walt, brought her smack into Sam's arms.

'We meet again,' Sam said.

'Small town,' Kelly countered.

He was a wonderful dancer. Sam seemed to do everything well. She let the sense of safety he created enfold her.

The harmony of the choir was sweet as a summer night. She put her head on his shoulder and swayed to the music.

Someone turned the lights low, and dozens of twinkling lights came on, inside and out. The quartet faded off, but the bass, piano, and violin played on. They moved from one song into the next without pausing. The music was lovely.

The idea of just hanging out for tonight and moving on was getting very twisted up in her head. After she'd left his office she'd figured that was the end of it. Now here they were in each other's arms. Every time they got around each other, the space between them became more . . . compact.

His body moved against hers as they danced. She felt his heat and his passion and his heart beating hard. She felt the wildness between them, and she let herself fall into it.

'You're making me crazy, Kelly,' he whispered in her ear. His breath was hot on her neck. He pressed his lips to the side of her neck. She felt her reason slipping away.

The last strains of 'You'd Be So Nice to Come Home To' ended. Kelly lifted her head to see the entire dance floor empty except for them. Smiling faces lined the edges of the room. Except for that not-so-happy frown on the face of devil-in-a-yellow-dress Lynnette.

If she didn't know better, she'd think it was a plot, this partner shuffling to get her with Sam. Kelly realized they'd played about three slow songs in a row.

Suddenly everyone started to clap. Now, that was too much. Someone flipped on a spotlight and craned it toward the piano. Kelly felt some relief. At least it wasn't shining on them. Sam kept his arm around her waist.

Much to Kelly's surprise, Cora Barnes, owner of Cora's Café, stepped up to the microphone. She had on a long, simple, coral-pink dress and wore a pink lily in her hair.

The bass picked up a deep beat, joined by the violin and piano for the opening bars. Cora's voice came rolling out like a velvet carpet. She sang an old standard love song, 'I'm in the Mood for Love.' People started to dance again.

Sam swept her up in his arms. Kelly was amazed, confused and, most of all, wanting to be held by Sam Grayson. She felt like she'd fallen down the rabbit hole and Paradise was her own personal Wonderland. As she leaned her cheek against Sam's shoulder, she felt fear come over her.

Why, now that she had what she'd wanted all her life being offered up to her, was she even hesitating?

She was tired of thinking. Tired of hiding and tired of being lonely. Being in Sam's arms and listening to Cora's magical voice was enough to make it all fade away.

Kelly sang 'I'm in the Mood for Love' softly.

The full moon was shining through the trees as Sam pulled the truck to a stop by Paradise Park. 'We used to skinny-dip in the pond here when I was in high school,' Sam said.

'Was that the plan tonight? I think I ate too much.'

Sam leaned forward in the seat of the truck and looked out of the windshield at the stars against the October night sky. It was crystal clear, and the chill crept in right away, as soon as the heat shut off.

'Plus, I'm sorry to tell you, Sam, but it's bitchin' cold out there,' Kelly continued.

'No skinny-dipping. We can just talk.' Talking was his thing. He was a lawyer. He could do this. Why had he brought her here?

'Your town puts on one hell of a church social.'

'Presbyterians take their Harvest Social very seriously.' Sam turned out the truck lights and grabbed a blanket from behind the seat. 'Let's get out and take a walk in the park.' Translation: *Let's get the hell out of this truck before I forget my resolve to have complete control where my love life is concerned. Do I need to remind myself what kind of pain I went through with Chelsea?* It was a long translation.

'Okay, but you'll have to loan me that blanket,' Kelly said. She got out on her own and danced around, rubbing her bare arms. 'I can see my breath. Where I come from we don't do cold, you know.'

'Here.' Sam came around and wrapped the car blanket around her. 'Do you want my jacket?'

'Nah, this is fine. But let's move.'

He wanted to keep her warm. More than that, he wanted to repair her past and let her have at least one night of Paradise magic before she ran off to some other town. She was like Cinderella at the ball tonight. Too bad he wasn't her Prince Charming, but at least he could be less of a toad before the clock struck midnight and she vanished.

He put his arm around her. They walked toward the slope of lawn. The grass was dewy and cool and soft as a carpet. Kelly stopped and took off her shoes. She let her tired feet sink into the grass. She ached from dancing and cleaning up and from being happy.

Sam took off his shoes and socks, too, not too gracefully though. He ended up hopping on one foot, until she laughed hard. She reached out to steady him. He took her hand and kissed it. 'Don't start with me, Grayson. If you start, I'll start.'

'I'm not starting. I'm just being nice.'

'Will you stop being so damn nice?'

'What are my other choices?'

'God, I don't know.'

'Okay, I'll sing.'

'You wouldn't, would you?'

Sam proceeded to sing 'Bicycle Built for Two' very loudly in his deep baritone voice.

'You are the Corn King. King Corn.' Kelly laughed until she thought she would pee, then she joined in.

They reached a small pond with benches and tables scattered around the edges. The moon gave everything a soft look. Sam zeroed in on one bench and as soon as she got close enough, pulled her into his lap. It was cold, and Kelly snuggled close. Because of the cold. Yes, that's it, the cold, she told herself.

'So. Do we talk about this thing?' Sam asked.

'Let's just not. Let's watch the lake and bask in the glow of the Presbyterians' harvest moon.'

She leaned close and her fragrance drifted into him. For someone who was cold, she felt like a wildfire against him. She leaned her head back and relaxed. He could feel her body in his arms, all warm and inviting.

'There's only one problem with this idea,' he said softly in her ear.

'What, you feel compelled to verbally dissect something?'

'No, that's not it.'

'What, then?' Kelly was getting slightly annoyed. She

squirmed out of his grasp and twisted around to look in his face.

'I seem to be unable to resist kissing you.'

'Well, damn you, Grayson, just do it.'

Sam did. He pulled her to him and kissed her hard, right on the lips first off. A smoldering, knock-your-good-sense-to-the-wall kiss that made her forget any hint of chill she'd felt before. He ran his fingers gently over her temple, across her cheek, and down her neck. Then his mouth followed every inch of the fingertip trail. Kelly slowly melted into his arms.

When his mouth moved back up and found hers full on, she knew she was in trouble. It was like someone had turned the heat up on the back burner *way* high. His kiss burned into her and made her ache – her breasts ached to be the next victim of that mouth of his, and so did the rest of her.

He kissed like a sensuous, hypnotic magician. Her pulse had reached her temples, and she could feel her body come alive in every hungry spot she had. The ache became intense. He kissed light, then deep, in a lingering way. Kelly made a tiny sound, a taste-of-heaven sound.

She touched his face, then looked into his dark blue eyes. The moon was reflected there. Kelly kissed him with all the emotion the night had given her. He responded to her with a tender, strong passion Kelly had never experienced before.

Kelly let the blanket drop as his mouth moved down her neck, kissed her shoulders, exploring the curve of her collarbone. His kisses drove her wilder than anything she'd ever experienced before.

She wanted him to take her right there in Paradise Park. She pushed him back against the bench and straddled his lap. Her arms wove around him. He took a gasping breath as she tilted her head and kissed him.

She felt the heat from his body; felt him throbbing through his jeans. His hand brushed lightly against her breasts, just across her nipples. She arched her back and made some animal noise she had never heard herself make before.

He slowly untied the string of her blouse and let it fall off her shoulders. The strapless pushed out of the way, he leaned down and took her breast, his tongue like magic, like stars inside her. The stars were all around her then. She pressed herself against him and felt the heat shoot through her. She shuddered and cried out his name, aching with the desire he had released, letting herself throb against his hardness.

The distant headlights of a car passed over them for a second, bringing Kelly out of her dream.

'Wait a minute, wait a minute. Oh, my *God!*' she squealed, sitting up suddenly. She climbed off him, dizzy and hot and . . . still throbbing.

'It is a damn good thing there are no streetlights here. What are we, *nuts*? We have known each other like, what, one week? And we're in the middle of a public park getting crazy?'

She tried for serious but felt too giddy to carry it off.

She was necking in the park, for pity's sake. She started laughing, and he laughed along with her. She flopped back down on the bench, pulling the blanket over her again.

Sam gathered her back into his arms and turned her toward him. 'You have a point there, but hey, we still have our clothes on,' he pulled up her blouse and retied its little drawstring, a pretty sexy act in itself. 'Almost on anyway.'

'Obviously we are sexually attracted to each other.' Kelly tried to sound serious, but Sam kept grinning.

'Obviously.'

'You must think . . .' She pulled the blanket closer around her.

'I think you are a fantastic, sexy woman with normal needs. I'm glad you feel free with me.' Sam toyed with her disheveled hair. 'So how long can we decently go without . . . you think? I'm just assuming we're on the same page here?'

'Yep, same page.' She pulled him into a kiss. Same page, all right. She wanted him bad.

Then she shoved him away. She'd better get herself together. Where would a night of hot sex with the town's favorite guy get her? Maybe tarred and feathered if they all thought she'd used him and thrown him away, because the chances of Sam's going forward into an actual relationship with her were extremely slim. She'd better do something about that right now.

'Five dates, I think. That would be a reasonably

proper amount of time, wouldn't it? Now that the initial edge is off,' Kelly offered, backing away from his tempting kiss an inch at a time on the bench. Brr, her end of the seat was cold.

'Whose edge is off?' He pulled her back, his mouth hot on her mouth, his tongue dancing with hers, until she agreed. The edge was definitely still there.

'Five dates. We have to do this right, because . . .'

'Because . . .' Sam said.

She kissed him back, mercilessly, then continued.

'Five dates, because we both live in this town now, and just because we're both starved for sex doesn't mean we should necessarily indulge ourselves. We should take some time to get to know each other, and we should get me a divorce.'

'We'll look into that Monday. What are you doing for the next five days?' he asked.

'Very clever. I should say four weeks, then, because there's a chance I'll be completely free of . . . former stuff by then.'

'So, what you are looking for is an old-fashioned courtship ritual?' Sam asked.

'Yes, I think that's it. Something befitting Paradise. Something in keeping with my delusions of small-town life. Are you up for that?'

'Oh, I'm up for it, all right. Four weeks it is, then,' Sam agreed, and she sealed it with another kiss.

'I'll pick you up tomorrow morning,' he mumbled into her mouth.

*

Kelly sat at her Hawaiian dressing table wrapped in a towel. She pictured herself going wild with Sam in the middle of Paradise Park and slapped her hand against her forehead.

What in the hell was she doing? She was still a married woman, for pity's sake. Of course, she'd given him a pretty good argument on that point. Three hours does not a marriage make. Its legality was a technicality she needed to repair.

Kelly thought about Raymond. One make-out session with Sexy Sam was hotter than her and Ray's entire two-year sex life. She'd thought that a few times on the ride home, but felt guilty and had put it aside. It was true, though. She realized her reasons for marrying Raymond had very little to do with passion and more to do with the stability she thought he gave her.

She was too tired to sort it all out tonight. Kelly brushed her hair with the brush from a pretty set Myrtle had dug up for her. It looked like old ivory but was really Bakelite. Smooth edges. It made her feel elegant.

She slipped her silkiest nightgown over her head and slid between the cool sheets. Kelly sank into the wonderful sensations of remembering Sam's touches. How hungry she was for loving touches.

Her head was filled with Sam Grayson, and she drifted into dreams of waltzing with Sam. Waltzing naked.

Sam sat outside Myrtle's in his Chevy for a very long time, his arms folded against the steering wheel, his head leaning on them. What the hell was he doing?

He'd had it all worked out in his head to just leave things with Kelly, enjoy her company, then move on. Then his more *basic* instincts got in the way.

He saw how the Paradise ladies had worked hard to get them together tonight. I mean, who sings 'I'm in the Mood for Love' at a church social? So the town thought she was his match. So he'd have to tell every single one of them they were wrong. They didn't know what *he* knew about her.

Sure, she was soft and smooth and wild, and it made his blood boil just thinking about the string on her blouse. So what? Damn, he was one confused man, and that was highly compounded by the fact he'd never had any woman turn him on like that before. The way she threw herself over him and let him take her all the way to throbbing all over him was just too damn sexy even to think about right now.

On the other hand, she didn't seem to scare off tonight. If she *were* on the edge of running, she wouldn't have agreed to a month of dating. Would she? Was she actually looking for a home? Sam's head told him she was an incredible flight risk. She was hiding out, not settling down.

But he did sense her strong desire to create some artificially perfect place. Paradise had that effect on lots of people. Maybe on him as well.

Sam whacked his head against his folded arms. She'd really put a wrench in his plans. He knew it wasn't macho, but he had a powerful longing to march down the aisle in a tuxedo, to carry his bride over the threshold, and to have a couple of kids climb all over him when he got home. He wanted to show up at a family Thanksgiving with a wife. His parents would love that.

And how would his parents feel about *Kelly* at the holiday table? Hi, Mom and Dad, here's my recently divorced, car-thief, tattooed, runaway wife.

Maybe Kelly was just a detour on his road to the altar. A test of his resolve. Attractions were one thing. Life mates were another. He had to hang on to his visions of what he wanted in a marriage.

Men were supposed to run screaming from that kind of commitment, and here he was aching for it. He had enjoyed his single time, but at thirty-two, his biological clock must be ticking. Shit, did men even have those?

Before he let his heart get wrenched out by letting Kelly get under his skin, maybe he'd test *her* resolve. If she wanted a courtship, he'd give her one hell of a cornball Paradise-driven courtship. If she stuck around for the end of it, he'd be surprised. If she bolted, he'd have learned something.

He'd know for sure that whatever part of him wanted to take home stray cats, fix them up, feed them, and give them a warm place to sleep was the part that needed to be locked up for good. It led him nowhere but Troubleville.

Most likely he was going to scare this stray cat right out of town, and he'd never see her again.

That would be real unfortunate if she ran, because he had never wanted a woman in his arms, in his bed, the way he wanted this one.

Sam started up the Chevy and drove a few blocks before he heard a car come up behind him. In his rearview mirror he caught the familiar look of Lynnette Stivers's black Trans Am.

What the hell was she up to now? His glimpses of her had become more frequent. Either Paradise really was a very small town or she was following him. Considering it was one o'clock in the morning, chances were she was up to her old tricks.

He hated to call Tom Blackwell again, the poor guy. It had to be totally humiliating for him, being in love with her and all.

The Trans Am turned down a side street. Heck, she wasn't hurting anyone. It could wait.

At nine o'clock on Sunday morning, Sam Grayson came through the door of the Hen House Beauty Parlor. Kelly was having her second cup of tea and she half dropped her cup into the saucer, causing it to clatter noisily.

'Sam! I wasn't expecting you so soon!'

'Uh-oh,' Myrtle said loudly. 'Did I forget to tell you Sam called to say he was coming over? It's Eastern Star Mother-Daughter Day, and my mind is in the clouds. You know we're only open two Sundays a year, and this is one of 'em.' Myrtle said all that without breaking her stride. She was doing Rhonda Pierson's hair in a foil, and Rhonda looked like an alien.

Sam was staring. Myrtle had on leopard leggings and a black turtleneck top – Kelly could see Sam was a little startled by both Rhonda and Myrtle.

'I'll be right out,' Kelly called from across the room. If ever a man needed an escape route, Sam was in need.

'Great, I'll . . . er . . . wait outside.' Sam backed out the door. The screen made its sprongy noise as he opened and shut it behind him.

As soon as he stepped back outside, Myrtle and her crew, Opal and Rhonda, and a few of the customers ran over to the window.

'Rayanne, come over here and check this out! Sam's such a kid at heart.'

'Geez, you guys, has it been that long since you saw a man around here?' Kelly grabbed her leather jacket and headed to the door. Then she stopped dead and stood holding the screen open wide, like her mouth.

There he stood on the sidewalk with a tandem bike and a large bouquet of daisies. He had on an old-fashioned tweed bicycle hat.

'Date number one!' Sam called.

Myrtle came over and put her arm around Kelly. 'He's smart, just not too subtle,' Myrtle said under her breath.

Kelly agreed. 'We might as well take an ad out in the *Paradise Pioneer: Local nutcase lawyer dates new girl in town.*'

She grabbed the strap of her shoulder bag and marched out the door, ready for anything.

'I thought you'd look sweet on a bicycle built for two,' Sam said as he handed her the daisies and kissed her cheek.

'Hold on, let me get my Brownie camera,' Myrtle hollered through the screen.

'Do Brownie cameras still exist?' Kelly asked. She and Sam posed for Myrtle, then waved goodbye and tried to get their act together. After some wobbly starts and flat-out falls, peppered by laughter coming from the Hen

House audience, they made a synchronized attempt.

'*One, two, three, go,*' Sam directed from the back. They jumped together, started pedaling madly, and were up! She heard clapping behind them.

'Hey, we work pretty well with each other, Miss *Applebee.*'

'That remains to be seen, Mr. Grayson. We haven't had our first fight yet.'

'Call me Sam, honey.'

Kelly craned around to give him a look, almost steering them into a tree. She straightened out abruptly as Sam started singing 'Bicycle Built for Two' again.

'What are you, nuts?' Kelly called over her shoulder.

They rolled along past neighbors and white picket fences until there were more hay fields than houses, and the road got bumpier. It took a really long time. Her butt was getting sore.

'Turn right here, Kelly.'

He directed her to a field with rolling grass hills surrounding a small lake. Willow trees bowed graceful branches into the calm water, the breeze lifting them like skirts.

They walked the bike to a picnic table. Sam proceeded to lay out a tablecloth, linen napkins, then china. Out came still-warm croissants wrapped in foil, fresh-squeezed orange juice, Brie, smoked honey ham, some kind of papaya chutney stuff, a very colorful melon and grape salad, and a wonderful-looking quiche.

'Quite the magician, Sam. Where did all this food come from?' Kelly asked suspiciously.

'Leftovers,' Sam replied. He slathered an open croissant with Brie and laid a piece of the fragrant ham across it with a smidgen of chutney, then offered Kelly a bite.

'From what, the social? This stuff comes from deeply gourmet roots, Sam.' Kelly shook her head.

'I confess. My mother's cook packed it for me.'

'Your mother's cook. I'm going to try and not think about that right now, okay?'

'Don't hold it against me.'

'We'll get to that part later.'

They spent the morning sitting side by side, talking and feeding each other the delights of the picnic basket. The sun warmed her back, and she fell into timelessness with him. It was the magical place couples go when they are falling in love with each other. A place she'd never been with Raymond.

Kelly was cautious as to how much she revealed about herself: her unhappy childhood, running away at sixteen, even working in L.A., she skimmed over most of it. She listened very carefully to Sam's family stories. No alcoholic parent, no abuse, no divorce, just Sam and his two younger sisters and two parents who actually cared. A tear slid down Kelly's cheek. Sam caught it with his fingertip.

'Where does this come from?'

'You, describing the family I will never have.' Two more tears rolled down. She put her head against his shoulder and breathed deeply to calm herself. The pain twisted way down deep within her.

'You could start your own, you know, be the first part of a new family; give your kids what you never had.'

'That sounds grand, but I would have to learn how. My only pictures of normal family life come from *Leave It To Beaver* reruns.'

'That's not a bad start,' Sam said. 'June and Ward were pretty tight. She just needed to get out of the kitchen more.'

'Yeah, and what was Ward doing in the garage all the time, anyway? Working out? I liked *Ozzie and Harriet*. They laughed it off more, and the sex was better,' Kelly said. She reached for a piece of melon and smiled a goofy smile at Sam.

'Oh so that's what all those fade-out scenes were in Ozzie and Harriet's TV scripts – sex?'

'Of course, didn't you know?'

'You have a wonderful sense of humor, Kelly, and a very loving heart. That's unusual for someone who's been through what you have. It could have made you very bitter.'

'Thank you, Sam.' She fed him a melon ball and he licked at her fingers.

'Four more dates,' he garbled through the melon. 'No, four *weeks*. Augh. Do we get to neck?'

'Yes.' She bent forward and let him kiss her. His kiss had a big hunger underneath it.

'But that's it.' She pushed him away. 'We can date as much as we like in that four weeks, though.'

'How about a daily double?' Sam took her hand and kissed her fingers one at a time.

'I suppose.' Kelly started to lose her speaking ability. He was getting her really hot again.

'Good, because that plan is already in effect, I just needed the green light from you. We might as well get to know as much of each other as we can. That didn't come out just right, did it?'

'Never mind, Ozzie.' She kissed him again. 'I'll just torture you a while longer.'

'I knew you would.'

He ran his hands lightly over her arms, slowly moving up to her face, her temples, and her lips. She moved up against him, intoxicated by his touches. His kisses were even better than last night. He seemed to be . . . learning her.

Sam finally stopped and sat up. He obviously needed a break from her relentless torture. She sat beside him and remembered once again they were in public when she saw an older couple walking down by the lake path. They glanced up at Sam and Kelly, smiled, and waved. Kelly picked a leaf out of Sam's hair.

'What is this place, Sam?'

'It used to be an old homestead. Fish Trap Lake. The property on the rise over there is Red Miller's cousin's place. That couple you saw are probably bordering neighbors.'

'It's beautiful. Is this where you Paradise High boys take your dates to make out?'

'Damn, what a good idea! I can't believe we never thought about it. Mostly, we all went to the Doggie Drive-in outside Lynden.'

'The Doggie Drive-in. That is, like, whacked.'

'Hey, the old guy named it for his dog.'

'Okay, I'm not even gonna go there. It's out of the *Ozzie and Harriet* realm.'

'Time to pack it up, Harriet, we've got to get ready for part two of today.'

She helped him pack up the basket, and after wobbly starts, their two-seater cruised down the road. They worked in rhythm with each other. The soothing motion of the bike helped Kelly quiet some of the thoughts racing through her head.

She'd said too much about her life. Normal people didn't like to hear about someone's hippie mother and her drug problems. He was quiet behind her. No singing.

Sam delivered Kelly to Myrtle's and gave her a proper porch kiss. Enough to make steam in her veins. He retrieved the daisy bouquet from the front basket on the bike.

'Pick you up at five. Got any Western gear?' He held out the flowers.

'Just jeans,' Kelly answered, puzzled. She took the flowers.

'What are you, about a size six?'

'Ten. Real women are not size six.' She threw a handful of wilted daisies at him.

'Shoes?'

'Seven and a half.'

'Them's some mighty dainty feet, ma'am.'

Kelly threw another handful of flowers at him. Sam

walked bowlegged to the bike and mounted it like a horse. She couldn't stop laughing.

'That's too much horse for you, cowboy!'

Sam wrestled the bike into the back of his pick-up, making horse noises, hollering, 'Whoa, there, Gluepot!'

Kelly waved and went in the door. Myrtle had been watching from the front window, of course, and clucked like a hen, slapping her knee, overcome by her own laughter.

'Sam always was a clown. Didn't I tell you he was just the ticket?'

Kelly plunked down on a vinyl chair. 'He is just too good to be true. He deserves someone better than me.' Kelly's voice cracked, then she burst out crying.

Myrtle glanced quickly over Kelly's shoulder as one customer leaned forward slowly from underneath the dryer. It was Lynnette Stivers, and Myrtle was sure she saw a smirk creep over Lynnette's hard features. Myrtle knew what she had to do. She grabbed a box of Kleenex.

'Nonsense, honey. Now take this and march over to the house.' She sounded like a drill sergeant, but that's what the girl needed right now. Kelly snuffled her way to the connecting house door obediently.

As soon as she was gone, Myrtle flipped up the dryer hood on Lynnette and plucked a curler from her blonde head.

'Ouch!'

'Well, you are toast for sure, Miss Stivers. Now, I'm sure your mama is waitin' for you to get all dolled up for

Eastern Star tonight. It's late. I'm gonna close up. You best be gettin' along. The curlers are on the house.'

Myrtle figured if Lynnette hadn't been so stunned, she might have had something to say back. All she did do was raise one drawn-on eyebrow at Myrtle, grab up her white purse, stick on her white sunglasses, and stalk out the door, curlers bouncing.

'Don't you give me the evil eye, Lynnette Stivers, you're lucky I don't put a curse on you! I'm an old witch, ya know!' Myrtle cackled as Lynnette drove off in her black Trans Am. 'That woman is trouble on fat tires,' she said out loud, as the other two customers clapped and cheered.

'Okay, gals, fun's over. Opal, you take over in here, I have to go see to Kelly,' Myrtle said. She steamrolled through the connecting door to take care of one hysterical former city gal. 'Must be a bad planet,' Myrtle mumbled to herself.

Myrtle sat down next to Kelly on her red sculptured mohair sofa. 'What is it, child?'

'I don't deserve him. He's too good for me,' she sobbed out.

Myrtle put her arm around Kelly. 'Honey, that is not true. You are just used to being treated badly. Think of him as a gift the cosmos sent you to make up for all the bad times.'

Kelly would have laughed, but she couldn't speak anymore. She cried like a baby against Myrtle's shoulder. She was a married woman with a suitcase of drug money, in love with the boy next door who was just too good to be true. She should leave Paradise and let Sam have a good life with someone's second cousin. But she was really starting to love it here. Paradise.

Myrtle handed her a Kleenex from her smock pocket. She rubbed Kelly's back and offered silent comfort. When Kelly calmed down a little, Myrtle went into the kitchen and fixed them each a cup of hot chocolate and a plate of Oreos. They sat and twisted cookie tops off, eating the double stuff in the middle. Kelly finally curled up under a blanket and napped on the sofa.

When she woke up a short while later, Myrtle was in the kitchen making fried egg sandwiches. There, perched on the chrome and red vinyl dinette chair sat Fred Hansen, the man Myrtle had danced with at the social.

Myrtle winked at Kelly, and right in front of Fred, reminded her that Fred had been a widower for five years now and they had a great friendship with occasional sex but neither cared to get married. Fred was set in his ways, she'd said. Fred nodded amicably throughout Myrtle's frank talk.

'Feeling better, sweetie?' Myrtle motioned her in and patted the barstool seat beside her.

'Very much. Hi, Fred. Are you golfing today?'

'If you want to call that cow pasture a golf course, you bet,' Fred replied. 'But first me and the boys are going to hit the driving range and improve our distance some. You know I occasionally take eighteen holes with Sam Grayson's dad.'

Kelly shifted closer to the table, suddenly interested. 'Is that so? What's he like?'

'Well, you'd never know Hank had all that money. He sings bass in the local theater group musical. The guy did a hell of a singing Frenchman in *South Pacific* last year. He's a regular sort of guy. Gives a lot back to the town.

'Built a swimming pool for the high school. Course, Sam was a champ swimmer, and they all said his daddy built it for him. That's kids, though. They forget the pool stayed behind after Sam left.'

'His mother came from Texas and taught us all a thing or two about Southern hospitality,' Myrtle chimed in. 'Sam's daddy met her in college, then brought her up here to his family. I hear tell her own folks were dirt poor, and her daddy was a drinker. She turned out mighty refined for all that.

'She used to teach art at the high school, before her children were born. She and Hank lost their firstborn son to meningitis. You can see how precious Sam was to them. He was next born after that loss.'

Myrtle kept up her pace. She was truly a gossip factory. 'They built the medical center as a remembrance to their lost baby, then replaced it ten years ago with the new center. She raised funds for that first center like a woman possessed. I think she transferred her grief into fundraising. Of course, if there had been a proper medical center here before, her first baby might have lived.'

'My goodness, how do you know so much about them?' Kelly asked.

Myrtle struck a familiar Bette Davis pose with one hand on her hip. 'Darlin', what else do women in a small town do but talk and gossip to their hairdresser?'

'Where did they get all that money in the first place?' Kelly asked.

'Sam's granddaddy was a banker,' Fred said. 'He made some good land deals. They managed through the Depression pretty well. He must have stashed his own money in a mattress instead of at his bank. Most likely he saw it coming and ducked.'

Kelly felt a chill tingle over her at the thought of money stashed under the bed. Myrtle looked at her funny.

'Well, that's enough gossip for today, ladies. My nine iron needs a warm-up, and so do I.' Fred leaned over and gave Myrtle a kiss, then took Kelly's hand in his and looked into her face.

'You're a wonderful gal, Kelly. Sam would be lucky to have you,' he said.

'Thank you, Fred.' Kelly smiled. She wished she could believe it herself.

As Fred left, Kelly walked slowly upstairs and drew herself a hot bath in the claw-footed tub. Tiredness seeped into her, despite the nap. She slipped out of her clothes and let them fall in a heap on the floor. The tub filled, and she added a few capfuls of lavender-scented oil.

She stepped into the bath and sank into the warmth. Kelly drifted into the feeling of Sam's arms around her.

Paradise had *so much* to give her. *Sam* had so much

to give her. How did she even get to that thought? She'd come here a week ago to hide out. She'd come straight from a wedding. She sure hadn't planned on getting involved with anyone.

Kelly pulled Myrtle's sea sponge into the bath, then set it on her forehead, letting the hot water drip over her closed eyes.

If she wanted Sam, or Paradise, or both, somehow she was going to have to set it all straight.

Tomorrow she would make some calls and figure out exactly what Raymond was up to, and whether he went on the honeymoon without her. It would help speed up the divorce if she could tell Sam exactly where he was. Divorce? Heck, they were only married three hours before she knocked him out and bolted; she could probably have Sam get the whole thing annulled.

Monday morning she'd call Caroline Prosser. Caroline was the closest thing to a good friend she had in L.A. She'd tell Sam what she found out afterward.

Caroline could find out where Raymond was. He might have already filed for divorce himself and done that thing where he published it in the paper. And even if he hadn't, she could be a free, unmarried woman in, what, ninety days?

A slow smile spread over Kelly's face, and she sank deeper into the water, returning to her more pleasant thoughts of Sam's arms around her and his fabulous kisses. Yes, that man could kiss the socks off a schoolmarm.

At five o'clock a delivery boy came to the door

carrying boxes from Duncan's Western Wear. He handed Kelly several large packages and grinned nervously as he waited for a tip, eyeing Kelly in her bathrobe.

Kelly scrounged in the bottom of her purse and came up with $2.50 in change.

Seeming pleased, the boy said, 'Thanks, ma'am,' and ran off.

He acted like that was probably the largest tip he had ever received. You're not in L.A. anymore, Dorothy, she realized.

She found Myrtle, and together they ripped into the brown-paper-wrapped boxes like kids. Inside one was a beautiful turquoise Western shirt with white embroidery and silver decorations.

Another box held the hat to match, and the third box had a pair of turquoise boots trimmed in silver and white.

Inside one of the boots they found a gray felt jewelry box. Kelly opened it and took out a stunning turquoise and silver necklace, very tasteful, not too gaudy, and a pair of earrings to match.

'My, my, my. Sam sure does know how to treat a lady,' Myrtle said. She held the shirt up to Kelly's front. 'This is a wonderful color on you.'

'It is beautiful, but do people actually dress like this? We aren't in Texas, you know.' Kelly giggled.

'Well, normally we don't get too gussied up in Paradise, so my guess is you are going to the Grant County Fair and Rodeo, dear. It's about forty miles east of here. You better hurry up, now. Sam seems to be the prompt type.'

'Okay. Let's get me all gussied up.'

Racing upstairs, Kelly got the basics on with her own jeans and called Myrtle up for inspection. The boots fit like a glove – thank goodness, because her feet weren't used to much but Keds and sandals lately. The slim boot toes reminded her of the ten pairs of Charles Jourdan high heels she'd left behind in Raymond's L.A. closet.

God, she missed those shoes. There were some benefits in working in the wholesale garment market, and getting wholesale prices from the shoe rep was definitely one of them. When she got the divorce she would ask for her shoes back.

'Looks like it was made for you.' Myrtle primped the shirt collar and turned Kelly to the full-length mirror.

'I look like Annie Oakley!' Kelly laughed at her reflection. 'I can't actually wear this, can I?'

'You'll be the queen of the rodeo. You can borrow my old six-shooter if you like. It has no bullets, but it looks scary. That ought to keep Sam in line.'

'That's assuming I want to keep him in line.' Kelly winked, and they both elbowed each other.

'*All* young men need keeping in line in my opinion, including Sam Grayson.' Myrtle smiled and helped Kelly fasten the silver necklace around her neck. They stood back for the full effect.

Myrtle reached over and took one of Kelly's hands. 'Just be kind to yourself, sweet cakes, and don't let anyone treat you badly. You get to choose now. You're a grown woman, not a child who has no say in how she is treated.' Myrtle gave Kelly a big hug.

'Quit it, you're going to make me cry again,' Kelly said.

Myrtle pulled a Kleenex out of her pocket and wiped Kelly's misty eyes.

'Then my makeup will run all over my face, and Sam will run away when he opens the door. You can only do that to a new man once.'

The doorbell rang on cue, and the two women raced downstairs like wild kids. Kelly took a deep breath and swung the door open.

There stood Sam, handsome as the devil in his Western duds. He was all in tan, with a dark brown suede jacket, brown boots, and hat. He tipped his hat back on his head and held out a bouquet of white roses and daisies.

'You look good enough to ride sidesaddle on my favorite horse, Wild Hair. These are for you, ma'am,' he offered.

'That is the second person that called me ma'am today. Am I looking matronly? Don't answer that. And you don't really have a horse out there, do you, Sam?' Kelly peered over his shoulder, half-expecting to see a couple of horses tied up waiting. 'Because I don't do horse, Sam Grayson.'

'Just horsepower. Excuse me, Myrtle, she needs kissing.' Sam took off Kelly's hat for a minute. Myrtle pretended to look away, but watched out of the corner of her eye as Sam gathered Kelly up and kissed her good.

'Mmm, thank you for the wonderful ... presents, Sam,' Kelly said breathlessly. She stepped back and steadied herself, somewhat embarrassed to be kissed in front of Myrtle. She took her hat back and popped it on her head. 'Okay, cowboy. Let's hit the road. We have a rodeo to get to.'

'How'd you guess?' Sam kidded.

Myrtle sang 'Happy Trails' after them.

Sam drove the Chevy straight down the east highway to a place that glowed in the dark called the Starlight Diner. It looked like a railroad car, but Sam gave her a diner history lesson. He said most railcar diners were actually built to look like they rode the rails, but they never really did.

He almost had to drag her out of the truck in her turquoise duds, but oddly enough, the place was filled with people similarly attired. Kelly felt absolutely tame after seeing a few gold lamé Western outfits on some middle-aged ladies with big, big hair.

Even so, Sam and Kelly turned every head in the joint. Man, she'd love to know what stories people were making up about the two of them.

Sam was attentive and polite. He didn't order onions and didn't fawn too much. But she felt constant eyes on them.

It's hard to bite into a double cheeseburger with everything but onions while you're being stared at. She did it anyway, because she was starved. Kelly hadn't eaten since the early-morning picnic Sam had provided. She washed it down with the best chocolate shake she'd had in her life. Once again, even the towns around Paradise provided her with fabulous food.

A real live Wurlitzer jukebox played country music. 'I Fall to Pieces' came on; Kelly thought that only Patsy Cline could sing it that good. Kelly was done falling to pieces. Now she was going to pick them up and put herself together. Whatever that looked like.

If that included Sam, that was great. If not, they were still her pieces. She'd have to guard her heart against the obvious Grayson charms until she knew for sure he wasn't just playing some game. Maybe he liked edgy girls from big cities with problems. The gossip on his Philly fiancée pointed to that.

Or maybe Sam Grayson made his parents nuts by dallying with bad girls. Seemed like he was a little old for that sort of thing, but it was a well-established fact in Kelly's book of knowledge that men never grew up. It was only a matter of what age they stuck at: two or seventeen or thirty.

Question was, was she a bad girl? She'd come from bad, but more of a mess-bad than real-bad. She'd always kept to one relationship at a time, and really, those were few and far between. Sure, she'd lived with Raymond for a few years, but she did decide to marry him finally. Dumb as that was.

Kelly straightened herself up and looked Sam in the eye across the table of the booth. If she'd lived a bad life, that life was over. Paradise was going to give her a new life. She slurped the rest of her milk shake down to the dregs.

'So, did Paradise fall under a curse back in 1955 and just get stuck there forever? Have we time-traveled into the Starlight Diner? When we leave the city limits are we never going to find Paradise again? Will it vanish in the mist?'

'I know the way back.' Sam stirred his coffee.

'Back from time travel, from curse, or from the rodeo?'

'All of the above. Want a bite of pie? Blackberry-blueberry. Starlight special.'

'I'm willing to try anything.' Kelly stabbed her fork in Sam's pie and hauled out a big hunk.

Sam slipped his hand warmly into hers on the way out the door. 'They'll get used to it pretty soon, Kelly. I intend to be seen with you in all the best greasy spoons, if you're willing.'

When they got to the pickup, he pulled her closer and pressed her up against the side of the truck. She kissed him lightly across his lips.

'Let's give 'em something to talk about,' he said.

'Happy to oblige, cowboy,'

He took off his hat, then hers, and set them on the hood. He kissed her deeply, softly, and passionately, all at once. Their bodies melded together. She was warm and so full of desire, and she surrendered to his kiss like she had the night before, for the first time today. That made him hot for her all over again. Sam pulled back and looked into her eyes. He leaned close to her ear.

'I'd like to get to know you much more, Kelly Atwood-Applebee. Let's take a drive to the rodeo, and you can tell me all your secrets. You tell me yours, I'll tell you mine.'

Sam just hoped she didn't have too many more secrets. He was still wrestling with the ones she'd already told him.

Back in the Chevy, driving toward the Grant County Fair and Rodeo, Sam listened to Kelly talk about how she wanted to settle herself down and the dream she'd always had about a perfect town, just like in the movies. How she knew you weren't supposed to say stuff like that to a guy, but he'd asked, and she might as well get it over with so he could bolt if he didn't like what he heard. That made him laugh, considering it was she who was most likely to bolt.

She talked about houses, and her white-farmhouse-with-the-red-and-white-kitchen fantasy. They talked about art, about wanting to go to Italy and Paris and see the museums.

He told her he had a minor in art history, and she told him she secretly wanted to try painting someday.

Sam was listening. She talked like she wanted to stay put, but he still wasn't sure. He *was* really enjoying her company.

When he'd picked her up at the Hen House there had been a sense of distance in her. Like she'd put up the safety circle again. It bothered him that she sometimes took two steps backward with her emotions when he got too close. Too close to some old pain, probably.

Kelly was strong, though. She was a clear thinker,

and he liked that. She was passionate, and he liked that, too. He was listening, but he could smell the faint scent of lavender, and his body and mind drifted into the desire that was burning inside him, the desire to make love to this strong yet fragile woman.

S am could see the lights of a Ferris wheel and hear the announcements over the rodeo loudspeaker in the distance. He'd managed to convince Kelly to appear in public in her Annie Oakley duds once again, and they hiked from their distant parking spot holding hands, into the crowded fair, together.

The night was warm. He was with a very beautiful woman who turned into a kid as soon as they crossed the gate into the Grant County Fair and Rodeo.

First, Kelly made a beeline for the caramel corn and bought a huge bag to share with Sam, then Sam took her to the 4-H tents full of prize pigs and chickens. Kelly took a liking to the strange speckled breeds with fancy topknots and decided she would have chickens someday to complement the white farmhouse.

Sam watched the pleasure on Kelly's face. She actually squealed with delight over the lambs and again over a handmade quilt. He slipped the quilt maker's card in his pocket when she wasn't looking. Maybe someday he'd wrap her up naked in patchwork.

It wasn't often a man got to see his date get really

excited over small things. His life to this point contained jaded women who stayed cool and unruffled at all times. *Jaded* was such an old word for young women, and Kelly, for all her hard knocks, was not jaded.

At the arts and crafts tent Sam bought Kelly a painting of black and white chickens since she couldn't have a real one at Myrtle's.

Then they headed for the beer garden, where folks were dancing to polka music. The ladies wore dresses with huge petticoats. The men wore string ties.

After one beer, Sam convinced Kelly to polka with him. They swirled around the dance floor, Kelly following as best as a greenhorn could. The music ended, and they started back to the table, laughing hard from her lame attempts to two-step.

'Where the heck did you learn to polka, Sam?'

'It's a required subject at Paradise High. That and animal husbandry.'

'Polka 101. Did you get an A? Of course you did.'

Sam stopped dead in his tracks, and Kelly ran right into his back.

'Ow!' she said, still laughing.

'Sorry,' he apologized, but she noticed he had stopped laughing. He took her arm and walked her back to their table rather quickly. She sat down and looked at him.

'What's up, Sam?' she asked, but Sam didn't have time to answer. A tall, slender blonde was standing right in front of them with a look on her face that explained Sam's reaction – Lynnette.

'Sam Grayson. Aren't you going to introduce me to

your friend?' The blonde in the bright red Western jumpsuit put her hands on her hips. A tall man in a sheriff's uniform came up behind Lynnette. This could be interesting, Kelly thought.

'Kelly Applebee, this is Lynnette Stivers. We went to high school together.' Sam had an odd stance as he introduced Lynnette, but Kelly stuck out her hand in greeting.

'Actually, we've met. At Cora's, remember?' Kelly smiled, sort of.

Lynnette ignored her and her hand. Sam broke the silence.

'And this is Tom Blackwell. He's the sheriff in Paradise. How's it going, Tom? Anything exciting?'

'Hey, Sam. Just the usual. Kids tipping over headstones at the graveyard. We make 'em do community service and pull lots of weeds. We never used to get caught at stuff like these kids do, right, Sam? Nice to meet you, Kelly.' Tom reached around his stone-statue of a date and shook Kelly's hand.

'Haven't I seen you somewhere before?' Lynnette asked as she surveyed every inch of Kelly's face.

'Yes, at Cora's, *remember*?' Kelly said again. Boy, this chick was missing a few feathers.

Lynnette stepped back as Sam walked behind Kelly's chair and put his hands on her shoulders.

'No, I've seen you somewhere else. Like in a magazine.'

'She just has one of those lovable faces. Are you going to ride the broncs this year, Tom?'

'I'm getting too old to go flyin' off some wild horse, Sam. Besides, I have my hands full with Lynnette, here.'

Lynnette looked at Sam and laughed a short laugh. 'Too old for that, too, aren't you, Tom?' Lynnette went on. 'Well, Miss Applebee, you've got yourself quite a catch, honey, and rich, too, but I'm sure you know that, now, don't you? You must be very pleased. You've caught the elusive Sam Grayson in your little web, and you've only been in town a few days! Why, you must be a talented little thing.'

No one laughed. Tom Blackwell got a sad, far-away look on his face, then tipped his hat to Sam and Kelly.

'We have to be heading over to the sheriff's charity booth for our shift. Come on, Lynnette.' He gently took her arm. She jerked away and stalked off ahead of him. Kelly shuddered.

'Well, now, I'll be sure and invite Miss Stivers out for a day of shopping and tea real soon,' Kelly joked.

'We dated our senior year. She was put out that I didn't marry her then, and it got worse when I came back to town,' Sam said. 'But she's harmless.'

'Oh, I see. Are there any more former girlfriends lurking about I should watch out for?' Kelly stood in front of him with her hands on her hips, in a stance similar to the one Lynnette had taken.

'You're beautiful when you're jealous.' Sam put his arms out to her, and she stepped into his warmth.

'I guess you're right. It is a little early for full possession.'

'Possession is nine-tenths of the law, Kelly.' Sam held her tightly.

'What does that mean, anyway?'

'It means this is our second official date, and we have less than four weeks to go before I can quit being a gentleman, and I am so very pleased about that, and yes, you've caught me in your web.' He tipped her chin up with his finger and kissed her tenderly, right there beneath the colored lights of the beer garden.

'Let's go up on the Ferris wheel and watch the sun go down,' Sam suggested.

Kelly agreed, and they walked over to the rides.

The sky was pink and lavender with evening light. The sights and sounds of the fair surrounded them like a colorful dream: the delighted squeals of children as they rode the carousel horses, the rhythmic voices of the carnival barkers, and the tinny music of the kiddy rides. They got in line at the Ferris wheel. When their turn came up, she saw Sam whisper something to the attendant and slip him a bill.

'Bribing the help, Sam? I suppose he's going to strand us up there, and you will have to climb down to save me by turning the crank back on? He's going to set you up to play hero?'

'Sam Grayson, attorney at law, to the rescue!' He held the bar for her as they sat in their swaying cart.

Kelly held on tightly as the first rush of movement caught her by surprise.

'Ooooh. I forgot to tell you I'm sort of ... ride-impaired!'

'This is as tame as it gets, city kid, so we'll overcome your terror together.'

He wrapped one arm around her, and she snuggled into him. He was such a teddy bear, for a guy with such a great body. Hard but soft, Kelly thought.

Predictably, after once around, the Ferris wheel paused with Sam and Kelly at the top. The sun was just giving a final color show. Scarlet and pink streaked the sky. The moon was already up, almost full, and pale in the last light. Two or three stars sparkled around the moon.

Sam kissed her – first on her neck, then her earlobe, then his lips settled on hers. His kiss deepened. It was like whooshing up on the Ferris wheel. It caught her and moved her so much her heart ached.

She moved back and looked in his eyes. There in those deep blues was the promise of a better future. She touched his cheek gently and kissed each of his eyes.

'Kelly, you'd be damn easy to fall in love with,' Sam whispered.

She ruffled his hair and played with the dark brown curls around his forehead.

'Thank you, Sam. You're like a special gift.'

'And you haven't even unwrapped me yet.' He took her hand, kissed the palm and each fingertip. Kelly leaned her head on his shoulder and watched the dark blue night descend and the moon brighten.

The ride began to move again, and Kelly looked down on the tiny scene below them. Something caught her attention. Partially hidden at the back of a row of booths, staring straight up at them, was Lynnette Stivers in her red Western gear. She was gone when they reached the bottom.

Sam had to help her out because her legs were wobbly. It was more than the Ferris wheel ride making her shaky.

She decided not to mention Lynnette. Why spoil their lovely time with a discussion of an old high school girlfriend?

Instead she let Sam feed her purple cotton candy. He tried to win her a blue and white china teapot she said she wanted to take home to Myrtle. Capable as he was, the breeze had kicked up, and the dancing balloons just wouldn't hold still for his darts. But after about twenty dollars, the barker awarded him the teapot for a three-in-a-row balloon score.

Sam decided to cure Kelly of some of her unreasonable fears and bought her a ticket on the pony rides. He put her aboard an actual horse, the only one on the track, and Sam cheered from the platform as she trotted around the ring, bouncing on her ass unmercifully.

'Post! Post!' He cried from across the ring, making very odd up-and-down movements with his body.

'What post? What the hell is post?' She laughed so hard she almost fell off. At the end of the ride he helped her down and caught her in his arms.

'Ouch,' she said. But then she saw something that startled her. Over Sam's shoulder, off under the trees, stood Lynnette again, watching them. She ducked behind a tree trunk when Kelly glanced in her direction.

'Sam, I think Lynnette is following us. This is the second time I've seen her.'

'She's kind of hard to miss in that neon red and gold number,' Sam joked.

'I'm serious. What's up with her, anyway?'

'I kind of thought she'd recovered.' Sam and Kelly walked to a nearby bench, and he continued his story.

'Lynnette always took things more seriously than I did. She used to talk about getting married. I told her we were too young, and that I had college and law school ahead of me.'

Kelly watched Sam tell his story. She started to get the sense he didn't get how crazy Lynnette was. Sometimes being new in town gave you a clearer perspective than that of people who had grown up there. And Kelly had a much clearer perspective.

'She said she would wait for me,' he went on. 'I kept trying to tell her not to, but she wouldn't listen. We broke up over that, and over her jealous fits.

'She didn't seem to actually grasp that we had broken up since I didn't get involved with anyone, but we were just about to graduate and I figured, why start something up when I was leaving?

'She hung around me, called me all the time. I was friendly, but I knew I was leaving four days after graduation.'

'What happened when you left?'

'She waited. Years. My mom told me, when word got out I was engaged, she went kind of nuts. She climbed up on the high school water tower in her negligee and tried to scrub our initials off with Comet. Tom Blackwell got the job of getting her down. He was a deputy sheriff then.'

'And what's up with him?'

'He sees something in her I don't, I guess. He's been waiting for her to snap out of it. She's supposed to be on some kind of medication. She works at Tom's office now doing data entry and filing.'

'Wow. I think she stopped taking her happy pills. She treats Tom pretty badly. Why does he put up with it?'

'I think he really loves her.'

'Maybe you should talk to Tom.'

'I was hoping she would eventually accept the fact that I'm not interested in her and turn to him.' He smiled at Kelly and reached for her hand.

Kelly figured she'd plow ahead, since Sam was talking. She wanted to know one more thing. 'What happened to your engagement, Sam?'

Sam let go of her hand and ran his hand through his hair in a nervous gesture. 'Chelsea Westheimer. She had a drinking problem I didn't know about. I ended up being the lawyer assigned to defend her when she was picked up for driving under the influence – reckless endangerment. She'd gotten into an accident. Her family disowned her. And she had to have a public defender – me.

'Unfortunately, she had a prior conviction I didn't know about. She was sentenced for a year, but she got out in six months.'

'Oh, my God, Sam. That must have been bad.'

'She got a particularly hard judge. Not that I disagree with the penalties for driving under the influence. We had already broken up before it happened. Of course, I figured for a long time that's *why* it happened, but that's not the case.' He got up and paced in front of the bench. 'I came back home after that. I wanted to work where I could do some good instead of . . .'

'It wasn't your fault, Sam.'

'You think you know the person you're with and then she just blows you out of the water.' Sam's face looked hard.

Kelly's stomach flipped. She stood up and pulled Sam into her.

'I know exactly what you're talking about. But let's just forget about the past and be together. How about we head over to the rodeo now?' she said.

'Sounds just fine,' Sam replied. 'Seeing a few boys rope their calves sounds relaxing.'

'Right. Just don't ask me to do that, okay?'

'I promise. This time. You could be a champ. You've got the moves. You were a natural on that horse.'

'Hog-tie 101, huh? You'll have to teach me that one, Sam.' They walked toward the brightly lit arena and the cheering crowd.

Kelly was quiet during the ride home. Sam put in a soft jazz CD. His mind was working on the problems surrounding them. First, he'd have to call Tom Blackwell tomorrow and have a chat with him about Lynnette for sure this time.

Second, Kelly was married. He'd have to call his college buddy Peter Brody in L.A. and see if Peter could file the divorce papers down there. The clear choice was to get the marriage annulled, although the prior cohabitation might complicate that.

Third, he was having way too many feelings about her. This dating thing was supposed to be a way to clear his head, to get his instincts to shut up and his common sense to take over. It was supposed to be about testing her resolve to stay in town and not run like a scared rabbit.

Trouble was, it was turning out different than he'd expected. He was falling in love with her, spiky hair, tattoo, and all.

It's not like he was a problem-free perfect catch; he had history, too. Sure, he wasn't married, and he hadn't stolen a car, but he had baggage. Like Lynnette.

'Kelly, are you upset about this Lynnette thing?' Sam asked quietly.

'No, I'm just worn out. Sam, you've worn me out: picnics, bicycles, horses. Geez, I better start working out at . . . where do people work out in Paradise?'

'I have a lap pool in my apartment. Want to come up and see my pool?'

'Get real, Grayson. You live on the seventh floor of your building.'

'Steel-beam construction with special reinforcements.'

'This I will have to see . . . but not tonight. Besides, you know we could never stop if we were alone in your apartment. *And* we have more than three date weeks to go. No welshing on our deal.'

'The Welsh are a proud and noble people who have been much maligned. Take Dylan Thomas.'

'Dylan Thomas was an alcoholic poet who died of liver disease. Okay, he was really good when he sobered up. See, I went to college, too.'

'You did? You never talked about it.'

'Oh, sure, Mr. Degrees-Up-His-Ying-Yang, I went to night school at a community college, and got my A.A. in business. Big deal.'

'Yin-Yang.' Sam grinned.

'Quiet in the Ivy League peanut gallery, please.'

'In many ways you're much smarter than I am, Kelly,' Sam said.

That minute they pulled up in front of Myrtle's. The drive home had gone by so quickly.

'And don't you forget it, cowboy.' Kelly put her hat on and gave it a tip back. Sam got out and came around, opened her door. He escorted her to the front porch, carrying her teapot and the chicken picture. Setting them all down on the steps, he leaned her up against the doorpost.

'I'll call you tomorrow.' He kissed her like he wanted to take her right there against the Hen House's porch.

'Thank you for a wonderful day, Sam.'

'My . . . pleasure.' He let her go. She could feel his *pleasure* pressing through his cowboy pants.

'You know, these outfits could come in handy later. After we do our getting-to-know-each-other deal.'

'I'll take that image home with me. Good night, Kelly.' Sam backed off toward his truck.

Kelly slipped inside the door. She was really exhausted. Her boots seemed to weigh her down as she climbed the stairs to her bed.

She wondered how long it would be before Sam lost interest in her with all her history. No man wants to deal with a woman loaded with problems, and he didn't even know half of them. Sure, he was attracted to her, but she didn't have what it took to be Mrs. Grayson, that was for sure.

Her idea to date for a while and get to know each other had more to do with seeing if he'd stick around once he knew all about her than being concerned about the small town they both now lived in. She'd let him make love to her tomorrow if she thought he'd be around for her the day after. It was about time she wised up before she got hurt again.

Sam Grayson was going to find himself some cultured girl who would fit with the rest of his cultured family.

Well, hell, the other thing was she was sick of even thinking about the fact she was married. How long would it take to get her marriage to Raymond annulled, a month? She'd better get the ball rolling and get Sam some information.

She managed to fold things across a chair, slip into a nightgown, and brush her teeth. Then she fell into bed and let sleep overtake her. 'Tomorrow,' she whispered to herself.

*

Deep in the shadows, Lynnette watched Sam's truck fade out into the distance. Good, he dropped her off. No nookie for Kelly-girl tonight, she thought. Lynnette crammed her black Trans Am into gear and turned toward home. She'd go see Tom Blackwell just to keep her from thinking about it. He always stayed up to watch Jay Leno. Every night. Tom wasn't a bad guy, he just wasn't Sam. And Sam was her objective.

'Caroline Prosser, please.'

'May I tell her who's calling?'

'Kelly Ap— Atwood.' She stumbled over her new and old name. The receptionist put her on hold with Mozart, which did nothing to calm her nerves.

'Kelly? Where have you been? I've been trying to reach you.' Caroline talked in low, intense tones as if someone were listening.

'I know, I'm sorry, I should've called you sooner. I just needed a break. Marrying Raymond was a big, big mistake. So listen. I want to get my marriage to Raymond annulled very quietly. We were only together for three hours after the ceremony, and I don't think that counts, but you tell me. Do I have to get the whole big divorce? Can I do this without ticking Raymond off any more than necessary? Do you know where he is?'

Kelly took a breath for the first time since she'd launched into her story. As soon as she did, Caroline broke in.

'Where in the hell are you?'

'In a town you've never heard of. I really just need to know where he is. Have you seen him?' Kelly continued.

'You are not going to need an annulment, Kelly. Or a divorce.'

'Caroline, listen to me! I don't want to be married to Raymond.'

'Listen to *me*. You're not married to Raymond. Raymond is dead.'

A cold-blooded chill ran from the bottom of Kelly's stomach all the way up to her head. She sat down on the side of the bed and tried not to be ill.

'Kelly? Are you okay? He was murdered on the day you left town. You need a good criminal lawyer, hon, and I can testify on your behalf that you called asking for information about a divorce, which means you really didn't know, right? Kelly?'

'What happened? He *can't* have been murdered. Did he OD? When I ran out he had a suitcase full of coke. I found out he was into drugs, Caroline.'

'Try not to say anything more, Kelly. Just write down everything you remember and turn yourself in.'

'What for?' Kelly's chill took over her entire body.

'They think *you* killed him. Now, listen, I can get you lined up with a good criminal attorney. Craig Templeton is in our firm.'

'I'll call you back, Caroline.'

'It will look better if you turn yourself in, Kelly. Just talk to Craig first.'

'I'll call back.' Kelly hung up the phone and ran to the bathroom. She got violently ill until there was nothing left to be ill with, then steadied herself, splashed her face with cold water, and brushed her teeth.

The chill took over again, so she went back in her room and slipped into bed, wrapping herself into a cocoon of blankets.

A black, dark feeling crawled over her. The kind she used to get as a kid listening to her mom's drunken fights with whatever man she was with that week. She shook uncontrollably. Her perfect town, her lovely romance, her calm, no-pressure job and life, her . . . Sam. It was all over.

She closed her eyes and cried a sad, quiet cry. She even cried for Raymond, whom she had liked enough at one time to live with and marry. Raymond had been so very alive and charming in his expensive, lying way. Poor Raymond.

Who would want to kill him anyway? As she calmed down, Kelly began to go over the memories of that day.

Pictures of the men in the hallway flashed in her mind: Raymond out cold in the apartment with a suitcase full of drugs, and how they had dumped out her bags like completely crazy people.

And she had their money. They were going to want that money. And she could identify them. They were going to want *her*.

Myrtle Crabtree was teasing Alice Hutchinson's gray hair into a bouffant for Alice's church choir rehearsal. Alice was a widow, and there was a tenor she had her eye on. Every Monday Alice felt compelled to have a set and comb-out. She was the only person Myrtle let in on Mondays besides Opal; her right-hand cleanup, sterilize, and answer phones, in-training-on-hair gal.

Myrtle took one look at Kelly and laid down her rattail comb. 'Opal, take over for me, hon, Mrs. H., I have a little emergency to take care of. Don't overdo that back comb, she's about ready for shaping.' Mrs. H. smiled amiably, and Opal popped her gum as she took up the comb.

Myrtle got up real close to Kelly and took her hand.

'Mercy, those nails of yours are a mess. Howz about we see if we can't pretty you up a bit.' She winked and kept hold of Kelly's hand, guiding her to the back room nail station. Kelly sat down and laid her hands out on the table. They were shaking so badly, Myrtle got a steamy towel out of the warmer and set it over them.

'We'll soak 'em for a while. What's up, darlin'? You look like roadkill. Let's do your hair while you're here, too.'

'Raymond is dead, and they think I killed him. They are looking for me. I have a huge amount of money in a briefcase upstairs that I found in Raymond's car.' A tear rolled down Kelly's cheek, and her mouth quivered. 'Everything I wished for is gone, Myrtle.'

'Well, you didn't kill him, did you?' Myrtle stated more than asked. She ignored the money bit. She filed that away for later.

'No. I knocked him out, but I swear he was still alive when I left the apartment. They want me to turn myself in.' Kelly sat at the edge of the seat nervously.

'Who the heck is *they*?' Myrtle took Kelly's hand and started gently working back the cuticles on her nails with a soft cloth. 'Your nails look like you've been shucking oysters.'

'I spoke to a paralegal friend of mine in L.A.'

'Did you tell her where you were?'

'No.'

'In my opinion, if no one knows where you are, and you didn't kill him, then I would say sit tight. They are bound to find the real killers.

'Did I ever tell you about my second husband Edgar? He was always mixed up with the wrong sort. But what a sax player. He could make that thing wail so good you'd think you were doin' the nasty with it.' Myrtle started buffing like crazy at Kelly's ridges.

'One time he disappeared for a week, and the cops came to see if I had done him in and, you know, buried his body in the cellar or something?'

'Lieutenant Michael Reilly. Lord, what a looker. He and I hit it off right away, and they stopped snooping around after that. Turned out Edgar was playing for a jazz band in St. Louis. He gave me the St. Louis blues.' Myrtle cackled and started singing.

'What if Caroline has caller ID? They could trace me back here through the phone number.'

'You said this gal was your friend. Maybe she will put a lid on it for you. That's the risk you're gonna take if you do it this way.

'Who the hell is looking for Kelly Atwood-Applebee

in this little truck stop of a town? Nobody. Besides, you are missing one important fact, missy. You are no longer a married woman.

'If you keep on with your quiet life, I say you could be Mrs. Grayson by next spring, and nobody is looking for her! It'll all blow over, anyway. One less drug dealer in L.A., ya know. Those cops aren't going to waste much time on that.

'So let's put some shine on these nails and get you all pretty for Sam. Time to take a different tack.'

'And what about the money, Myrtle?'

'We'll let that stew for a while. We'll think about it tomorrow. Find it a good home or something. It's been up there this long, it'll keep.' Myrtle held up a bottle of nail polish. 'How about Get My Man Red?'

'How about I'm Screwed Pink?' Kelly flopped back against the chair.

'You are not screwed. You are a free woman, and you ain't done nothin' anyway! Let's do a foil thing on your hair and pick up the highlights. Whadda ya say, sweetie?'

Kelly sighed. There were flaws in Myrtle's plan, but the idea of continuing on her present course, staying in Paradise, using her new name, and putting the past behind her . . . well, that tugged on her like a lifeline.

'Okay, Myrtle, you talked me into it. For at least the rest of today. Do the foil, and let's put some red on my nails. Here. Panic Red. That's perfect.'

*

Sam flipped over the desk calendar page. It was Monday. He sat back, slowly sipped his Cora coffee out of his stainless-steel and black rubber travel cup, and started reading through the details of Red's brother Herschel Miller's property dispute. Looked like the boundary lines had been defined by a row of Gravenstein apple trees in 1902.

Herschel wasn't going to be too happy about the fact that Mabel Thompson found the corner post under an old tomato can in the northwest section. Heck, maybe he could go over there and get the two of them to agree to share the cut-through road like civilized people.

What a weekend it had been. Eight days ago all he had on his mind was work and finding a wife. Now he was about to put in a call to Peter Brody in L.A. so he could pull Kelly Atwood out of a can of worms. She'd mixed up all his well-laid plans.

Life probably was so much easier in the old days. You'd meet some girl in high school or college. Get married by twenty-one, have three kids, coach Little League on Saturday, go to church on Sunday, and have a roasted chicken for dinner with mashed potatoes and gravy.

Couldn't life just be that way? Sam took the pencil from behind his ear, set down Herschel's papers, and drew a square on his legal pad. It was his future vegetable garden so he could pick fresh beans for supper. He'd planned out tiny rows of cabbages and potatoes. Very orderly.

Who was he kidding? Life just didn't *do* that

anymore. There were complications. There were problems. Tomatoes sometimes were ruined with the blight. People were unpredictable. His whole job was straightening out the messes people got into when their emotions ran high.

Why did people make such bad decisions? Seemed like it was his fate to fix things up after the decisions were made. Look at Kelly. She'd probably had it in her head Raymond was an okay guy. From what she'd told him he ran his showroom well, made good money, treated her decently – at least before the marriage ceremony. Why wouldn't she go ahead and marry him after two years?

Some decisions looked good, but turned out bad. Sam drew in a house beside the garden, and an orchard of pear and apple trees dotting the south portion of his imaginary property.

The real problem was what he was going to do with his feelings for Kelly. She was beautiful, sexy, and desirable. But could she hoe a row of corn? Even more important, would she stay in Paradise long enough to get through a single season, or would she blow out with the first frost?

Hell, she probably had a suitcase packed and ready under the bed. She was a runaway.

He picked up the phone and dialed. He'd waited long enough. Surely Peter had rolled into his office by now. Peter was a late-in type, what with getting his kids off to school. Sam really wanted to get this over with.

'Sam, you old country boy, what's new in Paradise?' Peter Brody's familiar booming voice was on the phone.

Sam put his feet up on his desk and leaned back in his office chair. 'Paradise is good, Pete. How's your family? How's Fran?'

'We're going nuts in this apartment while our house is being finished. The kids are climbing the walls. But work is good, life is good. What's up?'

'I've got a client up here that needs to divorce her badass husband. It's in your county, and I thought I'd do the paperwork for her and send it down to you. I need some particulars.'

'I can fax you the statutes. Long and complicated. California, you know. What's the story?'

Sam hesitated.

'So you're sleeping with her?'

'Worse. I'm not. We're dating.' Damn Peter. He'd known Sam too long.

'Damn. Well, fax me her file. I'll get right on it.'

'That'd be very good, Pete. It's possible she can file for an annulment, but there's two years of cohabitation to factor in. You read it over and we'll talk.' Sam hit the call button for Faith as he wrapped up his call with Peter. She came in just as he hung up.

'Faith, can you please fax this down to Peter Brody at this number?' He thumbed through his Rolodex, pulled out Peter's card, and handed it to her, along with Kelly's file.

Faith flipped the card between her fingers nonchalantly and held the file under her arm. 'Did you have a nice weekend? Wasn't that Presbyterian social something?'

'Oh, it was something, all right. "I'm in the Mood for Love"?'

'Cora's idea.'

'Is there no way to call off the troops?'

'I have no idea to what you are referring, Mr. Grayson. We all just want to see you happy in Paradise.'

'Thank you, Faith, I'll keep that in mind.'

Faith smiled and marched out to her desk.

He set down his pencil, took up his coffee and Herschel's case again. He'd just have to find out exactly what Kelly Atwood wanted out of life. Cautiously, with as much wisdom as possible, he'd slowly get to know her. This whole goofy courtship deal would give him plenty of time to do that. The next few weeks would tell him a lot. If she was still around at the end of that time, he'd be surprised.

She wanted to see him. She'd tell him what she found out. She had to tell him, she just had to. He deserved to know the truth. But it might sound better if she wore her black dress. Kelly shimmied into the spandex tank dress she had brought with her from L.A. The highlights Myrtle had foiled into her hair lightened up her face considerably.

Too bad all her best high heels were still in Raymond's apartment. She settled for a one-inch heel on a pair of black strappy sandals she'd picked up at Yeackle's Shoes.

Once again Stan Yeackle had great taste. They were also comfortable enough to take a good walk in. See,

Myrtle? Right shoes for the occasion. She was learning.

The October weather was doing Indian summer. She'd put on her black cashmere cardigan over the dress and was almost feeling too hot as she walked toward town.

Mrs. Palmer had given her Sunday and Mondays off until November, when the holiday rush would force them all to work longer hours. Kelly felt a laugh bubble up inside her. Paradise had no idea what a rat race holiday retail could be. Until you worked in a big department store in a city like L.A., you just didn't get it.

There were the stressed-out women and their unfortunate children dragged out for shopping. Kelly had made a pact with herself that when she had children, if she couldn't afford a sitter for a few hours of shopping, then she couldn't afford shopping. Of course, what did she know? She was twenty-eight and single.

Then there were the hours on your feet with no break in sight, the smile pasted on your face. It was one reason she'd finally gone into wholesale. Even though working retail had been a big step up from her tattoo parlor job she'd gotten in her early days.

It hadn't been so bad there. Her buddy the ex-army sergeant had kept a good eye on his seventeen-year-old apprentice. She'd slept in the back room and only had minimal problems with the customers, thanks to Sergeant Douglas.

Years later he told her when she'd come in his door with the HELP WANTED sign in her hand he figured if he didn't take her in, she'd get in real trouble.

Remembering that made Kelly feel lucky. Things could have been worse in her life. She'd get out of this mess with Raymond. She was innocent. If she could just hang tight, they'd find the guys who killed Raymond, surely.

She found herself in Sam's office so fast she forgot to work out how she was going to tell him.

'Hello, Miss Applebee, have a seat, won't you? I'll just pop in and tell Sam you're here.' Faith had blue jays on her sweatshirt today.

'He's not with a client, is he?' Kelly asked. She hadn't even thought of that.

'Heavens, no. He said something about heading out toward the Miller place for a while, but he's still here.'

Sam came out to get Kelly. She looked incredible. Black dress. Tight black dress. Her eyes shining. She pulled herself out of the chair and tugged her dress down a bit.

'I called, really I did. Myrtle said you were on your way over,' Sam said. 'Come on back, Kelly.'

'Your calling was not an issue, Sam.'

'I know, but women like it when you call.' Boy, she sounded odd today. 'I had a great time at the rodeo last night.'

'Me too. First time I'd ever seen a real live bronco rider,' Kelly said.

'You look great. You and Myrtle have some fun today?'

She blushed and said nothing.

Sam looked hard into her cat-like green eyes. She was damn nervous about something. He touched her arm. She brushed at her bangs with the other hand. Slowly he drew her into him. His arms wrapped around her softness. She leaned against his chest and he could hear her heart pounding.

'Long walk?' he said softly.

'Not too.'

He lifted her chin with his fingers and kissed her. She was delicious, fresh-air-cold lips. Soft red lips. He ran his fingers through her newly highlighted hair. Her jet-black hair now had reddish highlights. Still crazy. Silky to the touch. He felt suddenly overwhelmed by her. Lost in her. He kissed her again and let one hand run down her back. The sweater she wore was hot from the sun – and her warmth.

'Sam.' She said his name in a moan as he slid his hands all the way down her backside and pulled her toward him. Her arms were around his neck. Her body was burning against his. He felt the throb of his need for her.

'Sam, not here.'

'Not here. Yes. Not here,' he repeated. He eased himself from her. 'This is getting hard.'

'Sure is.' She started laughing.

He held her away from him by the shoulders. 'I was about to drive out toward Fish Trap Lake again. I have a client out there. Want to come?'

'You make house calls?'

'Yup. I take chickens for pay, too.'

'I'll come, but can we stop at Myrtle's and pick up my other shoes?'

'Sure. Let's get some fresh air. Clear our heads. Take a cold shower.'

Sam went to his closet door and swapped his suit coat for a brown leather jacket.

'Clever lawyer. Your doors hold many surprises.'

'You, too, I imagine.' He put his arm around her and got them both out of the office, into public. Maybe he could keep his hands off her better in public.

For Kelly, everywhere Sam had touched her was burning. Her lips were still on fire. She smiled at Faith as they walked by. When the elevator doors closed behind them she heard laughter tittering through the doors. Sounded like everyone knew what was going on.

She looked up at Sam. He had red lipstick smeared on his lips. 'Sam. Lipstick.'

'Shoot. I can't get away with anything.' He pulled out one of those white embroidered handkerchiefs and wiped at his mouth.

She smiled. He was sweet. Like clover honey. Like blackberry pie. She just couldn't mess with a sweet thing like Sam. She'd like to tell him the reason she wasn't married anymore, that Raymond was dead; the words echoed in her head and made her hurt inside. But what if he didn't believe her about Raymond? What if Sam believed she killed him?

Kelly just could not bear to see the doubt that would flash through him the minute she told him. She had to have just a little more time with him. It would mean the end of it with them, for sure, and she wasn't ready for the end.

She grasped for conversation that would keep her from thinking about it anymore. 'You said your parents were out of town, Sam. Where?'

'He and my mom are in Europe right now on a museum tour. Which reminds me, there's this benefit for the Seattle Art Museum this Saturday. I've been left holding the ticket bag. Would you like to go?'

'Swanky, eh?'

'Swanky as they come in the Northwest. It's a masquerade thing. Just masks. Myrtle has some kind of feather collection I'm sure you can dig into. I suppose it's short notice for getting a dress.'

'Don't sweat it, Prince Charming, Cinderella has her ways.' Kelly reached up and kissed Sam on the cheek just as the elevator opened. A couple and their boy just stared at them. The woman grinned broadly. They excused themselves past them and got in. Elevators.

The October sun heated her up until Kelly stripped off her sweater and tied it around her waist. Her sexy black dress lost much of its effect when teamed with the white Keds she'd made Sam stop at Myrtle's for. But as Myrtle always said, a girl's got to have the right shoes.

Kelly stood on a hill overlooking a red farmhouse and its surrounding property. Sam was in the distance standing in his quiet way. The two people with him were more animated. The woman waved her arms in the air a few times. The man paced a circle around something.

Sam kept his hands in the pockets of his brown leather jacket and nodded a lot.

Kelly let the breeze cool her bare arms. The leaves on the old maples looked rusted. A tall birch tree had vivid yellow leaves still on it even though a shower of them came down with every gust of wind.

The property was behind the lake they'd necked at on their tandem bike trip. Driving here she realized how far they'd ridden. It must be five miles out of town, so she had biked ten miles! Man, she'd have to stay in shape for these dates.

She turned in a circle like Julie Andrews in *The Sound of Music*. The hills were alive right now with the sound of two grown people bickering down the slope from her.

Behind her she could see Fish Trap Lake shimmering in the sun. The willows beside it looked more golden than she remembered from even a week ago. Above the lake she caught sight of an old house, quite large. Its white paint was peeling away. The upper window was broken out. It must be abandoned.

Sam came up behind her and put his arms around her.

'All done.'

'Did you solve their problem?'

'Yup.'

'Wanna go skinny-dipping?'

'Don't ask. I'd like to roll you right down this hill and do you in the grass. Hopefully your dress would remove itself on the way down.'

'Why, Henry. You devil.' She wound herself around him.

'Who told you my first name?' He kissed her neck.

'Ginny Palmer.' She pulled his shirt out of his pants and ran her hands up his broad, muscular back. His skin was warm as flannel. 'What's that house over there?' She used her head to point because her hands were busy. She'd really like to see him naked. Everywhere she touched she felt an amazingly hard body.

'The old Shipley place. Haunted.'

Sam gasped as her hands came around to his chest. She liked having that effect on him.

'Who owns it?'

'County. Should be torn down.'

'Tsk. That's a shame. It's a beautiful location.' She reached up and kissed him harder. She pressed her body into his until she felt him want her *bad*.

'Kelly.'

'Yes?'

'Not here.'

Kelly looked over Sam's shoulder and saw the two bickering people pointing at them and laughing. At least they were getting along now.

'Okay, let's walk over to the Shipley place and say hello to the ghosts,' Kelly said.

The late-afternoon sun gave everything a burnished golden glow. Kelly couldn't believe how huge the Shipley house was when they got right in front of it.

'Wow, this was something special. What happened?'

'The last of the family, three sisters, lived here all their lives. Spinsters. My mom knew them well. They were very active in town life and you see their names all over old newspapers and public buildings. The last one died about 1968. No living relatives, so the house reverted to the county. There was talk of fixing it up, but it just didn't happen.'

Kelly rubbed at a small windowpane on the front porch and peered inside. Wow. She could see a big fancy stairway. Good woodwork. The front door was boarded shut. She really wanted inside.

'There's someone on the county board that comes out and checks on it once a month. I know there's a back door. Careful,' Sam took her arm as they stepped over broken boards in the porch.

'I want in. Can you get a key?'

'Sure. I'll ask Tom Blackwell.'

Kelly walked backward next to Sam, looking at the treasure she'd found. There was something about the place that pulled at her. A huge old magnolia tree stood to one side. Sprays of roses that someone had planted long ago were giving their last blooms to the fall warmth. They draped over a broken-down trellis leaning against one side of the house.

If she could just clean up the past, she could make a new home here. The less of her old life that intruded into the new one, the better. Maybe she could get this whole Raymond thing straightened out before she had to tell him. Surely some progress would be made on the case soon. She turned around and grabbed Sam's hand as they walked. She gave him her best smile. He was something.

'Wanna have dinner at Cora's?' she asked.

'Can't. I teach swimming Mondays and Wednesdays at the high school pool.' Sam opened the truck door for her.

'Fine for you. Oh, well, I've got mice I have to train to whip me up a dress by Saturday.'

'I'll drop you at your wicked hairdresser's house.'

'She is wicked, isn't she? I love her for it.'

'She's been real good to you. I like that in a crazy old lady.' Sam started up the truck, and they drove toward town with the sun setting in front of them in bright October orange streaks.

Lynnette Stivers booted up the computer and tapped her red nails on the mouse. Her job doing data entry at Tom Blackwell's office was really coming in handy now.

She entered the sheriff's office password and accessed the West Coast Sheriff's Watch main website. After flipping through a few hoops, she got to the site for profiles.

A series of drawings and photos came up and Lynnette entered her qualifying data:

Kelly Applebee
Female, 5′ 8″
Short black hair, hazel green eyes
Approx. 28 years old
110 lbs

Files came up, and she began flicking through them one by one.

The old school clock on the sheriff's office wall ticked away the seconds. There must have been hundreds of faces, but Lynnette was real fast – this was her forté, snooping.

Fifteen minutes later she hit pay dirt. 'I knew it. I knew I'd seen that face before.' Lynnette hit the print button on the file with pure glee and waited for the page to emerge.

Tom Blackwell came through the swinging glass door just as the printer spat out the last of it. Lynnette hit two buttons on the computer and turned to the wall briefly to stuff the paper in her bag.

'Hi, Tom, honey, did you take that ratty little Skaggs boy back home? I doubt his mama cares what he's been stealing. She probably sent him for it. Twelve years old and he's just like his old man.'

'Yep, I took him home, and brought a bag of groceries, too. Her husband's run off, and she can't watch after Kenny and the two little ones at the same time. I stopped at the church and asked the reverend to give her a hand. She will probably pitch a fit, but it will help her through. He needs a person to help out in the day-care center, and she can bring the twins in for free.'

Lynnette took the time Tom was rambling on to gather herself. She grabbed up her bag, sauntered over to him, and gave him a little peck on the cheek at arm's length.

'Tom, you are too good to these people. A night in jail might straighten that boy out.'

'You can't put a twelve-year-old boy in jail, Lynnette.'

'I suppose not. I'm going home to rustle you up some supper, just like I promised. Don't be too late, now.' Lynnette's bleached blonde ponytail wagged as she walked out the door.

She jumped in the Trans Am and turned the keys to roll down the window. October and it was still hot.

Pulling the paper out of her bag, she smoothed it out and read the notice.

Wanted for the murder of Raymond Bianchi
Kelly Atwood Bianchi
Female
Height 5' 8"
Weight 110 lbs.
Hair: red
Eyes: hazel
Age: 28

Got most of it right, Lynnette thought. She must have changed her name and dyed her hair black.

So a lying, murdering bitch with roots was about to snare her Sam. In a pig's eye, sweetheart. Over my dead body, Kelly Atwood Bianchi Applebee.

Sam was hers. He always had been; he just needed to remember it. Now she had everything she needed to get him to come to her. She'd pick just the right moment. She'd show Sam what a mistake he was making. Again. He'd finally figure out that a nice local girl from his hometown was waiting for him. She'd keep him safe from these slick city tramps.

She laid the paper on the seat and started the car. A cloud of dust swirled up as she peeled out of the parking lot.

Tom looked through a crack in the metal blinds and saw the rear end of the Trans Am disappear down the street. That woman was up to something. An uneasy feeling crept up on him like a cold coming on. He sat down at his desk and looked at the stack of paperwork waiting for him. He'd better get over to her house for dinner tonight and keep an eye on her.

Better stop at Cora's and eat something on the way, too. Lynnette practically burned her kitchen down last time she tried to cook when one of these moods came over her. She was usually an amazing cook.

Hell, if she was inclined to make him dinner, he was glad for it, no matter what her mood. Maybe now that Sam had a good woman, Lynnette would come around. He'd like that. He could hope anyhow. He'd hoped a long time now. Tom shook his head and started in on his reports.

Sam gave Kelly one final, lingering kiss outside Myrtle's screen door. She walked in on air, floating past Fluffy the stuffed cat, giving it a pat. Myrtle just stared as she passed by, then went on humming 'Smoke Gets in Your Eyes.' The shop was closed, and Myrtle was puttering with her potions, as Kelly called them: hair conditioners that smelled like tropical fruit and all sorts of other mysterious things.

Suddenly Kelly had a wild idea and stepped up her pace. She wanted to go see Sam teach his swimmers. She wanted to go see him in a different setting.

After a quick shower, she changed into jeans and her favorite white T-shirt. She borrowed Myrtle's big red Chrysler Le-Huge-O and found the high school easily enough. She slipped in the door and crossed through the girls' locker area to a glassed-in overlook. She had a great view of Sam, and he was too absorbed in his young charges to notice her.

Sam's swimmers were all around him in the water and hanging off the side of the pool: a group of kids who looked to be about five. He took one at a time around in the water, then returned each of them to the side.

Kelly could see their little legs kicking up behind them. Sam was focused on giving directions to his pupil and each time he did, the child would either dip under the water or kick harder.

Then they all grouped up and did head bobs in a row. He had to retrieve one who dipped a little too deep. He pulled her up so calmly the child hardly noticed.

Kelly heard his laughter like a deep musical instrument. Sam was fun. He'd brought fun and passion into her life, possibly for the first time ever.

After a while they all popped out of the pool and

were swept up by mothers with towels to dry them off.

Sam stood on the side of the pool chatting with one mother. He had on one of those Speedo suits that showed off a physique she hadn't seen since she'd watched the 1988 summer Olympics when Greg Louganis dived to the gold medal. She'd been thirteen, and television and books had been her best friends.

It took her breath away seeing him. Kelly pressed her nose up against the glass and it fogged up where she was standing.

Sam retrieved some long noodle-like toys and handed them out to a new group of kids, slightly older. They all jumped in the pool with a colorful array of waving foam tubes.

She could watch him forever.

Myrtle was right, he was her reward for everything that had happened to her as a child, and beyond. She had finally gotten lucky. Kelly made up her mind right there, in the steamy, chlorinated air of the pool waiting area. She was going to make Sam Grayson her own.

In the parking lot she unlocked Myrtle's red 'dozer' and thought about how funny that was – locking the car in a town like Paradise.

Parked beside her was a classic black Trans Am. Kelly bent down to get a clear view of the person in the car. In it was classic blonde pain-in-the-ass Lynnette Stivers. Lynnette waved at her like a prom queen on a float and smiled a real weird smile.

*

Back at the Hen House, Myrtle was just finishing up making supper. 'Want some stir-fry?' She whipped a dish towel over her shoulder and tossed the contents of a metal wok with a wooden spoon.

Kelly got two bowls out of the cupboard and started setting the table. 'Myrtle, I have big news.'

'Spill it, girlfriend. You looked like the Cheshire cat earlier. Where'd you run off to?'

'I went to watch Sam teach swimming.'

'Awesome, isn't he? When he was a teenager he took Paradise High to state finals two years in a row. He won everything hands down. Diving, mostly, and butterfly.' Myrtle supplied one-sided demos while holding her spoon and dishing up stir-fry. 'The whole town used to go and watch him.'

'Okay, what's the catch with this guy? He can't be for real. This is a Stepford thing, right?'

'Sam has his flaws, I'm sure. I just can't think of any.' Myrtle handed her a pair of chopsticks, and they both dug into their bowls of veggies and chicken. Pausing, she held her chopsticks in mid-air for a moment. 'Oh, I remember now. He took Lynnette Stivers to home-coming and the prom his senior year.'

'I don't suppose they ended up homecoming king and queen?'

'You betcha. And Lynnette still seems to have herself stuck right at that moment in time when the rhinestone crown went on her head. Sam's done something good for Paradise with his high school glory. She's just stayed in a state of arrested development. That's a good one.'

Myrtle snorted up a storm laughing. 'And if she'd get arrested again, then maybe Tom Blackwell could just keep her locked up and make her see some sense. Get it?'

'You're a card, Myrtle. Guess what? I got invited to the ball by Prince Charming Grayson. Some shindig in Seattle, yet. We have a week to come up with a killer dress and a mask. It's a masked ball.'

'Honey, having you around is just too swell to tell. We're gonna gussie you up so good you'll be the belle of the ball.'

'Love that word. *Gussie.*' Kelly finished the last of her stir-fry and did the dishes for Myrtle while Myrtle dug out her box of feathered masks. Halloween was apparently Sister Myrtle the Witch's biggest deal. Of course, Kelly hadn't seen her do any other holiday so far.

One thing was for sure: Judging from the store windows and the Halloween decor selection at Nettie's Bazaar, the local dime store that outdid any Kmart on honeycomb foldout pumpkins, Paradise was a holiday-driven town. That suited her just fine.

It was red velvet, strapless, and gathered across the front into a sweetheart-shaped bodice. She'd spent some of her traveler's check money having it drop-kick shipped from the Macy's holiday catalogue. She put on the new, but fake, big jewelry, and sprayed a little Obsession cologne in her hair, her favorite trick. Yikes, she was hot. The mirror told her so. She went for the Wine & Roses Red lipstick, which had magenta undertones just like the velvet.

Myrtle solemnly handed her the red feather mask with gold trim. It was one Myrtle had bought in New Orleans during a Mardi Gras adventure.

The doorbell rang. Damn, that man was never late. She had a moment of doubt as to her choice of dress — they were supposed to be going slow, and she was dressed to press; just a shade north of streetwalker. Well, it was too late now.

Myrtle toyed with one last strand of Kelly's hair. They'd put gold glitter in it. Kelly gave Myrtle a hug, grabbed her beaded clutch, and walked slowly out to meet him, mask on. He'd been extremely busy all week, and so had she. They'd had coffee every morning before work, but everything else had gone on hold for an entire week.

Sam adjusted his studs and checked his black and gold cuff links. He checked his reflection in Myrtle's porch window for a second. The five-year-old black tux still looked decent.

A red blur danced behind the frosted glass door panes, and he changed his focus. Kelly opened Myrtle's front door slowly, and inch by inch revealed the red dress. They stared at each other silently for a moment, then Sam started laughing.

'What? Is my slip showing? Do I have spinach in my teeth?'

'Kelly, your city roots are showing. You look fabulous. I have never seen a woman in this town clean up so well.' Sam had to stop himself from laughing. Obviously he had left one detail out about their evening. He'd have to tell her later. Much later. Why spoil the moment?

Kelly unfolded a black evening coat – *thank God*, he thought – and he helped her slip it on.

'Your sense of humor escapes me at the moment, Sam, but nice save. I'd kiss you, but the red lips are deadly.'

He was standing behind her, and kissed her long, slender neck slowly. The scent of her filled his body with longing. She intoxicated him almost immediately. This beautiful, shapely woman poured into red velvet, her exotic perfume teasing him. He wanted her . . . tonight.

She turned and put her arms around his waist,

pulling him close. Her chin tipped up provocatively. Her luscious red lips parted. Then, instead of kissing him, she spoke.

'Where to, big boy?' A big red smile lit up her face.

'Tonight, we fly away and do the town.'

'And dinner will be where? Cora's? I bet you two cooked up a romantic table for two with candles and spaghetti like in *Lady and the Tramp*. Only tonight I'm the Tramp, right? I hope I didn't overdo it with the dress.'

Maybe he'd just let her figure it out when they got there. 'You look marvelous, and I will be able to spot you in the crowd. Actually, we're going to throw my family money around tonight. Are you up for an adventure?'

'Ready and able. Is our limo awaiting us?' She pointed toward the street, expecting Sam's usual Chevy pickup, but in its place was a dark green Jaguar XKE. 'Holy shit, Grayson, is that a '63? What else is up your sleeve?' Kelly blurted out.

'My elbow, eventually. Climb in, your chariot awaits.' Sam opened her door for her, and she slid down into the tan leather seat. Cars and women were both so sexy. He shut the door gently and rounded the car to the driver's seat. The night air was sultry, and he was burning for her. Sam revved up the XKE's temperamental engine and it purred like a tiger.

The skill of Sam's driving and the sweet handling of the car smoothed out the curves of the north hill area of town. If it was one thing Kelly liked, it was a good car.

She'd managed her first one at eighteen. A VW

Karmann Ghia. She and that car had been in love. It was her escape.

Kelly found herself in a part of Paradise she hadn't explored. They wound their way up, around, and down a long drive lined with tall poplar trees.

Out of beautifully arranged natural landscaping emerged a wood, stone, and glass structure of stunning design and proportion. Arts and Crafts meets that modern Swedish architect she couldn't remember at the moment.

'Anyone you know?' Kelly turned slowly and eyed Sam.

'This would be the folks' place, but don't worry, we're just going to borrow some transportation.'

'More transportation? So the Jag just won't do, huh? Boy, Sam, are there a few things you might have forgotten to mention about ol' Ozzie and Harriet, here?'

'Okay, they have lots of money. Besides his law practice my dad is a partner in a pharmaceutical company that came up with something useful and made them all a fortune. My parents are really decent rich people, though.'

'Of course you know that now I will have to break up with you so you don't think I am after your money.'

'Does that mean we *were* going steady?' Sam said with a smile.

'I guess it did, but that's all over now,' Kelly teased. Sam pulled around past the house and down another little driveway. A large barn came into view. He pulled up beside it.

'Oh, no, not another horse ride. I really didn't dress for it, Sam.'

'No horses, but before you break up with me, I better pin you to make the going steady official.'

Sam popped open the glove box in front of her, reached in, and pulled out a little black velvet box. He extended it toward her. Kelly's heart did a thump. She was a sucker for good jewelry.

After all, diamonds are a girl's best friend. She'd proven that when she decked Raymond. Oh, God. Why did she have to think of that now? It all came rushing back to her and made her head spin. She should tell him. But that would ruin their great evening. Her hands shook as she snapped open the box.

'Are you okay?'

'Little velvet boxes always have this effect on me.' Kelly was trying to joke her way back to steadiness. Inside lay a gold and diamond pin shaped like a daisy. She looked up slowly and smiled. He leaned forward and brushed her cheek with his lips, then whispered softly in her ear.

'You still look sweet, Kelly.'

He was a keeper, all right. She felt flustered suddenly. 'Okay, so we're going steady. Pin me properly, now.' Sam smiled while he unfastened the pin from its backing and slipped it onto the folds of her strapless gown. His hands slid beneath the fabric and pressed against her skin.

He looked intently into her eyes. Kelly could feel the emotion and need rise up in both of them. Heat settled right where his hands were touching her. She shifted her velvet-gowned self over his direction and let him kiss her full on her red-lipsticked mouth. She ran her hand gently up his temple and into his hair, deepening the kiss, saying what she wanted to say out loud, but couldn't seem to manage. This was going to be one long, hot evening.

Sam sat back in his bucket seat, stunned from the power of her kiss. She couldn't help but giggle at the lipstick transfer. She pointed to his mouth and laughed even more.

'I'm doomed to repeat this behavior, so I might as well surrender.' He took out his monogrammed handkerchief and blotted his mouth. 'Come on, my little Daisy Mae, let's go before I forget we have dinner reservations and lose myself in your red velvetness.'

'What's that sound, Sam?'

Exiting the car, Sam guided her down a flagstone path toward the barn. It was only one turn of the corner before she saw the noise was coming from an airplane engine warming up and that the 'barn' was a hangar with a plane inside. Around the back of the barn Kelly could see a single-lane runway with lights already on. She really was in the Twilight Zone now.

A sleek little Cessna prop plane opened its hatch and lowered a stairway, courtesy of a uniformed man with a neat white beard who looked about seventy-five. Santa's summer job. They ascended the stairs, where Santa saluted Sam with a quick movement.

'Welcome aboard, ma'am, sir. Right this way. The

weather is great. We should have a smooth ride.'

Kelly was speechless. There were six gray leather seats, and Sam motioned her into the center row, by the window. He took the aisle seat.

'Thanks, Cap'n Jack,' Sam said to Santa.

The flight was as smooth as the champagne she sipped out of a tall, elegant glass. ROEDERER'S CRYSTAL 1975, she read on the label, and it went down like liquid heaven.

She'd done some high-life time with Raymond, but this was by far the most elegant experience of her twenty-eight years. Sam had thought of everything, and waited on her attentively. She settled into her leather seat and gazed out at the stars.

'This is the best champagne I've ever tasted, Sam.'

'Nineteen seventy-five was a very good year for champagne.'

'Probably made up for the fashion blunders,' Kelly said. 'I used to cut out old magazine pictures of fashion models. I had a scrapbook that took up the slack time of my childhood. It was actually a pretty good time line of the styles at the time. My mom couldn't exactly afford Barbie and her fiscal holdings, ya know, so my paper dolls filled in.'

Sam leaned closer to her. He ran his fingertips over her right temple.

'I'll buy you a Barbie, sweetheart.'

'Just ply me with champagne and toys. I'm easy.'

'If you were easy, we would be in bed right now.'

'So, I'm *not* easy.' Kelly ran a few kisses down Sam's neck and made him wish she were.

The rest of the trip was a blur of champagne bubbles and kisses until Sam pointed out the lights of Seattle and the Space Needle.

Kelly wondered whether leaving Paradise was such a good idea. After all, she was still hiding out. But it was too late now. She swept all that aside for twinkling lights and gorgeous Sam. For tonight, she was going to forget about it all and be a princess at the ball.

Their landing was bumpy, but it only served to make the bubbles bounce in his bloodstream a little more. Captain Jack came out of the cockpit as soon as they had taxied down the runway.

'My apologies for the turbulence. We hit some heat wave action. I hope your flight was pleasant, sir, miss?' Captain Jack had an amused look on his face and handed a handkerchief to Sam. Sam figured he had red lipstick blotches strategically placed on his face and neck.

'Got my own, Captain, but thanks. Great flying, as always.' Sam took out his own handkerchief and did his usual repair work. Kelly smiled, pulled out her mirror, and reapplied the telltale red lipstick. He was doomed.

She was tipsy, and as they exited the plane she paused at the top of the stairs. He didn't want her to fly down facefirst, so Sam scooped her up in his arms and carried her to the waiting limo driver.

'Hello, there!' Kelly waved to the driver from her position in Sam's arms.

'Let's go straight to dinner, Marcus.' Sam gently slid Kelly into the Town Car's back seat, where she shifted her dress upward a bit and sank into the black leather comfort.

'Yes, sir. The traffic is pretty mild. We should be there in less than thirty minutes.' Marcus tipped his hat forward and closed the door behind Sam.

'How gallant of you, Sir Sam.'

'My pleasure, believe me. I'd carry you around all over town if it didn't draw such a crowd. Do you like seafood?' Sam helped her with her seat belt and got his own fastened.

'As long as it doesn't stare back at me.' Kelly giggled.

Their limo ride was over in a blink and Sam retrieved Kelly from the car gracefully. As they entered the restaurant, she noticed several other couples dressed to the teeth. She got some long stares, which she took as a compliment, hopefully.

They were ushered to a quiet corner table where several candles were lit and an orchid in a plastic box sat at her place. Sam helped her with her wrap, which the host whisked away. Then he pulled out the chair for her.

'Oh, Sam, this is lovely. Where are we anyway?'

'Palisades. I thought we'd have dinner before our main event. How does fried calamari and crab-stuffed mushrooms sound to start?'

'Bring 'em on, big boy, I'm starving.'

Sam was thoroughly amused with Kelly. She must have had some big nights out in L.A., working in the fashion world, but she always seemed to be experiencing everything for the first time.

He ordered appetizers when the waiter came around, and passed on the cocktails. They both needed to eat.

'Those glass pieces hanging from the ceiling are Chihuly. He's a local glass artist.'

'They're just beautiful. You sure know your art, Sam.'

'I was raised by collectors. I'm sure my nursery was post-modern. I think there was a Chagall print over my crib. *Circus Horseback Rider*, if I recall correctly.'

'More likely the original.'

'I swear it was only a signed lithograph.'

Kelly went on teasing him about art and his parents and money until the waiter arrived with artfully arranged appetizers.

She was stunning sitting across from him in red velvet. Her arms were slender and tan, and that dress hugged her in all the right places. He found himself enchanted by her movements and her chatter while she dragged her fried calamari in red bell pepper and mango chutney.

He offered her a bite of scampi sautéed in garlic and butter. She opened her mouth and hungrily accepted it. Sam savored the incredibly sensuous moments one at a time. He was in no rush. He knew she would be in his bed soon enough. There was no keeping the two of them from making love in the very near future. Their desire was mutual; he knew that. In the meantime, the journey was an extremely pleasurable one.

After mounds of appetizers, a wonderful salad, very flavorful Thai soup, and lobster, Sam had the waiter bring the house special dessert: crème brûlée. Kelly went crazy for it and licked her silver spoon to get the last bit.

Kelly was in heaven. Dessert heaven, man heaven, food heaven, all of those. Her head had stopped spinning after her fourth appetizer, and she was ready to go to the ball and boogie.

She gathered herself together nicely when it was time to get back in the limo with Marcus. Marcus whisked them downtown and let them out in front of the art museum.

As they emerged from the car, Kelly found herself surrounded by handsome men of all ages in their black and white tuxes. The women were wildly adorned, with feathers in their exotic hair designs, masks, beads dripping from everything, and every dress she saw seemed to be black.

The more she gathered her wits, the more black and white she saw. They entered through a courtyard to the main building, where a sign read: SEATTLE ART MUSEUM'S BLACK AND WHITE MASQUERADE BALL. BY INVITATION ONLY. PLEASE PRESENT YOUR CARDS TO THE STAFF.

Sam pulled two engraved cards from his jacket pocket, and they entered the room. She was in a black and white movie, and she was the living color. Her red dress was a major standout.

'A little detail you forgot to mention, Sam?'

Sam grinned sheepishly. 'Just one. But you look so fabulous, I didn't want to tell you.'

'Oh, well, I'll be the flashing red light leading people to their destination. *Clean up on aisle ten*. Now clue me in on the event, here.'

'It's a benefit to raise money for the museum. My parents are on the board of directors. We usually all go, but they're in Europe this year. End of story. Would you like to dance? The orchestra is right this way.' He led her to a room full of black-and-white-attired guests, where the orchestra was playing a waltz. Sam swept her onto the dance floor boldly.

'Whoa, did you take ballroom dancing as a side course in law school? You hid your talents at the church social, Sam.'

'Just hang on there, honey, I'll show you how to cut a rug.'

Wasn't this scene in some old movie where she was supposed to wear virgin white, but wore red instead? Oh, yes, *Jezebel*. My, she was wicked. She relaxed into his arms and let him take her spinning around the room.

He led her skillfully through the waltz. By the time they had circled the room once, all eyes were on the dashing man and his *woman in red*. What else in new? Kelly thought.

Sam drew her close to him for the end of the dance and kissed her gently on the cheek. Her blood was racing. Her heart beat a completely new way than she had ever experienced before. As the next song began, Kelly fell head over heels into the experience of being held close to Sam and letting the music take them over.

The song ended, and they parted momentarily. Sam took her hand in his and brought it to his lips for a soft kiss.

On the stage, a woman in a fabulous sequined black sheath stepped up to the microphone. The band began to play an old forties song she had always loved, and the singer's voice was mellow and sweet. Not as good as Cora, but good. 'For Sentimental Reasons,' was the song she sang.

Kelly was swept away on a sea of emotion. She surrendered herself to Sam, letting him lead her gracefully across the dance floor. Their bodies molded together passionately. His hand pressed warmly on her back with a lover's touch. She closed her eyes and swayed to the romantic song. When Sam kissed her, she practically swooned.

The band picked up with a more lively number, and the singer was joined by two other girls for an Andrews Sisters sound. Sam swung her out into a perfect spin, and she found herself hoofing it up like a genuine forties babe. Who knew she had it in her?

They danced until her feet surrendered. She leaned on Sam as they found a table. The low candles glowed on the black tablecloths and tiny silver stars were scattered over the tabletop.

He motioned for a waiter and ordered a couple of Cokes at her request. Caffeine and sugar, that was what she needed. When it arrived, she ordered another and downed the first very ungracefully.

'Don't get between a woman and her cola!' Sam handed his glass to her and sat back to watch her. She winked at him and let a satisfied sigh escape her lips, then sipped his drink more slowly.

'Oh, oh! Prince Charming, look over there. I see another Cinderella in red! Yippee! Wow, she has a feather boa, too. I can relax now.'

'You seem pretty relaxed already. I love dancing with you, Kelly.'

'This is simply maaaarvelous, Sam, and all for art's sake, you say?'

'Let's go upstairs in a few minutes. They're having a sale. It's work by little-known local artists. The museum buys the paintings, then sells them for a fund-raiser. My folks always scout out new talent and try and support the artist's work in the future.'

'Boy, I have done a lot of things, Sam, but this world is a new one on me.'

'It made me a very visual person, being raised to appreciate art.'

She watched him sit back in his chair and take in the whole picture of her with a look of *appreciation* on his face. So he was visual, huh?

Kelly gave him a quirky smile and reached out across the table. He met her touch and their fingers intertwined.

'I know it's still early, but I have a deep desire to have you all to myself at some point this evening, so drink up, dear, and come with me.' His voice was dark and tempting across the table.

She felt her resolve to have a full four weeks of dates evaporate like morning mist in the Seattle sunshine. In this case, it was moonlight, and she heard the words to 'Blue Moon' in the background.

She was tired of standing alone. All of her dreams were here in front of her. Sam, Paradise, and a life she had imagined a thousand times. Why not? she thought to herself. She drank the last sip of cola and rose up from the table.

'I'm all yours, Sam.' He got up and moved over to stand in front of her. He ran his hands softly down her bare arms and pulled her close to him. She looked up into his dark blue eyes.

'Those are the words I've been waiting for, Kelly.'

She put her arms around his waist and kissed him deeply. 'You're going to need that lipstick wiper again, Sam,' she whispered.

'Do your worst, darlin', I'm ready.'

'So am I, Sam, so am I.'

Sam let Kelly pick out a very striking Impressionist landscape – purples, greens, and vivid rose shades danced all over the canvas.

The painting somehow reflected the inner secret dialogue that danced between them. Each brush of her hand, each movement, sent a wave of heat over him. As they purchased their find and had the docent take the address to send it, he could feel the desire between them just under the surface, just under control enough to get through these tasks.

He finished up the sale and whisked her downstairs to the coat checkroom. It was early in the evening, and the line was minimal. Sam called Marcus on his cell phone while they waited for her wrap. Marcus was two blocks over with the limo.

As soon as they settled in, Kelly slipped her black velvet sling-back shoes off and twisted herself around so she was in Sam's arms.

Sam reached over and touched a button that sent a darkly tinted window sliding up between their compartment and Marcus. He saw Marcus wink in the rearview mirror before it sealed all the way. He was surrounded.

'Pretty smooth, Grayson. Is there a button for low music and another that makes this seat into a bed?'

Sam pushed one button and the music swelled up softly. He grinned. 'Haven't got the bed installed yet.'

'Sam, I know we promised to spend four whole weeks together before . . . and it's only been one week . . .' Kelly was stumbling over her words. 'I just want you to know I am usually a woman of strong conviction.'

'I'm crazy about you, Kelly.'

'You don't have to say that to get me in bed, you know.'

'I know.'

'Oh, very funny.'

'Kelly, I have only good thoughts about your virtue and conviction, but these condoms have a shelf life, you know?' He kissed her neck, and she arched so he could get more of it. That made him nuts.

'Mmmmmm ... and that is my last word on the subject,' she mumbled.

And it was. She leaned into his kisses for the next twenty minutes as they returned to the airfield.

They made a smooth limo exit and airplane entry, and Captain Jack seemed to know to make his appearance brief.

The lights of the cabin were suddenly dimmed off except for a golden strip of light along the floor runners.

They were off the ground quickly and off the ground with each other, floating above Seattle, lost in a long, burning embrace. Time was suspended as Sam slowly touched and stroked her body into a state of ecstasy in the strange and sweet darkness of the plane. The night stars were like a pathway leading them to the moment they would make love.

As the plane came in for a landing, they leaned back tenderly in each other's arms.

'My place?'

'Can we teletransport?'

'Next year.'

'Take me anywhere.' She meant it, too. She would have gladly become a mile-high-club member about twenty minutes ago, but as Sam reminded her, he wanted hours with her, and the flight was only a short one. Or, as had become their favorite phrase: not here.

Somehow they managed to get off the plane, climb

into the Jag, and arrive at the Grayson Building faster than she imagined possible.

They parked on the street, and Sam took her through a side door, then to an elevator. He inserted a key, the doors opened, and they stepped in. He pressed *P* – for penthouse, she assumed, 'cause it sure wasn't the parking level they stepped off into.

Two stained-glass Frank Lloyd Wright-style windows flanked the double entry doors. Knowing Sam, they were originals. Sam opened one side and invited her in with a sweeping gesture.

He reached a light switch and pulled up a dim, romantic light. His apartment was glorious. She walked into black and gold, with rich olive green accents. It was very open and spacious, and very sensuous. There was an Asian feeling to it.

Several sculptures reflected the soft light. Luminous jade carvings of two horses were lit by soft up-lights that glowed against the raw silk wall coverings. A painting that she swore was an original Edward Hopper hung over the black granite fireplace. It depicted a man in a very square office, looking out over the rooftops of an old city with low buildings.

'Is that what I think it is? I keep having to ask you that question.'

'It's called *Office in a Small City*. Perfect for me, isn't it? It was a gift from my parents. It's actually a copy, though. The original Hopper is in the Met.'

'Well, that's a relief. For a minute I thought you might be really stinking rich.'

'Very funny.' He came over and put his arms around her from behind. 'I can't help what I was born into. I hope it didn't scare you off tonight. It's pretty rare that I'm forced to flaunt it.'

'Hey, as long as you don't sleep in a coffin during the day, I think we're all right. *Renounce your fortune and run away with me, Rodriguo. Your parents will never approve of our match.*' She put her hand to her brow melodramatically.

'Actually, they are extremely cool people and just want to see me happily m-m-m-m . . .'

'Married?' Kelly filled in the word Sam was stuttering over and it hit her like a splash of ice-cold water. Her body went stiff in his arms, and he felt it. He stepped back and grabbed her hand.

'I'm so sorry, it just slipped out.'

'No, no, it's okay, it's not you.'

It wasn't him. It was *her* and being wanted for *murder*. She had promised herself to tell Sam the truth, and she'd failed. She'd let herself fall into a game of omission.

She looked around the room at the burnished bronze wool sofa with its elegant black and green hand-painted pillows, and wanted to sink into it until she disappeared.

If she told him, all of this, all the magic of this evening would vanish like a ghost. The ghost of her dead husband. She just couldn't make love to him with this sick feeling overtaking her. She would be sealing all her lies . . . with a kiss.

'Sam, I have to go home.'

Sam brought her close to him and held her hands together between his own. His warmth and strength were powerful. She wanted to close her eyes and pretend it all away except for him and this moment.

'Don't,' he whispered. His voice was deep with desire.

With great emotional effort, she pulled herself away, touched his cheek, turned, and ran out the door in her red velvet shame. She left her coat and clutch behind, bolted out the double doors, pushed the elevator button, which opened immediately, and got in.

When the doors closed behind her, she leaned on the wall and let the sobs that were stuck in her throat rise up and out. She heard herself wail a terrible, sad cry. The tears streamed down her face, and she had nothing to wipe them with. Damn, damn elevators.

Kelly stepped out of the building into a downpour. Those happy little clouds they'd flown through had darkened and rumbled up some lightning and thunder and a bucket dumping of rain. Perfect. She had a ten-block walk to Myrtle's house in fabulous shoes and a velvet dress.

She hiccuped through her tears and leaned against the Grayson Building like a stray cat. Damn dead Raymond. Damn him.

Sam poured himself two fingers of Scotch and let it slide down his throat in one smooth shot. He heard the rain pouring down outside and worried about Kelly. But there was no use chasing after her. She was a runaway.

Kelly was going to have to find her way back home herself this time. She just had to find her own way to end her running streak.

He set the glass down hard. She might come back. Just in case she did, he went over to the entry and sent the elevator back down. He would be here when she decided to have a real relationship.

Sam sat in his sleek black leather club chair and contemplated the disastrous ending to a beautiful evening. He rubbed his hand across his eyes and forehead in a strained gesture. He always went for the difficult ones, didn't he? What an optimist, always believing this one was going to be different.

Kelly *was* different. The difference was he was in love with this one.

Sam got up and did what he always did to relieve the stress of his relationships, or any other stress he managed to create in his life. He took his clothes off. He left a trail of tuxedo parts strewn across the room as he walked.

He dimmed the apartment lights even more, leaving just enough to see. He slid back a set of shoji screens at the far end of the living room and stepped onto the black stone surface surrounding his lap pool.

There were low, underwater lights that just barely illuminated the long, narrow pool. He dove noiselessly into the warm water and glided half the length before taking up a smooth stroke, then another.

Kelly took three steps out toward the sidewalk thinking the rain was letting up, only to have the sky open more violently and dump on her. She jumped back under the narrow eaves.

Thunder and lighting now came directly together with no room to count the seconds in between, which she had been mindlessly occupying herself doing in an attempt to stop her stupid thoughts. She jumped about a foot when the sky lit up around her.

Sam loved her. She was a grown woman, and they would work everything out. He would help her prove she hadn't killed Raymond, and they'd figure out what to do with the money under her bed. He would know she hadn't killed Raymond.

Suddenly she ached for him even more than before. She was in trouble. She and her soaking-wet velvet dress and the rain dripping off the end of her nose. She needed Sam.

Kelly turned around and went back through the door. Thank heavens it wasn't locked. She stepped into the elevator. Why was she forever crying or screaming in elevators? Her life transitions seemed to take place in elevators. Maybe this would be the last one.

The doors opened on the seventh floor and she walked quietly through Sam's front door. He was such a trusting person – he never locked any doors.

She was overwhelmed for a minute with her feelings for this amazing man. She took a deep breath and prepared herself for the confession she had practiced a hundred times. He would understand.

The lights were so low she had to wait for her eyes to adjust. As she slowly walked across the room, leaving soggy footprints all over the floor, she could hear the pouring rain outside, and a sound like splashing water over in the far corner. She approached as silently as possible.

Peering through the darkness past the open screens, she caught sight of Sam as he rounded the end of the dark pool and started toward the other end again.

His magnificent shoulders and back were revealed by the dancing underwater lights. She watched his power-ful strokes propel him through the water, letting her glimpse portions of his completely naked body. It was truly the most seductive thing she had ever seen in her life. His form was perfection. He hardly broke the water as he swam. She was mesmerized. Slipping into a dark corner, she leaned against the wall and watched him.

On his next turn, Sam lifted his head slightly and caught sight of her red dress. He stopped and came up to the end of the pool closest to her. She was shivering, soaking-wet, her hair hanging in dripping strands. She clung to the wall. Her eyes flashed wild as she met his gaze.

'Come here,' he commanded.

She came slowly over to him. He stood up waist high in the water on the built-in stone steps. He put his hands softly on her ankles and slid them down to her shoes.

She flinched at his first touch, and held on to the stair rails for support. With two swift moves he slid the shoes off her feet and threw them aside. Her wet velvet dress dripped all over him. He took one step up and ran his hands up her bare legs, then his mouth up her wild rose tattoo. She shivered – with pleasure this time, it seemed.

He let go and brought himself up next to her. She gasped and started to speak, but he put his fingers against her lips for a moment, then covered her mouth with a deep, probing kiss that said everything he was feeling. He left her for one second, reached his fallen clothes, and came back with his erection sheathed in a condom.

He unzipped her wet dress and peeled it off her. He looked into her eyes and saw hunger and need burning through her gaze. She leaned against his arms as he ran his mouth down her neck. With one hand he unhooked her black strapless bra. As it fell away he cupped her breast in his hand gently and circled it with his tongue.

He would have her. She would be his. A dark, heated blackness overcame him.

*

She let out a low moan as his mouth burned and teased her breasts. All she could do was feel. He slid her dress and panties all the way off and she reached down with one hand to step out of them.

Her touch moved up his muscular thigh and pressed against his throbbing, full-blown erection. She moved her gaze down his body to drink in the gloriousness of him.

She stroked him softly with her fingertips until a deep, primal sound escaped his lips. He dropped to his knees on the smooth black stone floor and let his hands and mouth caress her everywhere, holding her from behind, until she swayed with the pleasure and grabbed his shoulders, screaming his name.

He stood, picked her up in his arms, and stepped back down into the water.

Leaning up against the poolside he expertly and smoothly guided her, lowering her onto him until she felt the incredible heat and gloriousness of his manhood slide deep within her. She almost fainted with the pleasure, and leaned against his broad chest for a minute. Then she moved on him.

The water rushed around them. He held her and moved her until together they were like music.

The sound and sensations of their lovemaking rushed into her head and made her crazy, just crazy with lust. Their bodies were part of the water, and the water flowed with their movements.

He raised her and took her breast in his hot mouth,

and suddenly she was spinning into the darkness, stars exploding behind her eyes. As he held her she arched backward against him and let go of everything holding her back. She dug her fingernails into his strong shoulders and cried out his name again and again. At that moment, he howled like an animal as he reached his release, a throbbing explosion inside her that made her release come all over again. Then she fell back against him, and he held her close.

She sobbed and put her forehead against his shoulder, letting the tears slide down into the water. He put his arms around her, picked her up, and carried her out of the pool to a wooden platform covered with thick black towels.

He dried her off gently for a minute, then quickly dried himself and carried her to his bed.

They lay closely together in the dark. He stroked her hair and her forehead until she fell asleep in his arms all night long.

It was cold where the back of her body stuck out of the covers. Kelly opened one eye, then the other. Sam had most of the covers slung over him. Early-morning light filtered through the billowy silk curtains of Sam's bedroom windows.

She quietly pulled the silky cotton duvet around her shoulders and burrowed into his bed. Sam's warm back was against her, and she held very still, savoring the feel of him. His essence was all around her.

Whatever she supposed was the rightness or

wrongness of her actions, she didn't care right now. She would sort all that out in her mind later. All she knew at this moment was that she belonged here next to Sam. Like she was filling a space that was intended just for her. She went back to sleep pressed up against him.

There was a knock at the door that made both of them sit straight up in bed. Kelly instinctively clutched the covers to her front. Sam bolted out of bed naked.

He grabbed a pair of silk boxers out of a drawer, and danced into them, walking at the same time. A huge grin started across her mouth, and she stuffed her face in the pillow to laugh.

She heard him stop and probably look out the view hole to the hall, she guessed. There was a long silence. Then Sam opened the door. Now, who rated a peek at Sam in his boxers?

She stopped laughing and almost got up to find out, but he quickly reappeared in the bedroom carrying an enormous basket.

He stood there, basket in hand, and looked at her for a moment. He tipped his head to the right, then the left, as if trying to focus on her face. A very, very amused look came over him.

'Very funny, Grayson. Well, this is what I look like in the morning when I sleep on wet hair. What's with the basket?'

'It seems there are no secrets in Paradise.' He came over, set down the basket on the nightstand, and eased himself back into bed, taking her in his arms.

His kisses started softly against her neck, then turned sensual and hot. She wrapped her arms around his broad, muscular back and luxuriated in his passion until she was mindless.

They made love with the heat of the sun streaming in on them.

Sometime later, Kelly stretched languidly, rousing Sam from his half-draped-over-her position. He was toying with her wild hair.

'The basket?' she murmured.

'Here's the card.' He reached for it and read:

'To our two favorite friends. Life is a picnic, so eat! P.S. Don't worry about work for a while, you are on wellness leave.

Love, Myrtle, Dottie, Cora, and Mrs. P.'

'Boy, the old ladies in Paradise are a little different than what I am used to!'

'I assume this means I have their blessing to seduce you repeatedly.' Sam ran his hand down her side and over her hip.

'Not until I brush my teeth. Do you have a spare toothbrush? I seem to have no clothes, no shoes, and no equipment.'

'That will get you service around here for sure. There's a new one in the medicine cabinet.'

Kelly slid out of bed and padded naked to the adjoining bath.

'So tell me, what's in there? I'm starving,' she called through the door.

'Here's a list on the back of the card. Dottie's orange-currant scones, Cora sent a thermos of coffee, and homemade biscuits, and wild clover honey. Hey, I can think of a few uses for that. Mrs. P. put in fresh squeezed orange juice. Myrtle put in . . . a can of whipped cream. Hmmmm, I wonder what that's for?'

'I don't know whether to be grateful or mortified.' Kelly emerged from the bathroom naked and ran for the covers. 'Sam, I'm naked.'

'I noticed.' He warmed her. 'You can borrow my pajama tops like Claudette Colbert in *It Happened One Night*, or I can just keep you warm.'

'How about both?' Kelly reached over him and grabbed a pear out of the basket. Sam got up out of bed, letting her browse over his fine body once again. She hadn't noticed the muscles on his legs last night; they were amazing. And since he'd lost his silk boxers again – there was that great behind of his.

As he headed across the room he glanced behind him and caught her looking at him. He smiled and winked.

Sam managed to find her a pajama top and even set up their goodies enough to take a huge tray back to bed. The coffee was still steaming, and Kelly put whipped cream in hers.

She fed him bites of pear and a piece of scone with honey, which he licked off her fingers. Pretty soon she was deeply involved in his ability to devour honey and whipped cream off her midriff, and then Sam got very creative, and then she got very creative back, and then he got more creative. Between moans of pleasure, she begged him to stop.

The day moved into night and Kelly stood at the kitchen window, having reclaimed 'her' pajama top, to watch the sun slide behind the hills. She didn't care about anything anymore except being happy with Sam.

Sam came up behind her, wrapped his arms around her waist, and held her in his warmth. She could feel the strength of his bare chest. She had never felt this safe in her life. She turned around to face him and melted into his kiss, then put her cheek against his chest.

'Can we just stay here forever?' she murmured.

'Let's see, this is Sunday. I think we can have at least today without the outside world disturbing us.'

She lifted her face and looked in his eyes. 'Let's curl up in bed and watch old movies. You do like old movies, don't you?'

'Musical, Western, or drama?'

'Comedy . . . love, you know, chick movies.'

'I'm willing to sacrifice for a good cause. You check my film archives and see what's available.'

'Sam?'

'Yes?'

'Thank you.'

Sam kissed her again, slowly, lovingly, in answer. Then he took her hand and led her to the movie cabinet in his bedroom. She was amazed at the range of movies he had. He went back to the kitchen while she browsed.

Kelly decided to test Sam's resolve and picked *Music Man*, a nice sappy musical. She went over to the TV and started deciphering the remotes.

'That one with the purple buttons runs everything,' Sam called from the kitchen.

She heard popcorn beginning to pop. 'Psychic guy, huh?'

Sam rummaged in the freezer for ice cubes and clinked a few in two glasses. He pulled a couple sodas from the fridge and got a bowl for the popcorn. He leaned against the counter, waiting for the popcorn to finish.

He felt a deep satisfaction in his body. Their lovemaking was incredible. Maybe he had tamed the skittish cat at last. Now she was in his blood, and even thinking of her, her silky skin, her long legs, made his head rush and his body respond.

He wanted to see her in his bed every morning. For as long as he could, anyway. All he had to do was be cool and take it slow. Cats always stay where they're fed.

He took the popcorn out of the microwave and emptied the bag into the bowl. He was going to have to call out for some dinner pretty soon. Catnip and salmon. He balanced the soda glasses and bowl of popcorn in his arms and headed for the bedroom. The familiar strains of 'River City' were wafting out of his bedroom, his sister's favorite movie. Sacrifice. He groaned. Good cause. He kept walking.

*

'Sam, I have no clothes.' Kelly stood at the window wrapped in Sam's silk curtains as the Monday morning light streamed in beside her.

'I suppose people might talk if we took you out in the red velvet gown.'

'Not to mention I think it shrank.'

'Hmm, this is an interesting dilemma. How about a pair of my sweats and a sweatshirt?'

'Well, hell, that might get me out to your car and over to Myrtle's. Bring 'em on.'

Sam pulled a clean pair of gray sweats and his Penn State sweatshirt out of a dresser drawer. Kelly climbed into them, naked underneath.

'I don't think my clothes have ever been this happy.' Sam reached out for her.

'It's just a damn good thing they are big on me, 'cause I don't date guys that wear smaller sizes than I do. Okay, I'm all set. You've got your swim class tonight, and me, I'm . . .'

Kelly broke off from Sam's embrace and gathered her dried-out belongings up in one of his gym bags he loaned her. She'd finish her sentence, but what would she say? *I'm going to find out if I'm still wanted for murder?*

She watched Sam in his lawyerly dark olive suit make the rounds of his apartment: water the plants, turn on the answering machine, and get his briefcase. She liked being part of his routine.

She really needed to get back home to Myrtle's and think.

*

Back at the Hen House, Myrtle was just finishing up with the every-Monday comb-out on Alice.

'Hi, Mrs. Hutchinson, I hope you have a nice choir rehearsal tonight, and that tenor is going to ask you out for sure tonight, you look stunning.'

'Thanks, dear, and I hope you had a good roll in the sack with Sam. It's so nice to see you young folks being frisky.'

Oh, my God. Kelly didn't know what to say. Of course, here she was in Sam's clothes, including his college sweatshirt, and damn, everyone in town knew. Myrtle laughed silently until tears came down her cheeks.

Kelly went to the nail station and started stripping her old polish off. Two days in Sam's pool, in Sam's shower, and in Sam's bed had left her pretty much a wreck.

Myrtle finished with Alice in record time, sprayed her down, collected her check, and sent her out the door. Then she hurried over to Kelly.

'Spill it, girlfriend, I'm about to burst. Did you like the biscuits? And the whipped cream?' Myrtle sat down across from Kelly, grabbed up her hands, and started stripping red off her nails.

'Yes, everything was divine. Not very subtle, though, you guys are *so* bad.'

'The time for pussyfootin' around is over, dearie. Let's hear the story.'

Kelly told Myrtle the basic details, leaving out some

of the deliciously private variations on their weekend. After all, she did have some secrets worth keeping.

'I told you he was the one.'

'You were right. I've decided to marry him.'

Myrtle's eyes widened about up to her finely drawn eyebrows.

'Did he ask you?'

'No.'

'Well, I'll be a ring-tailed pheasant. It worked even better than we thought.'

'What worked?'

'Oh, all the matchmaking me and Dottie Williamson have been up to, you know.'

'Oh, that. Yes, it did, so give yourself a big pat on the back and paint my nails pink. Pink is a good nonexistent-engagement color.'

Kelly couldn't stop smiling. Her body was tired and ached in places she had forgotten about. She leaned back in the red leatherette chair and relaxed while Myrtle gabbed excitedly on about weddings and rings and photographers.

It all sounded great. A wonderful fantasy. She didn't even know why she'd said it, but after being made love to by Sam for two days she just felt like it was possible. She knew she was falling for him hard. The thought of him made her crazy and happy and warm all at the same time.

Too bad none of it was true. Her smile faded. Sam would never marry her. She was going to be found out, and he'd hate her. Then there was that pile of money under her bed. She was going to take a nap, get cleaned up, and go over to his office. It was time to come clean with Sam. She couldn't in any way justify not telling him that Raymond was dead.

Kelly showered, then lay down and slept a deep, middle-of-the-morning sleep.

She dreamed of a wedding dress, very floaty, with layers of silk organza and a beaded lace bodice. It was the kind of dress that made you look like a princess. There was a diamond crown in her hair, and her veils were floating on the summer breeze.

Sam stood at the altar waiting for her in a gray morning suit. He watched her come down the aisle by herself. When she came very close, he tucked one daisy into her bouquet. She looked down at it, then back to his face.

Sam became Raymond. Her dress turned into white leather, her veil was ripped, mud-stained high-heeled boots were on her feet. Her hair turned into black crow feathers.

She dropped her bouquet and backed away, then turned and ran down the white church runner, dropping black feathers all the way down the aisle. Her screams became a caw-caw-cawing.

Kelly's eyes stung with tears. She pulled the covers closer around her for a minute, then flung them off and got up. She was going to get ready.

She slipped into a silk camisole and matching panties from the back of her drawer and contemplated her closet. Her beige capri pants and a silk blouse would do. Some of the clothes she had packed for her honeymoon with Raymond. A little on the summery side, but still okay in this good weather they'd been having. Simple but sexy would be perfect. Her hair was trashed, but with some combing her new, softer waves sprang back to life.

Her hands shook as she buttoned the tiny buttons up her blouse front. She added a pair of beige sandals to let her peachy-pink-painted toenails show and threw her beige sweater over her shoulders. Her thoughts were racing as she dressed.

Before she went to Sam's she needed somewhere quiet and private to make a call to Caroline again. Kelly looked at Myrtle's statue of Mary that sat on a high dresser. She was made of shells with a beautifully painted face. Another New Orleans treasure.

'Give me strength,' she prayed out loud.

12

'How was the benefit? Grand as always?' Faith slid a cup of coffee onto Sam's desk and stood there waiting.

'It was the best one I've ever been to. Of course, I know that the entire town knows every detail of my life for the last two days, so I hardly need to fill you in, do I?'

'Hardly. *I* packed the basket.'

'Thank you. I live in a fishbowl, but thank you.'

'You're welcome. Bring my linens back in when you get a chance, will you?' Faith turned and exited, humming her way out the door.

Sam tried to focus on his work. He checked his schedule calendar. He straightened his desk up. He gave up and paced, staring out the window at Paradise. Faith knocked on the door and brought him the *Seattle Times*. She'd turned it to the society section. There on the pages of a large metropolitan newspaper was a picture of him in his tux and Kelly in her red dress.

'Son of prominent art philanthropist Samuel Grayson II had a ball at Seattle Art Museum benefit this Saturday with his Lady in Red.'

Shit! If Raymond Bianchi was smart and hired a private agency, he'd track Kelly down in no time after that picture. He had to do something. He couldn't let anything happen to her.

Faith knocked on the door and stuck her head in. 'Kelly's here.'

Sam strode out the office door quickly. Faith jumped out of the way. Kelly looked surprised – and smooth as silk in her beige outfit. He took her arm and pulled her into the office.

'Kelly, your picture, our picture, is in the paper. The Seattle paper.'

Kelly grabbed up the paper and stared. 'That's a good picture. Wow.'

'I don't know what kind of resources Raymond has, but he could possibly track you down from that photo. I think you should stay with me for a while.'

'Sam, there's something you need to know.'

Faith's voice came through the intercom, 'Sam, Peter Brody on line one. You asked me to tell you if his call came in.'

'Thanks, I'll take it.' Sam sat behind his desk and picked up the phone. 'This will be helpful. I'm glad you're here.' Sam pushed his phone line button. 'Pete, what've you got for me?'

Kelly was not glad. She felt sick. She curled up into one of the office chairs and watched Sam nodding to his friend. This must be his lawyer buddy from L.A. Would Brody know about her? She wanted to tell Sam herself. She was ready to tell him.

Sam had a look of concern on his face as he listened to his friend on the phone. That was normal. She knew the instant it happened – the instant normal changed to horrible. His eyes fastened on her, and he stopped answering his friend. His responses became short and curt. He said words like 'when?' and 'no' with a precision she'd never seen him use. All the time he never took his eyes off her.

Until the call was finished. He set the phone down deliberately. He lowered his gaze to his desk and stared at the leather blotter for a long, silent minute.

'Let me explain.'

'Don't. Don't talk.' He looked back up at her. 'First thing is, I want you to give me a dollar.'

'Why?' But she dug in her leather bag even while she asked it, and handed him a dollar.

'Good. I'll accept that as a retainer. Now I'm your lawyer. Nothing you say will go past these walls. It's called attorney-client privilege. But it's very important that you listen to me before you speak, okay?'

He was pale. She saw the strain in his face. A horrible chill ran through her. She wrapped her beige cashmere sweater around her and shivered. 'Yes,' she answered.

'Here is how this works. I can never knowingly let my client knowingly lie on the stand. If you are guilty, you must plead guilty, and it would be my job to *get* you to plead guilty. If you plan on claiming you didn't commit a crime, then I can never hear from you that you are anything but innocent. So don't tell me if you are guilty, tell me how you want to *plead*. Do you understand?' His fingers were laced together and his knuckles were white.

'I think so.' Kelly answered him slowly. 'If I were going to plead, I'd plead not guilty.'

'Okay, that's what you plead. From now on, as we talk, just tell me the story – just the events that occurred. Don't ever tell me if you committed this murder, all right?' Sam looked at her intently, waiting for an answer.

'Sam, I didn't do it. I came here to tell you.'

Sam pushed back in his chair and got up. He stood in the corner by his bookshelf looking at the wall for a minute, as if he couldn't bear to see her. Kelly felt tears coming. She breathed deeply and tried to steady herself.

'What, did you leave out a few details the last time we talked?'

'I didn't know he was dead when I came here asking for help on a divorce, remember? Then last Monday, after we'd talked, I called a friend of mine in L.A. to see about the divorce. She's a paralegal and I thought maybe if it was simple enough she could do it herself.

'She told me Raymond was dead, and that I was wanted for his murder. I knew *I* didn't kill him, so I waited to see if they'd find the real killers. I called her back today, but no progress has been made. Sam, please look at me.'

She realized he now knew she'd kept it from him for a week.

'Why didn't you tell me? What possible reason would you have?'

'Everything was so good. Somehow I just didn't want that to end.'

'So you found out Raymond was dead last Monday. Why didn't you turn yourself in?'

'I needed some time to think. If I turned myself in, then . . .'

'What?'

'Then the men who probably killed him would come after me. After I left Raymond I found a briefcase full of money in his car. I was halfway to Seattle before I found it. I figured I'd make a new start with it – or something. I wasn't sure what to do with it.' She twisted her hands together and watched for his reaction.

Sam leaned his head against the bookshelf on one hand. Kelly got up and came over to him. She put her hand on his shoulder. It was rock-hard. 'Sam, please listen to me. I was scared. I was confused. I didn't want to dump all this on you. I felt myself falling in love, and I wanted it to be wonderful.'

He turned and put his arms around her. She leaned her cheek against his unforgiving chest. She felt his anger burn through his gesture of kindness.

'Kelly.' His voice resonated through his chest to her ear. Rumbled into her. 'You need to turn yourself in to the police. I can afford the best lawyers on the West Coast. I can help with the case. I'm no criminal attorney, but I can do second chair.'

Kelly pushed herself away from him and sat down. She swiveled toward him. 'I'm not going to turn myself in, Sam. I'm not going to stand trial for Raymond's murder. I knocked him out; I didn't kill him. I left him alive.

'I ran into two men in the hallway. I'm betting they went looking for their money, and Raymond didn't have it. How did he die? Did he die of head wounds from the fall? Then we have a problem. I don't even know how he was killed. Do you?'

'Tell me the entire story again. Don't leave out anything. If you saw the men in the hall, you are a material witness. You can't clear yourself unless you bring in the evidence the police need to find the killers.'

'I'm not so worried about clearing myself. I know I didn't do it. But if I go back to L.A., even in jail, those guys will kill me, too. I can stay in Paradise. Even with the picture in the paper, it will be hard for them to find me.'

'You're thinking wrong. They *can* find *me*. My name is there in the paper next to your picture. I'm in the phone book, Kelly. Use the system to clear yourself. Turn in the money and yourself.'

'Can you promise me I won't be convicted?'

Sam felt a searing pain in his gut. He hung on to the bookcase and let the cold sweat pass over him. He couldn't promise her that. He'd seen people who should have walked free get convicted and people who should have been locked up walk away. He'd watched Chelsea get a jail sentence.

He fought all his cases with the ideals that his father gave him. Trusting that justice often was served, hoping his case wouldn't fall through any legal loopholes. He could fight a good fight, but there was never a guarantee.

He didn't answer her. He only knew she had to turn herself in. He couldn't accept any other alternative.

'Sam?'

Sam walked over to the door and opened it. He called Faith over and told her that the rest of the day would be spent in his office with Miss Atwood. Could she please hold his calls? All of them. Faith must have sensed trouble. She said she'd take care of it and could she bring in a pot of tea?

Everyone needs something to do when the pain starts. He agreed to the tea. He shut the door and realized he'd used Kelly's real name to Faith.

Kelly was standing at his window now. Looking out at Paradise.

'Are you going to turn me in, Sam?'

'As your attorney I can only advise you to turn yourself in, which I am doing. It's my job to protect you from past crimes. I would be breaching our attorney-client privilege if I turned you in, unless you told me you were about to murder someone. Hence the retainer. I'm now sworn.'

'Sam, surely you must see why I can't do that. Do you want to see me dead?'

'I want to see you cleared of murdering your husband.'

Myrtle stuck a long butcher knife into the fattest pumpkin. 'Somethin's up. I can feel it in my bones.' She cut jagged zigzags around the top.

'Oh, those old bones of yours are just worried. I think things are going very nicely.' Dottie Williamson scooped out the guts of the taller pumpkin with a long metal spoon and splatted them into a bowl.

'Faith said they were locked up in his office all day and she heard yelling. Mostly her.' Cora finished a particularly good eye on the smoothest side of a nice round pumpkin. She cleaned off her carving tool and pointed so the others could see.

'That's one good eye, there, Cora. Looks like Paul Newman.' Dottie wiped pumpkin guts off her cheek with one of Myrtle's pink dish towels. 'Myrtle, it's only been two weeks since Kelly came to town. Don't you think we're rushing things a bit?'

Myrtle wrenched the top off her pumpkin with one swift movement, then hacked at the connecting strings until it pulled free. 'We are talking about two people whose time has come. They're both ready for it; they both want the same things. They are both stubborn as mules. Keep runnin' around with a carrot tied to their tails and can't even see the big picture.' Myrtle handed over her pumpkin to Dottie for gutting and picked up a lopsided but large specimen.

'So how do you s'pose we get them to see that big picture, Myrtle?' Cora tilted back Paul Newman and gave a fine tune to her artwork.

'Plan B, ladies. Plan B. Dottie, Cora, can I get you two a refill on the peach daiquiris?'

'I believe that's a yes all around, hon.' Cora held up Paul for inspection.

'My, that's fine. You are a gifted artist, Cora.' Dottie passed the next cleaned-out pumpkin to her. 'Now make this one Joanne Woodward.'

Faith braved up and knocked on Sam's office door. Kelly had stalked out the door hours ago. The man couldn't shut himself up in there all night. 'Sam, I've got dinner for you. Cora sent it over.' She talked to the wood.

'It's Cora's night off.'

'She made it special for you. Now open up, I can't twist the knob with my hands full.'

Sam opened the door. He looked bad. His tie was gone, his shirt unbuttoned, his sleeves rolled up, his eyes red. She walked past him and put the covered plate on his desk along with silverware rolled in napkins and a bottle of beer.

'What's that for?'

'For drinking. It's Miller time.'

Sam laughed a short laugh. Faith saw law books scattered all over the office with sticky notes hanging out the edges.

'Now sit down and eat. I'm gonna stay here till you eat.' She plopped herself down in his client chair and popped open the diet soda she'd brought for herself.

'What's up, boss?' She took a sip and waited until he sat down and opened the cover of his dinner.

'Meat loaf, gravy, mashed potatoes. Green beans.'

'I've known you since you were six. I've worked for your dad for fifteen years and for you since you got back in town. I've read over all of Miss *Atwood*'s documents. You need someone to talk to, Sam. I'm it.'

'Pretty short story. Miss Atwood has problems.'

'Damn, I'd say. You know she didn't kill the guy. Why else would she have come to you for a divorce?'

'You know I can't talk about her case.'

'So, let's talk about something else. Let's talk about your love life.' Faith watched the bite of meat loaf pause in midair before Sam went ahead and ate it.

Kelly walked in the door like a bat-out-of-hell directly into *pumpkin* hell, formerly Myrtle's kitchen. Three women were cackling over shredded gourd innards and they all seemed to be . . . drunk.

'Ladies, are we having a good time?' Kelly laid her purse on the window seat cushion and sat down to watch. She was twisted up inside. She was bone weary. She could cry, but if she started, she'd never stop.

'Grab that blender and pour yourself a glass of Myrtle's famous fresh peach daiquiris, dear, they are divine, and you look like you could use one.' Dottie was blotty.

'None of you gals are driving, are you?'

'Nope. This here is our annual pumpkin night. Red Miller's Hardware Store has a competition for the best carving. Cora here's won three years running.' Myrtle was still understandable, but a little slurry around the edges.

'Oh, my God, it's Paul Newman and Joanne Woodward.' Kelly looked at the finished row of intricately carved pumpkins.

All the women screamed and slapped hands in the air. Kelly sat and watched the circus.

'I got his picture off the spaghetti sauce jar. For Joanne I just winged it.' Cora was obviously the best at holding her peach daiquiris.

'You're an extremely talented carver, Cora. Where'd you learn that?'

'Honey, I went to chef school in California. I took ice carving. You should see what I can do with an electric knife and a block of ice.' Cora beamed.

'Wow,' was all Kelly could say. It always amazed her to discover another layer to a Paradise resident. Everyone had a past. Everyone was more than they seemed. Maybe she fit in here better than she thought.

'Siddown and pull up a pumpkin, Kell, we'll have a gabfest and tell you all about life.' Myrtle handed her a large pumpkin and a large spoon. 'Clean the guts outta this one.'

'Okay, but I get a crack at carving, too. Not to challenge your winning streak, Cora. Just for fun.'

'Don't worry, hon, there's room for another winner in this town. Fun is what it's all about. Let's have some fun, right, girls?'

They all screeched and hollered and laughed again. These old women were nuts. Kelly got handed a Howdy Doody glass full of peach daiquiri. It was so delicious she forgot it was rum-laced and tossed the entire thing down.

'Slow down, there, honey, this stuff packs quite a punch.' Cora patted her shoulder.

A half hour later Kelly sat back and looked at her intricately carved pumpkin. Three old women stood behind her chair.

'That there is the most beautiful thing I've ever seen. Kelly, you are an artist. Working in that tattoo parlor really gave you skills.' Cora pointed at a particularly well done portion.

'Isn't that the old Shipley place?' Dottie asked.

'It is,' Kelly answered. 'See the twin turrets, and over here the magnolia tree?'

'Looks haunted even on a pumpkin,' Myrtle said.

'I think the spirits are friendly. When I was there, I felt it.'

'Now we're talking Halloween talk. I think we oughta go up there and turn it into a haunted house for the town kids this year.'

'We've only got a couple of weeks, Myrtle, how could we?' Kelly said.

'It's not condemned or anything, is it?' Dottie sat down and picked up her spiced tea.

Kelly laughed at Dottie. She'd decided to sober up a while back and made everyone tea. They'd all eaten the chicken Kievs Cora brought with her and moved on to Dottie's chocolate brownies washed down with spiced tea. The smells of peach and pumpkin and cinnamon and orange tea, and the wonderful tastes and that whole *female* experience was making Kelly forget all her troubles.

These women had lived through the death of spouses, through poverty, joy, and sorrow. Dottie had been married to the same man for fifty-one years. Cora had recovered from the loss of her wonderful husband ten years ago and remarried. She had five children who grew up into great people. She used to sing with a big band in the fifties. They'd all three worked hard to make themselves a life.

She felt more determined than ever to let the situation with Raymond go away. Turning herself in could only result in her having to leave this wonderful place and these wonderful people.

'Two weeks is plenty. We can do it. We'll get everyone to pitch in,' Kelly heard herself say out loud. 'But, ladies, I have another problem, and I need your help.'

'We were wondering when you'd get to it. Lay it out, girl, we're ready to take on the devil and tie his tail in a knot. We want you here with us, and no man's gonna get in the way.' Myrtle had stood up to make this speech. Her red apron was festooned with strands of pumpkin and an occasional seed. She whammed a wooden spoon on the table for emphasis. The other two applauded wildly.

Damn, she was in for it now. Kelly grabbed another brownie and started in telling her story.

13

He was in love with a wanted woman. Her perfume still lingered in his office. He felt her haunting him. He needed her to be free of the shadow of her past so they could have a future. He was going to have to talk her out of her fears. But how could he if she was right?

She'd run out the door after an hour of going over the details of the day she'd left Raymond. She'd left when Sam had tried once more to convince her to turn herself in.

Maybe she was packing up right now. She could leave Paradise and go hide out somewhere else. He could lose her forever.

He stood at his window and looked over the town of Paradise, almost hidden in the darkness of night. A few lights gave off a golden glow on Main Street.

She came back once after running away from him. He thought about their lovemaking. It was spectacular and wild and loving all at the same time. The intimacy that happened right away with them, even just watching movies together, was so unusual. He felt so alive with her. She was like a fire in his heart.

She came back once; she'd come back again.

Sam distracted himself making order in his office. He stacked up the law books he'd spent hours going through, and piled up all his documentation in his desk in-box. Faith had stayed late talking to him and finally, working together, they'd created some files and done some Internet research.

What if she was right, what if they convicted her? He'd seen it happen before. He let his mind slip to a horrible picture of Kelly in prison. He'd seen the harshness of prison. He'd visited Chelsea there a few times, and it had changed her forever. He couldn't let that happen to Kelly.

Even if he appealed her case, she could be held for months, even years. They'd probably try her for first-degree murder. Sam had deliberately not told her how Raymond had died. A murder involving a gun, that couldn't go any lower than second-degree.

It wouldn't jeopardize his law license to let her go on living here without dealing with it, because he'd be violating attorney-client privilege if he revealed anything about her case to the police – or to anyone. They might come up with some leads in the case if he could buy her some time – and for himself – to prepare her case.

According to Faith, the entire town was ready to hide Kelly forever. That Rat Pack of four old women who actually knew all the details of Kelly's status had already sworn their secrecy.

Raymond sure wouldn't be after her. That left the

two men and their money. Could they track her down from the picture in the *Times*? Possibly. The money was a problem. But the police didn't know it existed. Apparently only Kelly, Myrtle, and dead Raymond knew it existed. Plus the two drug traders and ... himself.

Everyone in Paradise knew she was innocent. He did, too. He knew it with all his heart. He wanted to give her the home she'd always been looking for – in Paradise.

He'd finally met the stray cat of his dreams – Kelly Atwood ... Bianchi ... Applebee ... whatever. She wasn't the domesticated cat he'd imagined a hundred times, curled up by the home fires, but she was his. Scraggly, wild, and in trouble.

He couldn't think anymore. He'd justified himself into a knot. Somehow it still felt wrong. He had ethics and they were being stretched thin. He grabbed his jacket and walked out, locking the office door behind him.

It was midnight. He'd get some sleep and come at it fresh tomorrow. He just wished Kelly was in his bed tonight, safe in his arms.

He felt what that would be like and it made him ache for her so bad his body hurt. His body and his mind. He pressed the elevator button, stepped inside, slid his key in the lock, and hit *P*. The doors closed. The lights were dim. He kept the building on minimal lighting after eleven to cut the power consumption.

There was one way to keep Kelly safe. One way to have her with him so he didn't ache for her every minute, and one way to buy her some time. He'd marry her. A change of name would do her good. Sam smiled – Kelly Atwood Bianchi Applebee Grayson. It had a ring to it.

The elevator doors opened and he walked across to his front door. He better hang on – he was in for a bumpy ride.

Kelly woke up a blonde, thanks to Myrtle and the pumpkin-party gals. Even her eyebrows had been bleached. She threw off the covers and ran to the dressing table. Her hair had grown past her ears and now she had a feathery cap of blonde spikes with blonder highlights. She was a double-process girl.

Myrtle said she needed a new look. More like a new disguise, Kelly figured. Kelly was filled with a new kind of resolve. She was going to beat this. The past was going to fade like morning fog and leave her in the clear.

She showered quickly and wrapped herself in a huge beach towel she'd found amongst the linens.

Her whole wardrobe looked different on her. She settled on red, as usual: red bra, tight red T-shirt, and her jeans. Wow, on a blonde, red was *pow*.

This just might work. She didn't look like herself at all. She peered in the full-length closet door mirror. Her once-gaunt face had filled out softer. She must have put on ten pounds with all this great food in Paradise. She'd never eaten this well in her life. Somehow, it looked fine. Her bust line definitely benefited from the extra. Not bad. She smirked at herself in the mirror. She needed to stay strong.

She dressed in a flash and ran downstairs. It was early morning, and Myrtle was still in her Chinese silk pajamas. They were turquoise and lined with flannel and really warm. Kelly knew because Myrtle had given her a red pair.

She had work to do. The haunted house project had been launched last night along with her hair, and it was going to keep her very busy.

'Mornin',' she said to Myrtle. She brought over the coffee percolator and poured Myrtle a refill.

'Mornin'. Damn, you're a good blonde. I did a fine, fine job, if I do say so myself. No one would know you from Eve. Glad you're up early. That's good. I've been thinkin' on your problems.'

Kelly brought her cup of coffee over to the table and sat next to Myrtle. 'I'm sorry I dumped it all on you last night.'

'Don't think twice about it. We'll get it ironed out.' Myrtle handed Kelly a piece of toast with cheese melted on it and went on talking. 'So now, here's what I've come up with. It seems to me that ol' Ray or someone else was going to spend this money on bad things that would get sold to bad people – that would get into the hands of a bunch of mixed-up kids after a spell. Then some mama down in Los Angeles would be wringin' her hands, tryin' to figure out how to get her kid back on track, and she'd be missin' work worryin' and lookin' for that kid. Are you followin' me here?'

'Yes,' Kelly said, listening intently.

'What say we send a donation to that Boys and Girls

Club down there that keeps those kids busy and off the streets, so that mama can keep a roof over her kid's head?' Myrtle propped her elbow on the table and tapped her chin for a while with her long purple acrylic nails.

'That sounds great, but how do we send a pile of money to them? That's a problem.'

'That's the truth. How about this? I'll take the money to Willard Gibbs at the bank. He won't blink an eye me comin' in there with a briefcase of money. I know things about him, he knows things about me. We'll get it turned into a check.'

'Damn, you're good, Myrtle.' Kelly swallowed her coffee and stared, amazed at the interweavings of Paradise society.

'You get the address, and we'll have a mailing party. Now, when we stick this in the mailbox, you, missy, are going to say goodbye to the old days. You can't let the past push around your present, or your future, neither. Take it from me, I should know.' Myrtle winked.

'Myrtle, I love you. Will you marry me?'

'We've been all through this. You're meant for someone else.' Myrtle poked her in fun.

Kelly patted Myrtle's arm. 'I wish you'd been my mom, Myrtle.'

'We play the hand we're dealt. But you're here now, and we have lots of time to make up for it. If I'd had a daughter, I'd hope she'd be just like you. Full of spit and vinegar.'

'Quit it, or I'll start blubbering.'

'Well, it's true.' Myrtle took Kelly's hand, then patted it vigorously. 'Hey, we're comin' up on your first holiday season in Paradise. We do it up big around here.'

'Speaking of, I've got to round up help for the haunted Shipley house project. I figure Ginny and Will, and even Robert and who knows who else. We'll get a work party up there this weekend.'

'Just the thing to take your mind off everything.' Myrtle got up and put her cup in the sink. 'I better get myself fixed up. Eleanor Palmer's coming in for a beehive at eight-thirty. She's an early bird, too.'

'Good, you keep Eleanor busy while I get the rest of the Palmers jazzed up. Maybe we'll make this haunted house project a benefit to fix up the Shipley house and make it usable to the community.'

'That's one grand idea. It's a short time to pull something together, but you're young. You can do it. Heck, it's already spooky as hell up there, just patch up the busted spots and set up some sound effects. You can borrow ol' Fluffy if ya like.'

'Thanks, hon.' Kelly kissed her on the cheek. 'I've got to get to work. I left you some hot water.'

'Decent of you.' Myrtle's voice drifted as she went up the stairs. 'Get my Not Just a Waitress red lipstick out of the tray in the salon. It goes just perfect with that shirt.'

Kelly washed out the two coffee cups and set them in Myrtle's dish drainer. What if she'd grown up in a nice house here in Paradise as someone else's child? With parents and a family and cousins and one school and church socials? Who would she be? Would she be the girl of Sam's dreams?

She probably wouldn't be wanted for murder.

Kelly wondered for a moment who Sam would be when she heard from him again. Her lawyer, or her lover, or neither of those.

She decided she wasn't going to allow herself to think about it. She'd go crazy. This wasn't the first time she'd had to find the grit to make it through alone. She'd just throw herself into the Shipley house project. Fixing something up would feel good right now.

The dining room was straight out of Dickens's *Great Expectations*. The furniture was draped with white sheets, and the cobwebs were too numerous and authentic to remove: candelabras and cobwebs for Miss Havisham's wedding dinner. At least there wasn't any old food petrified on the table. Kelly had set ten places of the Shipley sisters' Limoges china for the ten cheese-cloth ghosts supplied by Nettie's Bazaar. She thought it looked pretty spooky – in a funny way. Will had strung the ghosts up to the ceiling so they appeared to float.

Kelly looked down her clipboard checklist for Fire Safety and scribbled a note to herself. She'd have to get Red Miller to replace the candles with battery-operated ones.

The town had really jumped on her haunted house project. There had to be thirty people here. It helped that everyone seemed to have five relatives to lend to the preparations. Plus Cora had sent sandwiches and apple cider for all.

She walked down the hall to the sweeping curved staircase and looked up to the second floor. The sound of pounding hammers and busy folks upstairs sounded very productive.

As she gazed upward she noticed someone had the brilliant idea of replacing the old portraits with fakes sporting realistic eyeballs that seemed to watch you as you climbed the stairs. Very clever.

Kelly continued down the hallway to the front entrance. The double door to the outside porch was now unboarded, repaired, and wide-open. She checked it off her list. The porch was actually the biggest problem. It needed some real carpentry work, and Red Miller couldn't get away till tomorrow.

Maybe his brother Herschel, who'd wandered over from his place across the way, could do it. Heck, maybe she'd get him working with Mabel Thompson. She seemed perfectly capable of swinging a hammer. They could work out their legal differences with tools. It would be cheaper than going to court.

She stood on the wide old porch and looked out over the land. This must have been grand at one time. Rocking on the porch watching the sun go down.

It had been a long day, and the sun was three o'clockish. She wished for a chair. But she knew if she sat down and rested, her mind would travel to Sam. Mrs. Palmer had given her time off to work on the house, which meant she'd been up here almost every day, away from morning coffee at Cora's – and away from Sam.

She hadn't answered his daily messages, despite being set upon by a quartet of concerned Paradise matrons. She was . . . busy.

Maybe she'd tackle the blackberries rambling up the side posts before dark. Where were those clippers?

A figure came toward the house, but the sun glared in her eyes and she could only see his outline. Hopefully it was someone with carpentry skills.

Sam. It was Sam. He strode straight up to her and grabbed her and kissed her. She dropped her clipboard. His mouth was hot on hers, and finally she wrapped her own arms around him in return. He came for her. He came.

He let her go enough to look in her face.

'Oh, my God, you're a blonde.'

'I'm in disguise.'

'Not bad. Why haven't you returned my calls?'

'How'd you know where I was?'

'You're talking Paradise, here. Did you think I'd just forget about you? I want you back in my bed.'

'So it's sex, then?'

'Damn straight. I can't get enough of you.'

'That'll do for now, I guess.' Kelly breathed in the scent of him. His flannel shirt was as smooth and warm as an embrace. She wanted to crawl inside it with him. Tears welled up in her eyes and spilled down her face.

He pulled her back to him and let her put her head on his chest. It felt so good.

'Kelly, I'm not saying I agree with the way you are handling your problem, but while we figure it out, I want to be with you.'

'I'd like that, Sam,' she said, letting her tears dry against his soft shirt. Then she straightened herself up. She wasn't going to cry anymore.

He handed her his handkerchief. 'I've been working on your case. But there's been no change.'

'Oh.' She didn't want to talk about it. 'I'm sorry I've been avoiding you. But now I need you. Did you bring a hammer?' she asked. She blew her nose on his embroidered-with-a-G linen handkerchief and handed it back to him. He smiled at her and shook his head. She did need him, for more than hammering nails; but she didn't want it to show too much.

'I heard all about your Shipley haunted house project.'

'Great idea, isn't it? It's keeping me out of trouble.' She backed out of his arms and put a little distance between them. She watched him accept that and not react.

'I'm all for that. I've got a toolbox in the truck,' he said in a very even tone.

'What? Are you telling me rich-boy lawyer can pound nails?'

'Honey, give me some power tools and move over.'

Kelly found that rather sexy. Of course, whatever Sam did was sexy. He just was. She stood back a step and took him in. His wavy brown hair and blue-jay blue eyes were enough already. Combined with that body? Stage-two sexy. Add his mind and his down-home upscale ways? Bingo, we have a winner, as old Fred would say on Bingo nights at the grange hall.

If she thought Sam was a catch before, after she watched him single-handedly rebuild the front porch with a circular saw, a pile of boards, and a hammer . . . well, any lawyer who could do that made her feel like she'd hit the big Vegas jackpot. Now she wanted his children.

Every time she was around Sam she fell harder. She held the ends of the boards for him while he cut. She handed him nails. They worked hard together and stood back to admire the job together, just as the sun lowered toward the horizon all orange and red and pink.

'It's just a damn good thing the joists were solid. If you've got good joists, it's easy.' Sam wiped the sweat off his brow with the flannel shirt he'd tossed off earlier.

He had on one of those tank T-shirts that Kelly usually thought of on old guys. The way Sam's muscles flexed around in that thing, she'd never get that former image again. He smelled like sawdust. She just couldn't take it anymore. She wanted him, and she didn't want to hold herself back another minute. She flipped off the shop light they'd set up.

Kelly came over to him and slid her whole body against him. She pinned him against a porch column.

'Just *do me*.' She pressed her newfound, rounder breasts into him and squirmed.

'Damn, woman. You sure know how to get a guy hot and bothered.' He ran his hands up her back and under her shirt.

She could feel his pulse quicken as she mouthed his neck and spread her hands across his chest. The porch was dark, and they were in the shadows. Inside she could hear voices of people still working. They became a blur as Sam touched her.

His thumbs pressed into her nipples through her thin bra. He made circles. She could feel the heat and hardness of his desire pressing against her.

'Sam.'

The porch lights flicked on. They jumped away from each other. Kelly combed through her hair with her fingers.

Will Palmer stepped out.

'Look at this porch! Great work out here, you two,' Will said.

Ginny was right behind him. 'We'll all be back after church tomorrow to finish decorating,' Ginny said. 'We've got raffle tickets left over from the church social, and Mrs. Palmer called the *Pioneer* to place an ad for the haunted house. A reporter will be coming out tomorrow to take a few pictures. It's just looking great, Kelly!' Will hooked Ginny's arm and pulled her along. He whispered in Ginny's ear as they walked away. Ginny grinned and waved goodbye.

Kelly could just imagine what Will said, and it was probably all true. She managed some parting words. 'Thanks so much, everyone, this'll be really fun. I'll see you tomorrow.'

' 'Bye, Sam,' Ginny said with that *tone* in her voice.

'Good night, Ginny, Will,' Sam called.

A stream of people started coming out the door and departing. Kelly thanked each one. The last person, Robert Palmer, asked if they wanted to lock up and handed them the key. He looked a little disgruntled to see Sam on the porch with Kelly, but went away whistling.

When the last car drove out of the driveway, Sam turned to Kelly. His mouth found hers, and he knew she felt the demand of his passion for her. She didn't run or push him away this time. She stayed put. He undid the top button of her jeans and slid his hand inside. The cold night air went hot on him.

'Sam, not here.'

'Yes, here. Now.' He picked her up, carried her through the double doors, down the hall, through several passages to the kitchen. He gently lowered her onto the counter. The room was only slightly lit – enough for him to see her wanting him. Sam kissed her deeply, then pulled her red T-shirt up and over her head.

The room disappeared around him, and a blur of passionate kisses and touches replaced it. He had her undressed except for her red bra and panties. She wrapped her legs around him and let him press into her. His heat was unrelenting.

He moved his mouth between and all over her breasts. She leaned back and moaned as he ran his fingers inside her silk panties and buried them deep in her wet, throbbing heat. She took all the pleasure he was giving her and let herself go to it.

She cried his name. She opened her eyes. He was watching her as she released and throbbed around his fingers.

He reached into his pocket for a condom, then his jeans were gone and he was covered and he moved into her and they fit together madly and deeply. Her legs wrapped around him, and she leaned back against the smooth counter.

He ran his tongue over her breast, and reached down to touch her gently with the pad of his thumb as he moved himself wet and smooth into her heat for a very long time, taking her farther into pleasure.

He could feel her on the edge of her climax. His strength peaked as he thrust deeply into her one last time. She leaned into him harder and screamed her release from deep in her throat. He joined her.

They leaned against each other in the remaining heat of their loving, fingers running over each other's backs, kisses trailing everywhere.

'Kelly.'

'Oh, Sam, it's so good.'

'I love you, Kelly. I love you.'

'I love you, Sam.'

'From now on you'll sleep in my bed. Are we clear?'

'Yes, yes.'

'Was that a yes?'

She whispered in his ear, 'Yes, that was a yes.'

'There is one more thing.' Sam reached down to his

jeans. He rose, kissed her naked neck, and slipped a tiny black velvet box into her palm.

'More presents? I told you how these things make me nervous.' She popped open the lid to reveal a huge, glittering heart-shaped diamond ring. Her own heart stopped. She gasped for air. How could he do this?

'Will you marry me, Kelly?' He took her hand to his lips and kissed her softly in the center of her palm. Then he took the ring and slipped it on her finger.

'Somehow I always pictured myself with clothes on for this, and your pants are around your ankles.' She resorted to stall humor, as she always did when she fell apart.

'I want you with me. I've fallen in a bottomless pit of love. The only way out is to marry you.'

'I don't know what to say, Sam. I'm too stunned. I'm too naked.'

He found her red T-shirt and gently slipped it over her head, guiding her arms into it. It didn't help.

'Is that better?'

'No. Yes, no.'

'Very definitive.'

'It's all happened so quickly. How did we get to this place?' Kelly put her hand up to the light and stared at the ring. His hands were warm on the small of her back.

'How about you come back home with me in my extremely cool '56 Chevy and talk about it over dinner? Faith made beef bourguignon. All the women in town seem to think I need food when things are out of whack.'

'Out of whack. That's us, right?'

'No, that's me up until today. I kept trying to talk myself out of the fact that I fell in love with you in the first three days. Now come with me. I have things to whisper in your ear. And it's damn cold in here, in case you didn't notice. Bring that rock with you. We'll talk.'

The October night chill had descended, and it got damned cold all of a sudden. She slipped off the counter and groped for her jeans and other assorted clothes. The velvet box went in her front pocket. In case she wanted to put the ring back in. Was she nuts even considering this?

'Wait, Sam.'

He was jeaned up and ready. He came to her.

'Yes. The answer is yes. Yes, yes, yes.'

Kelly was rummaging in his fridge wearing his black silk boxer shorts and her red bra. He admired her curves from across the counter. She'd been working on the Shipley house and sleeping here with him at the apartment for three days now. It felt wonderful. It felt like what he wanted.

'Oh, my God, there's something alive back here! Oh, it's just olives staring at me with pimento pupils. Hey, there's actually enough stuff here for a decent omelet!'

Sam smiled at her backside. 'Can you cook? That's the thing with whirlwind courtships. There's some basic things we've neglected to find out about each other,' he said.

'More importantly, can *you* cook?' she replied, emerging from the fridge, shaking a limp scallion at him.

'I think there's a gourmet chef in me, waiting to spring to life. I just need an audience.'

'That's good. I love a man who can cook, because I really can't. Although Dottie has offered to teach me. Let's see, what else? I can see you're fairly clean. Not obsessive, are you?'

'I don't think so. Look in my junk drawer.' He pointed.

She opened the drawer, looked, and nodded with approval. 'Total disaster. Good. And what about kids?'

Sam gave her a funny look. Junk drawers to kids in one jump. 'We talked about that, remember?' he said. 'I suggested you start your own large and happy clan of kids with a good childhood. I'm picturing a pile of kids and dogs.'

'How many is a pile?' Kelly looked serious.

'Three . . . or four.'

'Dogs?'

'Two big ones.'

'Which, dogs or kids?' They both laughed. 'I think we can work with that,' she said, and came flying across the room to him and threw herself in his arms. 'I love you, Sam.'

He held her as she kissed his face all over. 'Now,' he said as he emerged from the kiss, 'we need to set a date for this thing, and dive into the mess – china, cake, swatches, all that stuff. How soon can you move in here?'

'How about today?' Kelly said.

She surprised him – and he also felt a scallion in her hand when he reached for it.

'You'll have to make room in your closet, and all that, but I think we should try it out right away. Uh-oh, what about your parents? Will they be all right with this?' Kelly took a bite of the onion, chewed, and made a face. 'Oh, I went too fast, didn't I? Sorry.'

'Kelly, I've waited my whole life for this. Fast is not a problem. The onion you just ate isn't even a problem. We do need to call my parents in Italy, but they have waited a long time, too. They'll be thrilled.' Sam knew it was true because he knew they'd believe his heart.

He also knew there was one more thing to put on the to-do list. Clear his fiancée of a murder charge. Just a small detail.

Kelly seemed to be pretending it didn't exist. Sam figured he'd give her that gift for a while. He'd put Peter Brody on the watch down in L.A. Peter would call him the minute the case broke, and Sam could keep preparing her defense on his end, just in case. Above all, they needed to lie low if Kelly refused to turn herself in. Time was on their side. He needed time to get this solved.

Right now his heart was very happy. He gathered Kelly up and kissed her, scallion breath and all. They could deal with it all – one step at a time. 'How about a November wedding?' he whispered softly.

'Late November,' Kelly answered him. He pressed her against the refrigerator, tasted her neck, and decided breakfast could wait.

Lynnette thwacked the folded-up Wednesday morning *Paradise Pioneer* down on the counter at Cora's. She stared at the photo of Sam and Kelly spread all over the announcement page. The photo showed Sam picking up Kelly and carrying her over the threshold.

Local Couple Engaged in Haunted House. Sam looked great, but Kelly was blurry – and blonde.

The story talked about the peachy project Miss *Applebee* had cooked up at the Shipley house and the surprise announcement during one of the work parties. How nice of the press to cover the whole mess. They should have written: *Miss Atwood Bianchi Applebee, recently arrived murderer with possible mob connections, hoodwinks local hero, her next victim.*

Lynnette felt a cold chill, and a big pain ran through her neck and up to her temples. So now the bitch was a blonde. Great disguise. Something about that *really* bothered her.

She reached for her coffee and knocked it all over the paper. It puddled up and started to run over the counter. Cora came over with a bar rag and mopped up.

'Refill, Lynnette?'

'No thanks,' Lynnette snapped. She bolted up and stomped out the door. It was time. Why should that dye-job hussy be happy with Sam when she couldn't have him? Besides, Kelly Atwood would probably kill Sam in his sleep like she did her last husband.

Lynnette climbed in her Trans Am and took off like a shot aimed at the sheriff's office. Then she slowed down. Timing was critical. It had to be big, and public, and scandalous. That was the only way Sam would see the truth. Lynnette swung into the A&W drive-through and ordered a chocolate chip mint milk shake. *She thought better on dairy.*

*

Myrtle was making up the round bed with clean sheets when Kelly walked into the bedroom. She was amazed at Myrtle's flexibility.

'Myrtle, how do you stay so . . . limber?'

'Yoga. A bunch of us old gals meet at the grange hall every Thursday night. Seven-thirty. Remember? I tried to get you to go. Mrs. Armentrout bends us all like pretzels.

'Then I do my own twice a week with Guru Bob on my tape player. He's cute. What kind of mess have you gotten yourself into now, honey?'

'Oh, Myrtle.' Kelly couldn't help herself; she felt tears start streaming down her face. But these tears were different.

'And quit that crying, you'll look like a red-nosed reindeer.' She pulled a Kleenex out of her pocket, reached over, and wiped Kelly's eyes gently. It was a surprising gesture. Kelly reached for Myrtle's hand and gave it a squeeze of affection. 'Quit it now, or we'll all crack.'

'Myrtle, you've been so wonderful to me. You are the best mom I ever had. These are happy tears. I feel so lucky finding you, and finding Sam. Can you believe I'm engaged?'

'You deserved a break, sweetie. I just happened along. But nothing could have kept you and Sam apart. It was fate.'

'I almost believe you at this point.'

'You both looked so cute in the paper this mornin' just like that movie with what's-her-name's daughter . . .

you know, *An Officer and a Gentleman*. Him carrying you over the threshold of that haunted house. So romantic. I hope he wasn't *too* much of a gentleman; that boy has too many polite genes sometimes.'

Kelly smiled at her with genuine love. Myrtle was something else.

'Now come here and help me make this bed,' Myrtle said.

Kelly obeyed. 'I was a little worried about the newspaper photo, but I'm fuzzy, blonde, he's carrying me, and it's the *Paradise Pioneer*. I figure, hey, the only person that's going to see it and get crazy is Lynnette.'

'I'd steer clear of that filly for a week or two, that's for sure.' Myrtle straightened up and stretched herself around like a cat.

'Okay, on a lighter note, I'm here for my Halloween suit and – to get my stuff,' Kelly said. 'Sam asked me to move in.'

'I figured that was coming. I've got yer costume pressed and ready. Dottie did the pressing. She actually likes to iron. It's a peach of a costume, if I do say so myself. The three of us outdid ourselves this time.' Myrtle dusted off the back of her black velvet leggings and straightened up her crochet sweater with a big pumpkin appliquéd to the front. 'Me, I'm gonna be a witch this year. I'm gonna make a pot of coffee in the parlor. See ya later, alligator. Now clean yer room, will ya? It's a mess in here.'

Kelly gave her a real-live-replacement-mom hug. Myrtle patted her, then cruised out the door.

In a few minutes Kelly heard Myrtle's voice downstairs at the front door, loud as hell. 'Hey there, Sam, go get that girl shaped up. Get her outta my hair. She's messy as a pig in a mudhole. Hope you're ready to hire a maid!' She heard a loud smacking noise, and when Sam appeared in the doorway, he had a set of orange lip prints on his cheek.

He stood there leaning against the doorframe and just took her breath away. His hair was tousled from the wind: his short-sleeved polo shirt showed off his strong, muscular arms. He had a smile on his face that lit up his blue eyes, and suddenly she could see what her future children would look like. Yep, she was going to marry this one. She threw a black lace brassiere at him.

'Sam, hang this on the door, will you?'

He hung the black bra on the outside knob and shut the door. She sat on the floor with the sunlight playing on her wild hair, her green eyes enticing him. Sam moved to where she was, knelt, and kissed her, lowering her underneath him into a soft pile of clothes.

She responded to him with warmth and passion. He had never known a woman to move his heart so thoroughly, so quickly. He was going to marry this one.

The Shipley house glowed eerily in the darkness of Halloween night. Shrieks shattered the steady stream of organ music. Outside, the October wind added just enough of a howl through the old house to be truly authentic. Kelly was pleased.

She had dressed herself as the ghost of Elvira Shipley, one of the three sisters who last owned the house. She wafted from room to room scaring the daylights out of everyone – including a pack of high school kids.

Occasionally she'd take up a chair in the dining room and hold very still until someone came in the room, then she'd come to life and pour tea. Even a few adults gave a scream.

This was probably the most fun she'd had in, oh, ever. Not once in her entire childhood had her mother ever gotten it together to make her a costume or participate in any classroom party. But at least her own love of school got her up and onto the bus every morning, wherever they were at the time. Kelly learned to shop the local Goodwill early in life, and probably part of her fashion sense came from being inventive with other people's castoffs.

Well, that was the past. This was now. She'd forgiven her mother for her inability to cope with life long ago. Now Kelly just needed to learn to cope with her own. And for once, she just might have gotten lucky.

Sam couldn't believe the amount of work Kelly and the others had accomplished.

He walked through the main floor. This house really was quite amazing. The fireplaces were white marble. The front parlor had deep window seats. The faded wallpaper and old wide-trim molding just added to the haunted feeling

The kitchen, his favorite spot in the house, was huge.

The cabinets were dated cream-colored metal with black handles. The sisters probably did it over in about 1950. There was a pantry and a keeping room attached, big enough to create an open kitchen and family room. Sam suddenly had a vision of what it could become.

The wind was really kicking up. He hoped the power would hold. Kelly didn't know the famous Paradise blackout history. They had power outages quite often around here. Maybe he'd better get a flashlight.

'Sam, we need some more hot cider. Turn up the heat on that pot, will you?' His favorite ghost came flittering up behind him. 'Love your costume. What are you, a gentleman cowboy?'

'Yep, string tie, black hat, and boots are all a fella needs to get by around here.'

'If that's all you had on, we'd be upstairs in the four-poster bed. Of course, we've had some fun right here, haven't we, cowboy?' Kelly moved up closer to him. 'I'd kiss you, but the white stuff on my face will smear on that great jacket.'

'I'll consider myself kissed. The jacket came from my granddad. The original gentleman cowboy of 1944.' He stroked her satin-covered arm gently and kissed a couple of fingertips. 'Your haunting is a big success. Most of the town has passed through here today.'

'We've collected a bundle.'

'Happy Halloween, Kelly. It's our first.' He put his arms through her many gauzy panels and found her lovely body wrapped in the silky gown. Smooth. He ran his hands down her back and pulled her close.

The lights flickered. 'Oh, no,' Kelly said. 'We've got an hour left. At least all the candles are battery-powered, and we filled every hall sconce and chandelier with them. It won't go totally dark. Except in here.'

Total pitch-black surrounded her one second later. She heard some genuine screams from upstairs.

'Hold my hand, Kelly. The dining room is just behind that swinging door. We'll feel along the walls.'

'Don't let go, Sam.'

'I won't.'

Kelly held Sam's hand and arm tightly as they moved slowly toward the faint outline of light seeping under the dining-room door at the end of the room.

A shadowy figure entered the kitchen. Her eyes hadn't adjusted yet, and she couldn't identify who it was. 'Who's there?'

Sam turned. 'Who is it?'

The figure didn't answer, and in the dark they heard nothing further. Kelly thought the person probably left. Sam kept moving. He reached the door and swung it wide. Kelly looked back into the kitchen and caught the movement of someone fleeing the room. A dark cloak covered the figure's head.

'Sam—'

'I saw. Stick by me.'

The dining room's candelabras were glowing enough for Kelly to see around her.

'Kelly, sit here and wait. I'm going to see who that was. Scream if you need me.'

'Be careful, Sam.'

He vanished through to the kitchen. It couldn't be anything really dangerous – probably just a kid playing pranks. Kelly picked up the silver teapot she'd polished and poured some lukewarm cider into a paper cup. Maybe someone would wander in here.

The wind howled up through the slightly open window behind her. It gave her a deadly chill. The satin gown she wore was far from warm. She got up to shut the window. When she turned back, a woman stood in the doorway.

'Wow, great costume,' Kelly said. 'Would you like some cider? I'm sure the lights will be on soon. We've got a backup generator.'

The woman put her finger to her lips, gesturing Kelly to be silent. Her black garments floated around her. Kelly's throat constricted as a sound tried to escape. She stared in fascination and fear, backing herself into the far corner of the dining room.

The dark-cloaked figure moved silently through the room. Kelly slid herself behind one end of a huge china hutch. Fear coursed through her like an electric shock. What if Raymond's killer had found her?

The hood fell away. It was Lynnette. Lynnette, for crying out loud. She kept moving toward Kelly. Lynnette's face looked twisted in the light of the flickering fake candles.

'Trick or treat, Kelly, what a fun little event you've cooked up.'

'You startled me.' Kelly regained an ounce of her

senses. She wasn't going to let this bitch scare her. She was a city kid, after all. A tough city kid.

'Quite the masquerade. Love your new hair.' Lynnette's voice sounded odd.

'Thanks.' Kelly put a hard edge on her own voice. What did this woman want from her life, besides Sam? She stepped out of the corner and straightened herself up.

Lynnette had been walking toward Kelly one step at a time. 'Congratulations on your engagement. Enjoy it while you can, *Kelly*.'

'Thank you.' Sam's voice came from the far doorway, strong and loud. He strode over to Kelly. 'The Millers will have the generator going in a few minutes. Everyone's fine. They all think it's a great lark.' Sam took Kelly's arm and stood firmly beside her.

Lynnette looked like she had something to say but changed her mind. 'Good night, Sam,' she said, then turned quickly and made her exit.

'Sam, Sam, I – I thought she was someone else.'

'She is someone else. A woman who needs a new hobby. You're freezing.' Sam took off his brown wool cowboy jacket and wrapped her up in it. 'Damn, this room is cold.'

'Thanks, Sam. You're my hero anyhow. Thanks for chasing off the spookiest guest of all.'

'You're cute when you're scared out of your wits.'

'Oh, thanks. Let's go see to scaring our other guests a few more times, then we'll talk about that string-tie boot thing again.'

'Yes, ma'am.' Sam took Kelly's hand and led her through the dining room. The generator kicked in and the house lights dimly lit up. Kelly went ahead to waft up and down the stairs, which left Sam to brood. He'd talked to Tom already, but Tom couldn't watch Lynnette all the time. She was getting out of hand. Maybe she really wasn't so harmless. He'd have to keep an eye on his fiancée. A very close eye.

15

She was a country bride this time. A November country bride. She stood in front of the full-length mirror in the bride's room downstairs from the sanctuary. Who would have ever figured her for a church wedding? They'd chosen the Presbyterian church, where Sam had danced with her for the very first time.

Myrtle set a circle of daisies and tiny white roses on her head and fluffed her hair up around it.

'It's a damn masterpiece, if I do say so myself,' she said with a mouthful of bobby pins. Myrtle stuck them in randomly around Kelly's headpiece.

Kelly giggled when she noticed the turquoise cowboy boots under Myrtle's completely creative pretty-much-the-mother-of-the-bride dress. It was a Western-style suit of beige wool with turquoise braid trim. Her daisy and rose corsage was fastened in her red hair, and she had turquoise jewelry stacked around her neck.

'Hey, isn't that the jewelry Sam sent over for our rodeo date?'

'Yep – it's symbolic, ya see. I knew the moment I laid eyes on you in that Greyhound bus that you were Sam's bride. I knew you wouldn't mind if I borrowed it.'

'You are a meddling old woman, and I love you for it.'

'I do it so good, don't I?' Myrtle puffed up Kelly's skirt and stood back. 'You look like a regular princess.'

Kelly gazed at the reflection of herself. Her now-blonde curly hair made beautiful waves under her veil. The dress was a confection she and Myrtle and Dottie had created out of a *Vogue* pattern. Damn, they'd done good. The pure white organza had reembroidered cutwork lace daisies overlaid on every edge and layer. The full, transparent sleeves gathered at her wrists in a smooth flip-back French cuff.

It had a fifties feel. Pretty appropriate for a town that had stopped in time about then.

'Hey, Myrtle, check this out.' Kelly lifted up the multi-layered skirt enough to let her shoes show. 'Something borrowed.'

'My stars! You're a chip off the old block!' Myrtle chuckled and gazed at the white and yellow satin strappy sandals, each with a bunch of fake silk daisies stuck on the top.

There was a knock on the door. Evelyn Grayson poked her stylish head through the crack.

'Knock knock, can I come in? Oh, my heavens, you are a vision. You look like Grace Kelly.'

'Come in, come in.' Kelly lowered her skirts and turned to get a hug from Sam's mom. Evelyn looked simply elegant in a navy blue and white linen suit. Her short blonde hair was tucked under a beautiful blue straw hat Kelly pegged for French. It had a narrow white ribbon, and a corsage of daisies and roses tucked in the band. She had navy and white spectator pumps on and a mysterious white box in her hands.

Kelly had met Evelyn Grayson for the first time at Thanksgiving dinner with the family. She'd never forget their open arms and loving hearts as Sam introduced her.

'I have a little something for you, dear.' She held out the box and let Kelly open it. 'This was my grandmother's, and all of the women in this family have worn it on their wedding day.'

Kelly pulled out a luminous strand of pearls. Attached to the center was a small gold locket shaped like a heart. She opened it and saw a tiny picture of a man on one side and a woman on the other, in 1920s wedding clothes.

'She was a regular flapper, my grandma. And my grandpa had the best still in his county during Prohibition.' They all laughed, which helped push off the waves of tears that were gaining on Kelly. *I deserve this family, I do*, she told herself, while Evelyn fastened the pearls around her neck. She looked in the mirror and touched the long strand. They were perfect.

'Thank you so much, Evelyn, I can't tell you how much it means to me to have you all as family. I promise to be a good wife to Sam.'

'Well, we will get you some staff, dear.' Evelyn laughed, and elbowed Myrtle in the side gently. Myrtle disappeared into the corner for a minute and brought out a bottle of champagne. She popped the cork in one swift twisting thumb movement, and headed for a set of glasses set out on a table.

'Here's to the bride. May she grow big, fat, and wide with grandchildren for us!'

'Hey!' Kelly put her hands on her hips, then reached for the glass and shrugged.

'Here, here!' chimed in Evelyn. The sound of laughter wafted in from the hallway and joined theirs. There was a knock on the door. Sam's two sisters peeked in.

'Are you decent? Oh, wow.' Anne and Emily stared at Kelly from the door.

'Come on in, ladies. We're having a toast.'

They gave the sisters a bubbling glass and clinked their champagne flutes together, coming up with more absurd toasts each time.

'Here's to the bride, for not picking the ugliest dresses ever,' Anne chimed in.

The dark olive-green velvet and satin dresses were lovely on the beautiful Grayson sisters. Both Sam's two sisters had his dark hair and blue eyes.

Ginny Palmer came in. 'Here's the matron of honor. Cheers to you, Ginny.' Kelly hiccupped. 'Every one of you is married; I should just say the matrons of Paradise.'

The champagne was beginning to kick in. They all linked arms, dancing in a circle and singing 'Bicycle Built for Two.'

Virginia Redfield, the wedding coordinator for the church, knocked on the door, but no one heard her, so she walked in to see the dancing drunken bridal party.

'Ah-hem, they are ready for you, dear.'

'Oh, gosh. Somebody point me in the right direction. Evelyn and Myrtle, you have to go first, you're the mothers, right?' Kelly blithered.

'Yes, dear, don't you worry, we'll shove you down the aisle when it's time.' Virginia was used to nervous brides.

Evelyn and Myrtle gave Kelly a kiss on the cheek and disappeared. Kelly, Ginny, and the sisters picked up their bouquets – daisies and tiny white roses for the girls, and a beautiful bunch of white roses, daisies, stephanotis, and variegated ivy for Kelly. The ribbons trailed around them all as they rustled through the hallways toward the sanctuary.

The front door of the church was open. A rare November sun streamed in on them as they came from the hallway into the sanctuary entrance. Huge bouquets of daisies were everywhere – on the church steps, decorating the pews, and up front – where Kelly caught a glimpse of the most beautiful sight of all: Sam in his gray morning suit standing next to the minister, waiting for her.

She suddenly remembered her bad dream from a month ago – her hair turning into crow feathers, Sam turning into Raymond. Her stomach knotted up. Sam had moved forward with this wedding very quickly. It had been such a short time since they'd become officially engaged. He'd assured her that going through with the marriage would be a positive move in regard to the small matter of her being wanted for murder.

Fortunately for her, the entire town seemed to be determined to get them down the aisle. She'd put herself in their hands and shelled out quite a bit of her savings, but it was beautiful, and nothing was going to spoil this day.

Lynnette sat in the front seat of Tom's squad car, smug as a cat that ate the canary and got away with it. She clutched that damn computer printout in one hand and had her other hand tucked under her left armpit. She was strung tight as a wire. Tom could see that.

Tom had his hat pulled low on his forehead as they pulled up to the church. He had called in Gary Reese, his deputy, for backup. Probably for moral support more than anything.

Lynnette tapped her foot under the dash nervously. 'Let's go, Tom, before he actually marries that husband-killer.' Tom sighed, parked the car, opened his door, and got out, then adjusted his gun belt. Gary stepped up beside him in seconds, and they started up the church stairs. He must be crazy to do this. But there was no denying the truth of the matter.

Lynnette skipped up behind them. Tom was sure she was getting some kind of warped satisfaction out of the whole thing.

'I hate to do this, Gary, but suppose she really did kill this guy? I hope we are doing Sam a favor in the long run.'

'Nice timing – did your girlfriend think of that? Probably didn't get an invitation.' Gary glanced sideways and caught Lynnette's eye.

'I can hear you boys. Just do your job.' Lynnette marched behind them like a storm trooper, clutching the wanted notice.

Cora finished singing 'I Love You, for Sentimental Reasons,' to Lydia Peterson's piano accompaniment, and something surprising happened. Red Miller and his trio stepped up to the front, pulled out their instruments, and Henry Samuel Grayson Sr., stepped up beside Cora.

Sam was going to do Kelly in. He'd picked all the music and kept it a secret from her. Now she'd be crying for sure. Not only that, Red had a suit on.

The incredible voice of Sam's father filled the church as he sang 'Our Love Is Here To Stay.' Cora joined him on the chorus.

Kelly watched her bridesmaids go down the aisle in front of her, moving to the music.

She fairly floated on the arm of Walt Williamson. Dottie's husband had volunteered to give her away.

It felt so different this time. So special. She and Raymond were married in a civil ceremony. They'd both been so unemotional about it. Like a business deal.

It was an odd thought at the moment, but it struck her hard halfway down the aisle. She truly loved Sam. For the first time in her whole life she truly loved and was loved in return.

She passed Eleanor Palmer, who put a lace hankie to

her eye. There was Cora's extremely good-looking husband and several of her grown children.

There was Faith Gallagher and her husband, and so many familiar faces smiling at her she felt overwhelmed.

Dottie sat next to Myrtle on the bride's side. She just beamed at Kelly. Will Palmer stood at the front of the church.

She could feel her heart pounding against her lace bodice until Sam stepped over and took her hand, and she lost herself in his consuming blue eyes.

A wonderful calm fell over her as they stood together in front of the entire town of Paradise. Reverend Evans began to speak in his deep, soothing voice:

'Dear friends, we are gathered here today to witness the marriage of Sam and Kelly. While the marriage ceremony creates a sacred and solemn bond, it is also a joyous occasion, and I hope that you, Sam and Kelly, will remember this day as the highlight of your life together.

'Sam and Kelly, your marriage is intended to join you for life in a relationship so intimate and personal that it will change your whole being. It offers you the hope, and indeed the promise, of a love that is true and mature. To attain such love you will have to commit yourselves to each other freely and gladly for the sake of a richer and deeper life together.

'You have made it known that you want to be joined in marriage, and no one has shown any valid reason why you may not. If either of you know any lawful impediment why you should not be married, you are now to declare it.'

'Hold your horses there, Reverend.' Lynnette's shrill voice echoed through the church. Kelly turned to take in the sight of not only Sam's old girlfriend waving a piece of paper, stomping toward them, but the sheriff and his deputy right behind her.

A strange rush of fear tingled from her toes to her head, and the room seemed to darken. She felt herself weave, but Sam caught her arm. He looked in her eyes, and she saw pain.

'Lynnette Stivers, what in the hell are you doing?' Reverend Evans spoke out, and no one even looked shocked at his language.

'Saving Sam from marrying this black widow spider from L.A. that MURDERED her last husband!' Lynnette was shrieking like a banshee, and her long blonde hair had gone wild on her.

'Lynnette, you are out of your mind.' Sam was trying to keep his voice calm, but Kelly could see the veins in his neck throbbing. 'Tom, I hope you're here to stop her. Could you put her in lockup for the rest of the wedding? I'll send you a sympathy note every week for the rest of my life.'

'Lynnette Stivers, you stop dead in your tracks, or I'll yank that over-processed hair of yours out by its black roots!' Myrtle jumped up and placed herself in the aisle between Lynnette and Kelly, with her fists up in a boxing stance. Sam's father Hank took one broad step out into the aisle and grabbed Lynnette firmly by the upper arm. 'Tom, let's take this outside,' Hank said.

'Hank, I would love to oblige you, but for once

Lynnette has the law on her side.' Tom cleared his throat with a cough and read the warrant. 'Kelly Atwood, you are under arrest for the murder of Raymond Bianchi.' A horrible sound rippled through the church as everyone gasped at once. Then there was dead silence.

'I'm so sorry, Sam.' Kelly wanted to kill someone, all right: Lynnette Stivers.

'I'm sorry, too, Sam, but Lynnette's got the notice,' Tom said.

Hank grabbed the paper out of Lynnette's hand and handed it to Sam.

'I don't have to read it. I know. I'm her attorney.'

'She's innocent!' Myrtle yelled.

Kelly thought she would die right there, watching Sam's pain. His public humiliation. What had she done? It cut her like glass, and she shattered. She bowed her head and let out a small, horrible cry.

'That's not gonna do you any good now, you murdering, drug-dealing witch! You lied to every person in this town. You were just using the whole town of Paradise to hide from your drug ring friends!' Lynnette tried to get closer to her, and Kelly looked up just in time to see Myrtle land a right hook on Lynnette's jaw.

Lynnette went down hard. Deputy Reese was behind her and took a small step back, hooking his arms behind him in a stance of innocence as she thumped on her butt in front of him.

It seemed to quiet Lynnette some, and she sat on the floor, stunned. Kelly saw a tiny smirk cross Gary's face. It made her almost laugh through her tears for one second. Tom turned and gave Myrtle a sharp look, but didn't move.

'She didn't lie to us, you crazy bitch, we all knew. We all knew she was innocent,' Myrtle yelled at Lynnette.

Something snapped in Kelly. As she looked around at the scene, the sick humor of it caught up with her.

Here she was, happy at last, and the past just jerked all that away from her like a magician's trick. She had been assaulted with Lynnette's poisonous words, her wedding was spoiled, Sam was humiliated, and the whole town probably hated her. She looked around through her tears and saw her beloved Paradise, every pair of eyes upon her. Judgment day. Just like in her dream. Raymond's ghost come back to destroy her.

But it was her own fault. She'd tried to ignore the past and pretend it didn't exist. She'd led Sam into her denial. How could she have even thought of getting married without having the charges against her cleared up? Not for her own sake, but for Sam's, and for his family. His wonderful family.

She held her chin up and faced them all. 'Tom, let's get this over with.' Kelly held out her wrists.

'That won't be necessary. Let's just take a calm walk to the car, Miss Atwood.'

Myrtle positioned her body in front of Kelly. 'Over my dead body! This gal is innocent, I know for a fact.'

'Myrtle, it's no use. I have very bad wedding karma.'

Myrtle turned to her and stared hard. Then she looped her arm through Kelly's and stood by her side.

Sam stepped behind her and put his hands on her

shoulders. She could feel her emotions reach over to him.

'I'm sorry, Sam, you were right. If I'd listened to you, none of this would have happened,' she said, without looking at him.

Sam's mother came over and took Kelly's other arm in a gesture of support.

'I'll get you out of this, Kelly, I swear.' Sam's face was like hard granite. His anger was written all over it.

'You deserve better, Sam.' She turned and looked up at him.

'Don't talk like that. It's you I want.'

She'd lost everything now. Even the tiny ounce of self-respect she'd found when she left Raymond. The self-respect she'd been nurturing inside her during her time in Paradise.

Lynnette Stivers made a hasty exit out the front. At least she was gone.

Kelly started her walk and watched the whole church full of people stand up as she passed by with Myrtle, Sam's parents, and Sam, with the sheriff and deputy behind. Kelly walked back down the aisle, out the church doors, and down the outside stairs. The sun was bright around them.

'Don't you worry, I'll tell them what happened, we will have you out of there in two shakes of a lamb's tail, honey.' Myrtle steadied her on one side.

'Sweetheart, I have enough money to hire you the best lawyers, including Sam. I don't care what you did, we will fix it.' Evelyn squeezed her arm tighter, and handed her a small white handkerchief with a *G* embroidered on it. Kelly smiled a little as Tom opened the squad car door, and she gathered her wedding dress up to fit through the opening.

'Tell Sam I love him,' was all she could manage.

Sam took three strides and stepped up to her. He held her tight in his arms until Tom asked him to stop.

Tom helped her into the squad car. Myrtle stuffed her billowing wedding skirts in behind her. She looked back to see the most horrible sight she could ever imagine. Sam, with her wanted notice in his hand, his face white and angry, staring at her. Sam's father had his hand on Sam's shoulder, and Evelyn Grayson was crying.

Tom shut the door. Kelly leaned back against the seat and wept into Evelyn's handkerchief.

Sam stood behind the pulpit, surveying the shambles of his wedding day. It was a replay of Philadelphia. But this time worse, because he truly loved Kelly. He'd just watched the woman he loved be taken away in a squad car on her wedding day. He'd wanted so much for this day to be perfect for her.

Sam looked up from his pain to see his mother standing beside him. Myrtle was pacing in the back of the church. His father had gone to the downstairs hall to deal with the wedding guests.

'I'm sorry, Mom, I was a fool to let this wedding take place before the charge against Kelly was cleared up. She refused to turn herself in, and I let it continue.'

Evelyn put both hands on her hips. He knew he was in for it. 'You are not a fool, son. You've had it easy growing up here, Sam, but you know how to deal with trouble when it comes along. You always do the right thing. Even with Chelsea back in Philadelphia – and you can stop beating yourself up for that. You tried your damnedest to get her acquitted. She just gave up.' Evelyn put her hand on Sam's arm. 'Don't let Kelly give up, Sam.'

Sam leaned on the pulpit as if he were about to deliver a sermon. Then he pounded it with one fist. His voice boomed out in the empty church.

'I should have *made* her turn herself in. I should have contacted people and made sure she'd be safe. If I'd done that, maybe this day wouldn't have happened.'

'Sometimes trouble comes no matter what you do, Sam. The important thing is to stick by the people you love. I would have folded up my tent and stayed in the house forever after I lost my first child, but your father lit a fire under me and gave me something to focus on. He also stood by me every minute of that time; I was so depressed I never got out of bed for six months.'

'I know. Dad is a great guy.' Sam ran his hands through his hair and paced the space around the pulpit. 'Suppose I lose her case, and she ends up in prison for murder? I don't think I could stand that. I'd go crazy with her in there.'

'You're not twenty-five and fresh out of law school, and you know enough to get a team together to help. You are going to get Kelly out of this, Sam. She is the

first woman I have seen you be truly in love with.'
Evelyn came up beside him and put her hand on his
back. 'It's that simple, son.'

She was right. It was that simple. He loved Kelly
more than any woman he'd ever known. Everything had
been so easy for him growing up. Kelly's life had never
been easy until she came to Paradise. She came here to
start a new life. He knew her heart, because she'd given
it to him.

Now he needed two things. One was to let Kelly
know he was going to get her out of this, no matter what.
The other was the best criminal attorney he could find
in L.A. – Peter Brady.

Myrtle spoke up. 'Sam Grayson, we've gotta get yer
almost wife outta jail.'

'That is exactly what I'm going to do, starting with
you.' He stepped down and put his hand on her
shoulder gently. 'I need to get a message to Kelly. Can
you deliver it to her at the jail?' He turned to face his
mother. 'Mom, I'm also going to need the plane, and
could you take her some clothes, something warm? Just
get something from my . . . our place . . . please?'

His mother smiled as he added the *please* on the end
of his list. 'You are so much like your father. At least I
taught you both to be polite when you order me around.
I'm assuming you'll fly down to L.A.?'

'I need to meet with an attorney down there. I need
facts. Now let me write this message. Let's go in the
minister's office and find some paper.'

'I knew you wouldn't let her down, boy. We'll get

some bail together and get her outta that birdcage while you're gone.' Myrtle thumped him on the arm with affection and pulled a notepad and pen out of her large purse.

He started writing his note. 'Actually she will probably be extradited to L.A. in the morning. Once the L.A. cops know she's been . . . caught, they'll want her back in L.A. for questioning and a preliminary hearing.'

'You should go to her, Sam,' Evelyn said softly.

'I know, Mom, but every minute counts now. I have a better chance of getting her released from L.A. I can set up her defense from there. I'm not going to lose this time. I can't. I love her too much. I'll meet her down in L.A. Just tell her that.'

'I'll tell her.' Evelyn kissed her son on the cheek, and marched out of the church on a mission.

'That girl didn't murder anyone, Sam, and we gave all that drug money to charity, too,' Myrtle began.

Sam folded up the note. 'Tell me on the way out the door, Myrtle. I've got a plane to fly.'

16

Lynnette slid out of the sheriff's office coffee room quietly, looking around the main office for signs of life. First Tom, then Deputy Gary had been forced to leave the jail on police calls. What incredible luck.

About a half hour earlier she'd overheard Sam's mother and that crazy Myrtle Crabtree come in, and Tom telling them that Kelly didn't want to see anyone right now. They'd left some things for Kelly. She'd have to check that out.

Then Tom had gotten a dispatch call and told Lynnette she had to leave, too. She'd promised she would. She lied.

Lynnette had hidden in this room, waiting. Hoping she could slip in and talk to Kelly. She'd been plotting how to get Kelly in more trouble just in case she hadn't really killed her husband. If Kelly escaped, that would really incriminate her. So Lynnette figured she'd help that along by unlocking the door.

When Gary left, he didn't even notice she was still in the building.

Truly, she was having rare luck today. When she

searched through the things Sam's mom had insisted on leaving for poor Kelly, besides just a pile of clothes, she found Sam's note.

She opened the envelope and read it. Oh, he went on about his love and how he wouldn't let her down and that he'd gone off to L.A. to line up a criminal attorney. What a shame Kelly would never read it. Pretty soon Sam would forget all about Kelly.

Now was her golden opportunity to rub some salt in Kelly's wounds. Maybe she could get rid of her for good. Or at least make things worse.

Kelly closed her eyes and rubbed her forehead. She *would* have to pee at a time like this. Her dress was voluminous, and the toilet was sitting in the corner of the room, taunting her. She tried to gather herself up, but then there was the garter belt and all that Victoria's Secret snap-crotch stuff.

'Ah, the blushing bride. Aren't you just a sight?' Lynnette stood in the corridor of the two-cell block, leaning on the opposite wall.

'Shut up, Lynnette, and give me some privacy. Where's Tom anyway?'

'He had to run out on an emergency call, and so did the deputy. Looks like I'm in charge.' She jangled a set of keys in her hand.

What kind of idiot would leave Lynnette in charge of the jail? There had to be another story there. Neither Tom nor Gary would have done that. Kelly sat back down on the cot and actually had a moment of fear. On the other hand, she was from L.A. She could take Lynnette if she had to. She sat up straighter.

'What do you want from me, Lynnette?' Kelly made her voice sound strong.

'You know the whole town hates you now, and Sam has disappeared. No one will ever believe you didn't kill that guy, because you ran, and with his money, too.'

Kelly's stomach wrenched. 'I didn't kill him, not that I care what you think. The money was an accident.'

'Oh, an *accident* . . . very good. You know, Kelly, I feel sorry for you. They're going to charge you with first-degree murder, because you shot him and stole his money. You're going to spend the rest of your life in jail. You might as well forget about Sam. If you had any real love for him, you'd set him free of you so he could have a life while you rot in prison.'

Kelly slid into the far corner of the cot against the wall. She curled her legs up under her dress and wrapped her arms around her knees, shivering. Lynnette was right. Raymond had been shot. It would be first-degree.

'Now I'd say your life was over in Paradise, honey. If I were you, I'd bolt out of here and head for Canada. You could start over just like you tried to here.'

'Now, how could I do that, Lynnette? I'm in jail.'

'I might be inclined to open your cell and let you go to the ladies' room proper-like, and I might have to answer the phone while you're in there.'

'And why would you be inclined to do that for me, Lynnette?'

'Let's say it would be much better for me if you weren't around at all.'

Kelly thought about the alternatives for a few minutes. She had changed so much. She didn't feel like running, even if her life was over here. The past would always come back to haunt her no matter where she was, so she might as well get this all over with. There was a chance she'd be found innocent. There was even a chance she'd get Sam back.

What interested her most was the ladies' room. She smiled to herself.

'Okay, Lynnette, I really have to pee, and I'm going to have to about undress to do it. You go ahead and open the cell. But we're going to have to make this look good; otherwise, Tom won't believe I got away from you, you being a very intelligent woman and all.'

Lynnette looked at Kelly with one eyebrow arched high. 'Like what?'

'We're going to have to tie you up, of course. Get a pair of handcuffs, and we'll say I tricked you into the cell, whacked you on the head, and handcuffed you to the bars.'

'What about the whack?'

'Oh, I doubt anyone will examine your head. If they haven't already, then the chances are slim.'

'What? Whatever, I agree. We have to make it look good.' Lynnette fetched the handcuffs and unlocked the cell door. 'But I'll keep the key in my pocket, if you don't mind. You didn't murder your husband, did you?'

'Nope. How can you tell?'

'You just don't have the guts, girlfriend.'

'Thanks. Now sit on the bunk here, and we'll put one cuff on the bars, one on your wrist.' Amazingly, Lynnette did what she asked.

Kelly snapped the cuff on the bars, then on Lynnette's one wrist. She even slipped the key into Lynnette's blouse pocket. If Lynnette decided to get free, it would take some contortion time. Plus Kelly had a plan for ol' Lynnette, but by then Kelly was dancing to keep from peeing in her lacy lingerie.

'Thanks, Lynnette. I'll be out of your bad hair before you know it.'

'It's my pleasure to be rid of you. Now get out.' Lynnette positioned herself on the bunk in a dramatic way, then shifted herself around a few times to emphasize her plight.

''Bye, now,' Kelly called as she shot to the ladies' room in the outer office, peeled off her wedding petticoat, unsnapped a snap-crotch, and made it to the pot.

Whew. Thank God she wasn't having a period. As she sat in relief on the cold toilet seat, a horrible, wild, and amazing thought came to her. She hadn't had a period since the first few weeks she'd been in Paradise. In all the excitement she'd forgotten her cycle completely.

Oh, God, oh, *God*. Then there was the mild nausea that had bothered her, and the way her wedding dress seemed tight in the bust. No doubt about it. She was pregnant with Sam's baby.

It must have been the first time they made love – in

the pool. All that water, the condom must have slipped. She stomped her foot on the ground. Could her life get any worse? Here she was, in jail for murder, pregnant.

In the quiet of the small bathroom, she buttoned herself back up and calmed herself. She was, in fact, carrying the child of the man she loved. Whatever happened to her, she had that tiny seed of wonderfulness inside her.

She would beat this charge and make a new life for her and her baby. Even if Sam wouldn't have her, somewhere there was another Paradise.

Tom pushed open the glass door and stepped into a very quiet office. Damn, he didn't want to leave Lynnette with Kelly Atwood, but he'd had to answer that dispatch. At least Gary was in the office and would have made sure she left. Either that or respond to Kelly's screams, surely. Wouldn't you know the Pickets would choose tonight to get into a quarrel, which of course was called in by Old Lady McBay, their neighbor and resident busybody.

Then again, someone needed to remind the Pickets that life was too short for this kind of nonsense. He unhooked his gun belt and hung it on a special hook. He noticed the neatly folded pile of women's clothes with a pair of loafers on top still sitting on his desk. Things looked pretty calm and orderly here.

He was about to sit down at his desk when a loud moan came from the cell area, startling Tom into a run. He came to a standstill, and took in the sight of Lynnette

Stivers cuffed to the cell bar. Her other hand was pressed to her forehead in a melodramatic gesture.

'What happened here, Lynnette?' Tom paused for her explanation, not moving to unhook her. 'Where's Gary?'

'Ooohh. She tricked me, Tom. She hit me on the head and cuffed me up. Give me a hand out of here. We have to get after her. She's really proved she's guilty now, hasn't she? Tom, get me out of here, will ya?'

Something didn't ring true here. No woman would get the best of Lynnette, particularly the one who was about to marry her precious Sam. He turned his head to the sound of rustling silk. Kelly strolled into the hall easy as you please.

'Hi, Tom. I made some coffee. I figured we might be up for a while.' Kelly leaned against the break room doorframe with one shoulder, her arms crossed. 'Apparently, Gary had to leave and didn't notice Lynnette.'

Just as he figured. This should be interesting. 'Well, well, if it isn't my escaped prisoner. Shall we sit in the office and have a cup? Cream or sugar for you, Kelly?'

'*Tooooommmmm!* Watch out! She's a murderer!' Lynnette screeched, partly in surprise.

'I'll have both, please. *The keys are in her right blouse pocket, Tom.*' Kelly whispered that last part.

Tom turned around and strode over to Lynnette in the cell. 'Here, let me help you, honey.' When he got close enough to her, he reached over and popped the keys out of her pocket, then walked out of the cell, past

Kelly, and into the office area. 'This way, Miss Atwood.'

A shrill noise came from the hall. 'Tom Blackwell! Get back here! You can't leave me chained up here, come back here!'

'If you be quiet, I'll only take a fifteen-minute coffee break. Otherwise, it'll be a whole lot longer,' he hollered back.

'Don't listen to her, she's a lying murderer!'

Tom went to the break room coffeepot and poured out two thick white mugs of coffee. He poured a spoon of sugar and a packet of fake cream in for Kelly, and stirred. He came back in the office and they both sat next to Tom's desk in his old oak chairs. 'So, what's the story, Kelly?'

'Thanks.' She took the coffee and let it warm her hands. 'Miss Stivers offered me a chance to escape and staged this little scene for you. I let her play it out so I could get to a toilet that wasn't out in the center of a room. Sorry about that, I had to take off half my clothes to—'

'I get the picture. Did you hit her on the head, or did she hit herself?'

'Neither. As tempted as I was, she's injury-free. I'm no murderer, Tom. When I left my husband, he was still alive. A friend of mine in L.A. told me he died of a gunshot wound. I came here thinking he would be after me. I didn't find out he was dead until about a month ago. As for the money, it was in his car. I didn't know what to do with it for a while, but Myrtle and I finally donated it to a worthy cause.'

'Why didn't you come in and tell me, Kelly? Why not just clear your name?'

'I fell in love with Paradise. And with Sam. I didn't believe the justice system would give me a break. I just . . . didn't want to lose everything. But now I've lost it all anyway, so I might as well face it and clean up this mess I've made.' Kelly's voice cracked, and she took a deep sip of the hot coffee to keep from breaking down.

'Here's what we can do. If you waive extradition and save them the paperwork trouble, the L.A. prosecutor will probably send someone by morning to take you down there. I can put in a good word for you, Kelly. But you will probably have a few days in jail before they can set a preliminary hearing and hopefully get some bail set. Oh, Myrtle and Mrs. Grayson brought you some clothes and shoes here.' He patted the pile.

'They did? Did they say anything about Sam?' She lowered her eyes in pain.

'I've known Sam my whole life, Kelly. I've never seen him in love like this. Hang in there. He's probably doing everything he can to help your case right now.'

'I've really done it up, Tom. He begged me to turn myself in, but I wouldn't listen. He looked bad when we drove off. So did most of the town. I'm no murderer, and I'm no drug dealer – I've never had much interest in altering my reality; it was hard enough as it was.'

'I can relate to that.' Tom leaned back in his swivel chair and contemplated Lynnette in lockup. He'd cared for her in a big way. He probably still did. The best he could do for her was help her get straightened out. She was probably madder than a wet hen about now. No more than she deserved, though. Lynnette was going to need a serious mental health workup.

'All right, Kelly.' He got up out of his chair. 'I'd leave you your roommate in there, but I think she'd be bad company. How about you change your clothes in the ladies' room, and I'll go have a word with Lynnette.'

Kelly nodded. Tom walked toward the cell. Lynnette was quiet, but she was madder than a cat getting a bath. He could tell by the set of her jaw. However, Tom found himself in a rare position. The woman he'd wasted the better part of his life waiting around for was a captive audience, and he had reached the end of his patience with her antics.

'Lynnette, we're going to have a little chat. Things are going to be different between you and me when we're all through.'

Kelly sat in the back seat of the rented Ford Taurus, staring out the window at the gray, pounding rain. She felt all out of tears, but the rain expressed her feelings well enough. She put a protective arm around her middle. How was she going to take care of her baby in jail?

She pressed her hand up against the glass and watched the trees bend against the wind.

The policewoman was fairly kind, anyway. They would be getting to the Seattle airport soon, and make L.A. by late afternoon. Kelly was exhausted. She'd try and get some sleep on the plane.

*

Four hours later their flight landed in L.A. She and the policewoman exited the plane and headed down the corridor. Boy, she hoped her next escort would be plain-clothed also, instead of a uniformed cop for everyone to see. Plus, she was going to have to convince someone to let her find a rest room – she was having some trouble keeping her airline breakfast down.

People met their loved ones with hugs and kisses, and the crowd thinned a bit. Watching, she felt crushed inside, but took a deep breath, and raised her head. She was going to clear her name. Maybe even change it again, to Grayson this time, if Sam would still have her.

Sam was standing ten feet in front of her. Her head rushed with elation, and she quickened her step, only to have her companion take hold of her arm and hold her back.

Sam closed the distance between them and introduced himself to the policewoman.

Kelly never took her eyes off his face. He was serious, but there was something else in his face ... forgiveness, she hoped. The policewoman let go of her arm, and she went into his embrace. He didn't hesitate a minute to hold her, close. He put his mouth close to her ear.

'I love you. I love you, honey. Don't worry, we'll get out of this mess together.'

'Oh, Sam, I love you. I'm so sorry.' She let out a cry against his shoulder. She could feel tears running down her face. She wiped them away. 'What are you doing here?'

'Didn't you get my note?' He kissed her forehead and pushed back her hair lovingly.

'No, no. But Lynnette probably made sure I didn't.'

'You spent the whole night thinking I'd run off on you, then?'

Kelly touched his cheek softly. 'Yes, but I was hoping you might forgive me somewhere along the line.'

'I'd be here even if you were guilty, Kelly.' He turned to the policewoman, his arm around Kelly's waist. 'We're going to have to make some time here, the prosecuting attorney is meeting us downtown and sitting in while the police question you. Is that all right with you, Ms. Jones?'

'Sure thing. I hope the kid gets a break.'

Sam steered Kelly toward the exit signs, with Officer Jones on one side.

'Are you telling me I can get a hearing and not have to do any jail time?'

'I'm afraid there's going to be at least one night. After that I've got a hearing with the court set up for four o'clock tomorrow. It depends on if they set bail for you at that point. I'll do everything in my power to make sure they do, Kelly. I've had a friend of mine working on some of the leads I've gotten on Raymond's murder. It's a cold trail, but a pretty obvious one. You know, Kelly, if you hadn't run out on Raymond, you probably would have been killed along with him.'

She shivered, remembering that day. A hundred times she had thought about the two men in the hallway, their search through her suitcase. Sam's words gave her a cold chill.

'One more thing,' Sam said quietly. 'I'm pretty sure the reason Raymond married you was because he knew things were getting out of control and if you found out anything . . . well, a wife can testify against her husband, but her credibility comes into question. That, and it's a great front for the customs people saying you are on your honeymoon.'

'Marital motivation,' Kelly said dryly. Somehow that made perfect sense to her when she thought back to the circumstances surrounding their marriage.

As he walked into the courtroom, Sam could see the judge was tired, and on final hour of the day. That wasn't good, but they were lucky to get on the calendar, so they'd have to take what they got. The assistant deputy prosecuting attorney assigned to Kelly's case was young and fresh out of law school. During the police questioning last night the woman was a little shaky in her role as prosecutor rather than that overzealous rabidity that earmarks newly assigned attorneys, which was lucky for them. Peter Brody was sitting at the defense table with Kelly beside him. Sam knew Kelly's case was in good hands with Peter, but he decided to argue for bail himself. He just couldn't let anyone else do it.

Sleep had eluded him last night. He had paced Peter's house until Peter's wife Fran made him stop and eat something. Thinking of Kelly in a jail cell had made him crazy, just crazy.

Today Kelly looked so vulnerable. She was wearing clothes his mother had picked out for her and sent along: a simple white blouse, light blue cardigan sweater, and slim khaki tan skirt. She had no makeup on, and her hair was pulled back in a ponytail. He looked at her and could see the stress in her beautiful face. He hoped the judge would see innocence there, too.

He sat down at his place between Peter and Kelly and gave her a gentle touch just as Judge Kratt called the case.

'Bail hearing for Miss Kelly Atwood Bianchi ... what's your position on this, Miss Randolph?' the judge finished.

Miss Randolph stood up. 'Your Honor, the prosecutor asks that the defendant be held without bail pending trial. She's a known flight risk, there is drug trafficking involved in this case, and after hearing the police questioning last night we believe she very likely murdered Raymond Bianchi.'

So much for shaky. Miss Randolph looked over to the defense table and caught Sam's eye. She'd put on her dark grey power suit, and she had a glint in her eye. Sam sighed. He kept his hand on Kelly's arm and could feel the tension going through her body into his fingertips.

'And what have you got to say about this, Pete?' Judge Kratt was certainly being informal, Sam noticed.

Peter rose. 'Your Honor, Sam Grayson is admitted in the State of Washington and appears here today as associated counsel pro hac vice. He's been working on the case.' Peter indicated Sam's presence and handed some papers to the court clerk, who passed them up to the judge.

'The Court recognizes Sam Grayson. Make note of that please.' The clerk nodded in confirmation.

Sam stood up and addressed the judge. 'Your Honor, my client left town after a quarrel with her husband, who struck her across the face. Raymond Bianchi was in fact alive when she last saw him. I have submitted several affidavits that indicate she had no knowledge of Mr. Bianchi's death when she left L.A.'

Judge Kratt peered at Sam through his half glasses, looked down to his desktop, ruffled through some papers and read something. The time he took to do that was dead silent and made Sam's heart practically stop. He looked over to see Kelly clutching a shredded up tissue, her knuckles white.

'Mr. Grayson, just for the sake of argument, I might also conclude that your client left the state, changed her name and hid to avoid prosecution. I'm inclined to see her as a flight risk myself.'

'I will personally vouch for her continued appearance in court, Your Honor.'

'It's my understanding you are only assisting on this case due to a personal interest, Mr. Grayson, and that you are from Surrey County, in Washington, and are occasionally their interim prosecuting attorney. It seems to me you don't have the freedom to take on that responsibility. You may be needed in your own jurisdiction. Plus there is the matter of your personal relationship with the plaintiff. In truth, you should recuse yourself from any further involvement in this case.'

Sam turned to look at Kelly again. Yes, he had a personal relationship with the plaintiff, and he'd be damned if he'd see the woman he loved behind bars.

To his surprise, Kelly stood up and spoke to a policewoman, who then accompanied her out of the courtroom. She looked pale.

She was losing hope, he sensed.

Peter Brody stood up, abruptly. With his neatly trimmed beard and round physique he reminded Sam of an Irish bar keep rather than a top criminal attorney.

'Please excuse my client for a moment, Your Honor, while we continue.'

'Fine. Do continue, please, Pete,' the judge said.

'Now, Howard, let's come up with some kind of compromise here. Sam here has a sterling reputation, and we are working on some solid leads in this case. We don't want to see this girl in a holding cell for the next month while we wait for a court date. Besides, she's pregnant.'

Sam's mouth dropped open, and he stared with complete shock at Peter. 'How the hell would you know that?' For the moment, Sam forgot they were standing in front of a judge.

'She's thrown up four times since we've been here, sport, and I have three kids of my own. I know what a pregnant woman looks like.'

Sam practically climbed up the judge's bench and spoke. 'Your Honor, I've gotten to know Miss Atwood over the last couple of months. She came to our town to make a new life for herself. She didn't hide, she took a job, she organized a benefit for a community center and she agreed to marry a very public, well-known attorney in town. These were the actions of a person who had no idea she was wanted for a crime.'

Miss Randolph interrupted. 'Which could have been a very carefully devised plan on Miss Atwood's part, your honor.'

'Including getting pregnant?' Sam practically shouted.

'Why not? That's a nice touch,' Miss Randolph sneered.

'Counsel, please direct your comments to the bench. Miss Randolph, your position is noted. Please sit down.' Judge Kratt gave the prosecution a lifted eyebrow.

Sam took a deep breath. Don't let your opponent rile you into a shouting match. Judges hate that, even friendly ones. Focus on your own journey. Just like a swim meet. 'Your Honor, I met Kelly when she came to my office in hopes of obtaining a divorce. I've provided you with a stack of character references, and if I have to chain myself to Miss Atwood to make sure she shows up for a trial, which most likely won't take place once further evidence is brought forth, I will.'

'Further evidence of what sort?' The judge rested his chin on his folded hands.

'Two men were seen entering the victim's building by Miss Atwood at the exact time of the murder. Yesterday we did some preliminary sketches and are trying for a match. We believe these men killed Raymond Bianchi.' Sam had cooled himself down to a boiling simmer. His brain was spinning like a computer hard drive trying to come up with a way out of this for Kelly, and a way to get this wrapped up so he could talk to her now. His heart pounded with adrenaline, but he kept his words under control. He had an idea. He hoped to God it worked.

'If I might continue, Your Honor, instead of chaining myself to the defendant, Miss Atwood could be released to Mr. Brody's custody with a security bracelet. She'll stay in this jurisdiction and no one can say you didn't do your job.' Sam's blood was rushing in his head. He stared at the judge as if he were deciding a death sentence . . . Sam's.

'Well' – the judge looked amused – 'that puts a different light on things. What do you have to say, Pete?'

'I'd be more than willing to take responsibility for Miss Atwood, Howard.' Peter smiled.

'Your Honor, I object. This is all highly irregular.'

'Maybe so, Miss Randolph, but it's my courtroom. Your objection is noted.' The judge cleared his throat and turned to the clerk. 'Enter a minute order that Peter Brody, representative of the district court of L.A., will act as custodian to the defendant awaiting trial with an electronic monitor and is to keep her within city limits at all times, and report in daily. Bail is therefore waived.' He turned back to look at Peter and Sam. 'How's that, Pete? And don't call me Howard while I'm on the bench, Pete.'

'That sounds acceptable, Your Honor, Howard, sir.' Pete's eyes twinkled. Judge Kratt gave him the evil eye, but banged his gavel down, and declared it so.

'All rise,' the clerk said as the hearing concluded and the judge rose from the bench. Sam heard all he needed and was already halfway down the aisle. He jumped over a railing and through the door on his way to her.

'Kelly! Where are you?' His voice filled the entire echo chamber of a courthouse.

'Sam?'

He spotted her down the east hall, with the bailiff. In two seconds he was beside her, swept her off her feet, and spun her around.

'Echhh. Stop. Put me down slowly, you nut.'

'Now, listen. You have got to start telling me things as they occur. I want a daily account of your life for the *rest* of your life, understand?' He set her down and pulled her close to him. He tipped her chin up with his finger. 'Are you pregnant?'

'I'm pretty sure. How'd you figure that out?'

He kissed her on the mouth and held her close. The policewoman leaned up against the wall with a smirk on her face and crossed her arms.

'It was Peter, and his experiences with fatherhood. He just whacked me in the head and woke me up. Kelly, honey, are you okay? This isn't exactly where I want my pregnant wife, and how the hell did that happen anyway?'

'We didn't get to the wife part, Sam. Reverend Evans was rudely interrupted. As for *that*, I think it was a combination of pool water and passion. Are you asking me to marry you?'

'Will you marry me again, but all the way this time? We'll have Tom lock up Lynnette for the ceremony.'

'I will. But the town is going to hate me, Sam. I hurt their favorite son. I deceived them.'

'How did you deceive them? By being the person you always wanted to be? We'll deal with that as it comes. The judge cut us a deal. It's not the best, but better than cell time for sure.' He kissed her again. 'I love you, Mrs. Grayson. Now let's get you out of here.'

They headed off down the hall under the eye of the bailiff to fill out forms and formalize the judge's orders.

'*What?* I have to wear this thing until the trial? Doesn't it come in gold? It weighs a ton. I don't think these guys know what the term *ankle bracelet* is all about.'

'Very amusing. I've heard them all, you know, and worse.' The electronics specialist adjusted a timer and fastened the lock. 'There you go, you're wired for sound, now. You might want to avoid pantyhose, and I just set you for a four-hour delay so you can get to your designated house-arrest location. I hope that's enough. I put in extra time for traffic and dinner.'

'That's plenty. Thanks.' Sam glanced at his watch. 'I assume Mr. Brody has a release key for emergencies?'

'That's correct. Mr. Brody, as a representative of the court, you know your responsibilities. Don't forget your license to practice law is at stake here.'

'We'll all behave ourselves, Max,' Peter assured the man. 'Hopefully we can get this case wrapped up and dismissed before we even have to think about a trial.'

Kelly walked ahead of Pete and Sam as they left the room together. Kelly sighed and tried to pick up her left ankle with better agility. It wasn't that bad, it just threw off her balance a bit. She stumbled along the hall, moving toward a large crowd that had gathered in the entry area. Oh, great, an audience.

'There she is!' A voice rose out of the mass of people.

Damn it all to hell, she couldn't very well run away at this pace. She slipped behind Sam and tried to hide. He scooped her back out and pointed her toward the group, his hands on her shoulders.

'Sam, what the hell?' Then she saw Myrtle in a lime-green pantsuit, with her flaming red hair tied in a sixties patterned scarf.

'Oh, honey bun, we are all so glad to see you.' Myrtle threw her arms around Kelly and gave her a huge hug. Over Myrtle's shoulder she could see all the faces she had come to know and love, all the way from Paradise: Dottie and Walt Williamson, Reverend Evans, Cora, Ginny and Will, and even Red Miller. Everyone she knew, and some she didn't. Sam's parents led the way, with Sam's two sisters and their husbands right behind.

'What'd you do, shut down the whole town? Are you all here to lynch me?' she joked, but her voice cracked with the words. She was looking at about fifty folks in the courthouse now. These wonderful people came here for her. Never in her entire life had she experienced anything so moving. Sam and the people of Paradise were better than any dream she'd ever had before.

'No, honey, we came here to tell that judge you're the best gal we know, and to keep you outta jail!' Myrtle said. 'The Graysons packed us into one of their planes tighter than sardines – isn't that so, Walt,' Myrtle chortled, and gave Walt a squeeze. He smiled with delight.

'Are we too late? Did they set bail? Because we've got it.' Sam's dad stepped up and took Kelly's hand in his. 'Don't worry, dear, we will take you home, soon.'

Kelly brushed her tears away with her other hand. 'Hank, that means so much to me, I can't even tell you. Sam and Peter made arrangements for me to be out of jail until the trial.' She lifted the edge of her slacks and pointed at her ankle bracelet.

'That's barbaric!' Evelyn Grayson said angrily.

Sam put his arm around his mom. 'I'm really proud of you two. And all of you.' He raised his voice to include everyone. 'Thank you so much. It means so much to both of us that you would set aside your lives and fly down here. You've really shown Kelly what Paradise is all about. She has to come back now.' Sam turned to Kelly. 'Besides, you have a wedding to finish up. I seem to have gotten the girl in trouble, folks.'

Everyone's voice went up a notch, then a cheer crossed the room. Evelyn Grayson started to cry. Hank Grayson gave her his handkerchief and whacked Sam on the back. 'Way to go, boy.'

'Thanks, Dad, it was my pleasure.' Everyone laughed and cried and talked at once. Kelly did all those things three times over. This was the happiest day of her life. All she needed now was to be free of the past. It hung on her like the weight of the ankle bracelet.

'What'd I tell ya, honey? Paradise is your destiny. Come on, folks, we're in the big city now. Let's go out for Chinese food!' Myrtle linked arms with Sam and Kelly, and led the way out the door. 'By the way, your friend Pete there is quite a dish. Is he hitched?'

After finding a Chinese restaurant with an empty banquet room, and generously bribing the staff, the Paradise contingent managed to present Sam and Kelly with a wonderful feast. Kelly even managed to keep it down, but fatigue set in, and Sam almost had to carry her out to Peter's car. Besides that, her timer was running out, and she had to be at Pete's address by eight o'clock or turn into a pumpkin.

The next morning she found herself tucked into a twin bed covered with clean Toy Story sheets. She hardly remembered how she got here. She opened her eyes to discover three small people staring at her as if she were Goldilocks. She had Fran Brody's nightgown on. Thank heavens it was some modest flannel thing.

'What's your name anyway?'

'I let you sleep in my bed. Didja find Stinky in there?'

'Mommy says we aren't s'pose to bother you until you're awake. Are you awake now?'

So this was what Kelly was in for. She smiled big at them, and they stared even more.

'Children, get your little selves in here for breakfast before the dog eats it all.' Fran Brody shooed her little brood out of the room. 'I'm so sorry about that, dear. They'll be gone to school in a half hour. Let me know if you need anything.'

'A hacksaw?' Kelly managed a joke, even though she could feel morning sickness creeping up on her.

'Good one, dear. You look a little green. How about

some dry toast, a handful of saltines, and a cup of tea before you try and get up? I could hardly manage the first few hours without that.' Fran tidied up the room all around her as they talked, picking up stray cartoon underwear and legions of tiny Lego pieces.

'I'd like that. Thank you so much for taking me in.'

'My Peter is a good judge of character, and Sam is an old friend. They're both in the den plotting away like mystery writers. I'll tell Sam you're awake . . . after the crackers. We need to spare the little dears all we can, don't we?'

Kelly gave a laugh at the thought of Sam witnessing her green-to-the-gills morning behavior. 'I say let's give the little dears the full dose. It might sharpen their appreciation of us,' Kelly replied.

Fran laughed. 'You're right. I'll send him in with the tea and saltines. You have to start their training early.' Fran started out the door. 'Oh, Sam's mother left some clean clothes. Looks like Mrs. Grayson knows how to shop in L.A. I think you'll be quite pleased. They're hanging in there.' She pointed to the kids' closet on her way out.

Kelly made an attempt to rise, and so did her nausea. She decided to wait for the crackers. Fran brought her a tray in a few minutes, saying the men were too deep into it to disturb, and were on the phone. After a couple of dry crunchy moments washed down with warm tea, she managed to get herself up and going.

The kids' room had a connecting bathroom. She

showered, cursing her ankle bracelet all the time. Damn thing must be waterproof.

Wrapped in a large towel Fran had graciously laid out for her, she went to check out the clothes. They were indeed amazing. Hanging in Fran's kids' closet she found an elegant cream and beige skirt, a pair of slacks, several matching cashmere sweater sets, socks, a wonderful jacket just in case she ever went outside again, and two pairs of Charles Jourdan shoes, just her size. Evelyn must have consulted Myrtle.

Kelly rubbed the baby-soft leather shoes and remembered her days in the garment district. Cashmere and leather always took the sting away, then and now. Along with all of that was a soft gray cashmere wrap robe, a pair of man-style gray silk pajamas, seven pairs of lovely panties, and several matching bras. She must have consulted Sam for that one. Good thing Sam overestimated, because her bustline seemed to be expanding daily.

Man, her mother-in-law-to-be was a woman of infinite taste and wisdom. No wonder Sam was so special. Kelly dropped the towel over a tiny chair and slipped naked into the cashmere robe, just for the sake of pleasure. She needed some.

She heard the Brody children heading out the door, with Fran yelling goodbye to Sam and Peter. Fran must be on car pool duty. There was a knock at the bedroom door. Sam stuck his head in.

'Are you decent?'

'No.'

'Good.' He shut the door behind him and came over

to her. His embrace was better than cashmere. Warm and delicious. He slipped his hands under the robe and ran his hands from the top of her back, down and over her bottom. He pulled her into him, burying his face in her hair with a deep groan.

'Ohhh, Sam. Not here. Don't stop, though.'

'Peter is a wise man, and Fran just took the kids out to school. He says we have a good hour and a half.' He ran his mouth down her neck and up again.

'Sam, I've missed you so much.' The robe dropped to the floor. 'Are you all right with this baby thing? I mean, it was a surprise . . . ummmmm,' – she lost her train of thought – 'of sorts.' His mouth covered hers with an intense kiss, full of his desire for her.

'Kelly, I have never wanted any woman I know to carry my child, until you. Nothing happens by accident.' He picked her up in his arms. Her ankle bracelet clunked him in the thigh. 'Oww.'

'Crap.'

Sam only answered by kissing her left breast as he carried her over to the tiny bed. He lowered her onto the Toy Story sheets. She watched him undress. He unbuttoned his white shirt and peeled it off, revealing his wonderful muscled swimmer's chest. He unzipped his jeans and pushed them down slowly. His magnificent erection made her crazy.

She squirmed and locked her legs around his knees, whacking him with the bracelet again, pulling him onto her. He seemed to be beyond any pain she might have inflicted on him.

He held her so he could look into her eyes as he entered her. He could feel his emotion blend into their lovemaking, until their bodies melted into each other, lost in the heat of their passion. All the time he made love to her, he watched her. It excited him beyond endurance to see the pleasure she was experiencing with him. He touched her full, tender breasts lightly with the tip of his thumbs.

He moved gently and slowly in her until she reached her climax, arched against him, dug her fingers into his hips, pulling him deeper. He held back and she went wild under him, coming once more, even stronger. His entire body seemed to be on fire as he finally let go. She opened her eyes to meet his as he gave himself to her.

Afterward, he saw a few tears in the corner of her eyes, and brought his hand up to her temple to wipe them away. He cupped her against him, cradling her. He knew this was the moment he had waited for all his life. To really love a woman, to be loved in return, and to create a new life between them.

Sam held her for another hour, smoothing out the skin on her belly, talking to it. They tried to find a slight bulge there, but decided it was way too early.

She sighed, and snuggled up to him, covering him with the corners of her cashmere robe. Which was a good thing, because just about then Peter Brody knocked wildly on the door, then opened it.

'Pete. Say, bud, at least I'm not in the act, but don't mind if I don't get up.' Sam pulled a sheet over Kelly's naked body.

'I'm sorry, you two, but it's ten-thirty, and this is great news. Seems those two guys you bumped into in the hall that day were put in jail last night. Guess where? Paradise.'

'Sam, that means they almost found me. If Lynnette hadn't had me arrested, who knows what would have happened?' Kelly said.

'I guess we owe Lynnette a thank-you,' Sam said sarcastically.

'Tom Blackwell stopped them for speeding and just looking suspicious – last night, and when he ran a make on them they had priors, of course. I guess he and his deputy brought them in single-handedly. They found a gun in the car, and it turns out that gun was the one that shot Raymond. Forensics had a type on it already thanks to Sam's efforts getting all the physical evidence lined up.

'Your local sheriff got them to confess to Raymond's murder this morning. He said it was easy with some crazy girl named Lynnette being in the next cell, yelling all night. Congratulations, you have been cleared completely. I'm here to deactivate you, Kelly.'

Sam jumped up naked, whooped, slugged Peter in the arm, and shook his hand repeatedly. Kelly had enough of a moment to grab her robe and tie it up before Sam pulled her up and danced her around the room. They stepped on a few squeaky toys, and almost fell over a large Tickle-me Elmo.

'I'll let you get some clothes on before we get to the unlocking ceremony.' Pete whistled a lively tune as he left the room.

Sam got on his knees in front of Kelly and held on to her robe ties. 'Will you marry me again?'

'Of course I will. I do, I do! See?' She squealed and pulled him up. 'Now let me get dressed and get this thing off me. Better yet, let's get it off me now so I *can* get dressed.'

'I know a good locksmith,' he replied as he pulled his jeans and underwear back on and searched for his shirt. She admired his long, lean, muscular body as he stretched to pull the T-shirt over his head. My, my. That would keep her warm on winter nights.

Sam caught her staring, then came over and caressed her, running his hands under her robe.

'Cut that out, Grayson, I've got a date with key master Pete.'

'We've got a honeymoon to plan,' he said, nuzzling her neck again.

'Oh Sam, we can go on a trip later. Let's just stay home in Paradise.'

'Home in Paradise. That sounds good.' He turned her and kissed her a forever kiss.

Myrtle was waiting for her at Cora's to plan wedding number two. Well, three, if you count Raymond. How could a girl get married so many times in one year? She and Sam and the rest of the family had decided to have a December wedding, considering her condition.

As she walked down the sidewalk, the shopkeepers came out to wave or shake her hand. She took in the details of the town with even more gratitude than before. What a wonderful place to raise her children. She still wasn't showing, but she could feel the stirrings of her child within her.

Cora was behind the counter. 'Hey, there, Kelly, welcome home, honey! Did you see the paper?'

'Over here, Kelly,' Myrtle called.

Kelly walked over to the booth and slid in. 'Hi, Myrtle, what's in the paper this time?'

Myrtle held up the front page of the *Paradise Pioneer* for her to see:

PARADISE SWEETHEARTS REUNITED

SHERIFF BLACKWELL AND SAM GRAYSON

SOLVE BIG-CITY MURDER MYSTERY

Boy, Christine at the *Pioneer* was feeling creative. Kelly smiled.

'Yep, it's pretty excitin'. Most excitement we've had around here since Willard robbed his own bank.'

'What? And he still runs it?'

'He said he was testing his own security. I think he just always wanted to put a nylon stocking over his head and point a gun at his clerks.' Myrtle stirred her coffee calmly.

'I guess everyone in town has some kind of past.'

'Yup, we all do.'

Cora came over and gave Kelly a booth-hug. Kelly ordered a pot of peppermint tea. Her nausea was still nasty. Cora said that wasn't enough, and she'd bring her a decent breakfast.

'Hey, you two.' Evelyn Grayson came in the door looking like a fashion model from the fifties. Slim gray wool slacks, a matching sweater, and one tied over her shoulders. Kelly smiled at her warmly, and waved her over. Cora added lemon tea for Evelyn and gave her a hug, too, before heading for her kitchen.

'Honey, I'm so glad this is all over.'

'Me, too. Your whole family was wonderful. And Christine at the *Pioneer* printed up all the details of the case for the whole town to read. She made me sound even more innocent than I was,' Kelly said.

'You *were* completely innocent, and we knew it all along. Thank the stars Tom was on the ball and spotted those two crooks that were after our gal. 'Course they were going sixty down Main Street, and we just don't tolerate that sort of thing around here, but that good description you gave him really helped, Kelly. It's just a good thing he stuck them next to crazy Lynnette's cell. I hear she helped get a confession out of those thugs – she kept 'em up all night yammerin' and hollerin' for Tom to let her out. When the news came in about the gun the next mornin', Tom had 'em right where he wanted 'em. Weakened.' Myrtle snorted a laugh.

'I call that the best luck I've ever had besides getting on the bus and meeting you, Myrtle; and Sam, of course. And think about this. If Lynnette hadn't had me arrested, those two crooks would have tracked me down for sure.'

'We would have protected you.' Evelyn patted her hand.

'I know. Of course I now have the most beautiful clothes I've ever owned as a jailbird bonus. What did you do, Evelyn, buy out Bergdorf's? Those shoes were to die for.'

'I learned it all from Myrtle, you know – a woman needs the right shoes for the occasion.' Kelly looked around at Myrtle in her purple spandex leggings, sparkly sweater, and purple half boots, then back to Evelyn in her country club elegance. She laughed so hard Myrtle had to pat her on the back. Cora brought the tea, and she sipped some to stop herself.

'Now eat this up. You're eating for two now.' Cora put a plate of hash browns and a glass of root beer in front of her. 'This here's the only thing I could tolerate in my first months – potatoes and root beer. Give it a try.'

'Cora, I've been eating for two since I got here, and look where it's gotten me. I'm going to put on fifty pounds with this baby. But this looks great, so thanks.'

'We'll help you work it off,' Evelyn said. 'Yoga class, and lots of long walks with that grandbaby of mine. We'll get one of those buggies and roll him down Main Street every day.'

'I better get married first,' Kelly managed between bites. Suddenly she was starving.

The three women sat in lively conversation for another hour. By the time they were through, the wedding of the year had been set in stone. Evelyn Grayson was going to have a crack at this one, and nobody could stop her.

'It's settled, then. I have more money than I can

figure what to do with. You and Myrtle already spent bunches on the last wedding, so this one is mine. Just show up at the church. Better yet, we'll have you picked up.' Evelyn looked secretive and excited. Kelly cried a little, laughed more, and let her almost mother-in-law take charge. She also decided potatoes and root beer were her favorite combination from now on.

18

Christmas Eve morning was like a picture postcard in Paradise. A layer of snow covered all the lawns and rooftops, and more was falling.

Kelly couldn't sleep without Sam next to her. She looked out of the penthouse bedroom window over the entire town. Her town. It was her wedding day, again.

Her figure had rounded out quite a bit, and even though she said she'd be happy to squeeze into her November dress, Evelyn had found her another wedding dress anyhow. Something about the master plan and overall theme. If it made Evelyn happy, that was fine with Kelly.

She went in the walk-in closet and opened the protective fabric bag to look at the gown. The waist was high just in case her waistline had expanded. Tiny pearls and crystal beads sparkled on the beautiful pleated silk lace skirt. It was supple, and flowed around her like shimmering water.

The bodice was silk-velvet – it felt like heaven. Around the low neck and sleeve cuffs ran an edging of white feathers that made her look like the snow queen in a storybook she'd once read. For her hair there was a crown of crystals and pearls, with flows of netting all around.

She supposed that white wasn't too appropriate at this point, but no one seemed to mind. There was a white velvet cape with matching feathers – all to keep her warm on her mysterious trip to the church.

The wedding wasn't until four. Ten hours away. Nothing was going to stop this wedding. That was for sure. Not this time.

Sam must be sleeping peacefully at his parents' house – they came to the penthouse and took him captive last night. Sam's mother insisted he not see his bride until the wedding. They said it was about putting the suspense back in, and they both laughed while Sam patted her belly, and claimed, 'I've had enough surprises.'

But they insisted and told Kelly to be ready by two o'clock to be picked up for the wedding.

Kelly ran her hands over the two beautiful quilts that she and Sam had unwrapped yesterday. One from Dottie with crazy blue stars all over it, and one from the Grant County Fair and Rodeo they'd seen together. Sam had surprised her with that one. There were gifts all over the penthouse. Some had been waiting for them since the last wedding. Last night was the best Christmas she'd ever had, two days early. She was overwhelmed with the generosity of her friends.

By twelve o'clock, she had showered, eaten breakfast, eaten lunch – she was ravenously hungry these days – and was pacing in her formal maternity lingerie.

Myrtle was coming over to help dress her. The snow was wild outside, wind drifted it up against the sidewalks and cars, and she hadn't seen a car drive down the street for two hours. At least a foot of snow must have fallen in the last three hours.

She pressed her cheek against the windowpane and thought about crying. No one had called. The power had flickered a few times, and here she was a good two miles from the church.

Out of the corner of her eye she noticed a lone figure in the distance, trudging slowly through the storm. Great, it was probably Lynnette Stivers escaped from jail, coming to get her. No, it couldn't be her.

It made her smile thinking how funny it was that Tom Blackwell was keeping Lynnette locked up in the town jail. He'd had her cell done over and brought in a psychologist from Vancouver for twice-weekly sessions. He figured that was the only way Lynnette would get a clue.

As the figure got closer, she saw a bright orange hooded parka take form. Myrtle! Kelly threw on her wonderful cashmere robe and a pair of snow boots, then ran to the elevator. On the first floor she stuck her head out the building door and yelled, 'Myrtle! This way!'

Myrtle's head popped up from her trudge, and she crossed the street, heading for the sound. Safely in the entryway, she stomped the snow off her boots and shook.

'Merciful Snow Goddess, we have a blizzard. Look at you, you're practically nekked. Get upstairs, right now.'

Myrtle had a colorful backpack they dusted the snow off, then hopped in the elevator.

'You know, Myrtle, I used to have this thing with elevators. I haven't had to cry in one for ages. I think the curse is broken.'

'That's because we're watching out for ya now.' Myrtle gave her a cold hug, and they jumped out the elevator doors and into the warm penthouse.

They stripped off Myrtle's parka, boots, and hat by the doorway, revealing her red velvet jacket with rhinestone buttons over a full red velvet skirt. Wow.

'Myrtle, you came through this snow for me. I love you, you sweet old thing.' She hugged her, then shivered. 'Let's have some hot tea.'

'Honey, it's gonna take a miracle to get this wedding together today, but that's what we're gonna do. You brew up that tea. I'm gonna make some phone calls while the lines are still up.' Myrtle plopped down on the sofa with the portable phone and threw Sam's mohair blanket over her lap.

Kelly went to the kitchen and rummaged for the tea, snagged two bags, filled two mugs of her brand-new Portmeirion china with instant hot water from the sink, and let it brew. Modern life had its perks.

By that time, Myrtle had already finished one call and was on to another.

'Yep, that's the size of it. Can you do it in an hour? Okay, doll face, I love you, too, and tell your daughter she can have a free color and cut for this. 'Bye now.'

Kelly sat down beside her, setting their tea on the small table in front of them.

'I can make it, Myrtle, I'll just have to get married in snow gear. I've been walking about a mile or two a day anyway. Nothing is going to keep me from this wedding.'

'Looks like the storm is lettin' up some. Jake Jacobsen up on the hill says he can see it lifting, and there's less falling at his place now. Don't you worry, we'll get there one way or t'other. Now let's see about yer hair, there – I might have to put it up so the weather won't blow it all to poodle-doo.'

'Leave it to you to put the hair first.'

'Of course, darlin', of course.'

Sam zipped a silver ski coverall over his black tux and stuck a helmet on his head.

'Ready, Sis, Tad, Earl? Mom? Dad?' His parents and two sisters appeared from doorways and stairways. Under ski parkas and heavy boots you could see bits of red velvet sticking out.

His sisters had red roses in their hair and looked like angels. He knew better, but they looked pretty anyhow. Their two patient husbands stood behind them. Tad and Earl were great guys.

It was great to see his family troop up and get into the four-wheel-drive spirit. Nothing on earth, or out of the sky, was going to stop this wedding.

'We've got the plan, then, Dad, you pick up as many people as you can, get to the church, make sure the reverend is there, and make damn sure Lynnette Stivers isn't. I'll take the snowmobile over to Jacobsen's and help get the sleigh team hitched up. Then we'll get the bride and see you there. I love you all. Drive safe, Dad.'

'Son, I'm a skier. I've driven in worse. This is nothing. Okay, Grayson women, assorted spouses, let's get to a wedding!' His dad took the rear and gave his wife a kiss on the cheek over her shoulder. 'You look like a bride yourself, Evelyn. Will you marry me all over again?'

Evelyn gathered up the long skirt of her ice-blue wool suit and stuffed the last of it under her full-length quilted ice-blue down coat. She put the hood up, framing her face in white faux fur. She'd deliberately let a long pause go by. 'I suppose I would marry you all over again, Hank.' She smiled at her son as she walked out. Hank Grayson let out a sigh of relief.

'Onward, Sam, we've got a wedding to put on.' Evelyn burst out singing, guiding her daughters out the door: '*Onward Christian soldiers, marching on to church . . .*' She made up her own lyrics.

Sam waved them into the huge Suburban four-wheel drive and closed the door of his family home. The snowmobile started up easily. He waited for the Suburban to disappear down the drive, then took off toward the ridge. One-thirty, he thought. We are *going* to make it.

Lynnette pouted, screamed, paced, flirted, pretended to be ill, then pouted again, but Tom Blackwell ignored her completely.

'I've put three extra blankets in there with you, a sub sandwich, a bottle of water, a thermos of soup, and one of coffee. There's a wind-up camp light if the power goes off, I showed you how to use it. I'll be gone two hours. I've got a wedding to go to. Now, if you behave, I'll take you out for a nice steak after. I put a copy of *The Dance of Anger* in there for you to read. I found chapter three particularly enlightening. Don't forget to take your Prozac, sweetheart.'

'Eeeerrrrggggggggggggrrr. I'll get you for this, Tom,' she growled.

'No, you won't, dear. Read those nice romance books I got you. Maybe you'll get some better ideas in your head. Gary's here if you need anything else. 'Bye now, dear.' Tom walked out into the main office. Just like taming a wild horse. Feed it sugar and pretty soon it's yours.

'Gary, I appreciate this no end.'

'I figure I owe Sam and Kelly one – or two even.'

'Well, I owe you one now. I'll bring you some wedding cake.'

'Thanks, Tom. I got the snow chains on the squad car. It's just a few miles, anyway. Have a good time, man.'

Tom saluted his deputy as he put his hat on and pushed back the wind to get out the door.

'Two o'clock, Myrtle, we better get suited up and start walking.'

'Now, be patient, honey, it's not good for the baby to fret like that. Go potty again before you get all trussed up in your gown.' Myrtle mothered her.

'I've peed four times in the last hour, Myrtle, I'll keep.' Kelly was getting snappish. 'Are you going to tell me how we're going to get there?'

'Look outside. It's just driftin' down easy as you please now. The wind died off. We're sittin' pretty.'

'I'm putting this dress on now, Myrtle. I have silk long underwear pants to keep me warm. You let me know when it's time.'

'Sure thing. Now let me help you into that, there's twenty buttons down the back need some special attention.'

Myrtle helped get Kelly buttoned, tucked, and pinned.

'I'll carry your veil in my backpack until we get to the church. Listen! D'ya hear that? I knew ol' Jake wouldn't let me down!'

The sound of tinkling bells got stronger by the instant. Kelly flew to the window. There, coming down the street, was a wondrous red sleigh with two huge horses trotting through the snow.

'It's Santa!' Kelly laughed, opened the window a crack, and waved. Sure enough, the driver was dressed in a red velvet Santa suit, complete with white beard.

'Ho ho ho!' she heard him bellow. That had to be a sign! Santa in the plane, Santa in a sleigh. Beside him was Sam in a silver jumpsuit. Oh, well, she didn't care what he wore to this wedding.

Myrtle got Kelly's velvet cape over her and handed her a pair of red snow boots. That's what she'd carried in her pack through sleet and snow and cold. 'We'll save the dainty shoes for later, hon, ya gotta have the right shoes—'

'For the occasion. I know, Myrtle, ya taught me good.' Kelly and Myrtle went out the door and down the elevator.

Sam held open the outside door. 'Milady, your carriage awaits you.' He bowed, then straightened up. Kelly kissed him. He really was Prince Charming after all. He never even grazed through frogness.

'Prepare for lift-off, milady.' He swept her up into his arms. 'Wait here, Myrtle, you're next.'

'Like hell, I'm self-actualized, you wild man.' Myrtle zipped up her orange parka, donned her fuzzy hat, pulled the hood over it all, and marched through the snow. Sam gently set Kelly in the back seat of the sleigh and tucked her in properly. Then he went back, grabbed Myrtle, and swung her into the front compartment with the jolly driver.

'Whoa,' Myrtle whooped.

Sam climbed up next to Kelly.

'Giddyap!' Myrtle yelped.

'Myrtle Crabtree, I might as well give you the reins right now. On Prancer, on Dancer!' Jake clucked the horses into motion and gave Myrtle the reins.

'You're a widower, ain't ya, Jake?'

'Yep, I am, Myrtle, and it's been a long, long time.' Santa Jake put his arm around Myrtle's waist.

Kelly smiled at Sam, who kissed her full on the mouth. She'd left the red lipstick off this time. He'd get that later, anyway – when Reverend Evans said, 'You may now kiss the bride.'

The sky was snowy gray, but all along the way twinkling lights decorated the streets, and in the last stretch Kelly could see row upon row of people standing on the sidewalks, cheering them on.

Mr. and Mrs. Grayson, Sam's sisters, and the minister were standing on the church steps. She saw Tom Blackwell in the crowd. He tipped his hat to them, and Sam raised his hand. It was a signal, Kelly could tell. Lynnette was in a nice warm jail cell.

As they climbed out of the sleigh, Sam took her hand. The twinkling outside lights flickered and went out. She turned to see the church. It was completely dark inside.

'At least there's no thunderstorm, and no ghosts.' She sighed. 'Will you still marry me in the dark?'

'In the dark, in a park, I will marry you, I will!' he joked.

'Very funny, Sam-I-am.'

'Don't worry, folks, grab a light tube on your way in. Lydia, light all the candles up front.' In ten minutes, the reverend had the entire sanctuary lit with candles. They were in every window ledge, on every stand. It was glorious.

Huge stands of floral arrangements – red and white roses, white lilies, and tiny daisies – glowed in the candlelight. They filled every corner of the room.

On a tall table beside them was her bouquet. It was stunning: glittering crystal and satin trim, white roses, white lilies and orchids, and the miniature daisies. She fingered it and let the fragrance fill her with joy. The entire thing was amazing.

'Good Lord, did your parents knock over a florist's shop?'

'No, they just had the wholesale grower fly in the winter hothouse crop and had the local florist and her entire family employed for a week, I'm sure. They're having fun.' Sam had slipped out of his silver coverall and stood handsome as a GQ moment in his black tux. He handed her a single red rose, and she pinned it on his lapel. He pulled her in to him and kissed her with that kiss that had knocked her socks off the first time.

'We need five minutes, Mr. Groom. Can ya wait that long?' Myrtle got between them and pulled Kelly into a side room – the reverend's office. Kelly slipped off her mud boots with Myrtle's help, and slid on her Cinderella court shoes, all satiny white and beaded with crystals and pearls.

'Oh, Myrtle, they're beautiful. And just perfect for the occasion.' Kelly gave a little laugh, then started to cry.

'I know, I know, shoes have that same effect on me. Now bend down here and let me pin up yer head. There's no champagne for you this time, so you'll have to pull yourself together. Here's a Kleenex.'

Myrtle set her veil and headpiece in place, and Kelly finished with a dash of red lipstick: Marry Me Red. Myrtle had sent away for it special. Kelly put it on using the reverend's little wall mirror. She looked grand, probably the best of her three weddings. Myrtle had sprinkled Kelly's still-blonde hair with some wild crystalline hair glitter. She was glowing in every way possible.

'I never had a daughter, but if I did, I'd want her just like you, sweetie.' Myrtle pulled out a tissue for herself and dabbed at her eyes. 'I've got a present for ya. You can think about it if you want.' She pulled a folded-up paper out of her backpack. Kelly read it: Petition for Adoption.

'You want to adopt me?' Kelly felt a huge lump come up in her throat. 'Can we really do that?'

'So says the State of Washington, and a very cute lawyer that helped me draw the papers up. More like we'd adopt each other, really. I'd be your ma, you'd be my kid, and someday you'd inherit the Hen House, even. Then I'd be official grandma to your little one.'

'Oh, Myrtle, I'd be honored. I love you so much, now you're gonna make me cry for sure.' Both women broke down, and Myrtle's pocketful of Kleenexes soaked up the stray tears while they gave each other hugs.

'Now quit yer blubberin', and let's get this weddin' over with. You'll be namin' that baby before you get a ring on yer finger, for pity's sake.'

Myrtle and Kelly walked around to the back of the sanctuary. Kelly picked up her beautiful bouquet.

Sam's dad stood waiting, incredibly handsome in a black tux with a red rose in his lapel. 'I thought I'd give you a hand down the aisle this time, if you like. I'm going to keep an eye on you until this is all over.' He offered her his arm.

She took it and kissed his cheek, leaving a red lipstick mark. It looked almost as good on him as on Sam.

They listened as Lydia Peterson struck up a lovely classical piece on the piano. Her sister Mavis joined on harp, and Emily Grayson played her violin. Sam had picked out the piece they played. He said it was perfect – and short.

Sam's sister Anne and Ginny Palmer looked so amazing in their red velvet. It was a spectacle the likes of which Paradise would not see again, because she wasn't going to throw them a wedding *every* month!

When she reached the front, Hank let her go, Sam took her arm, and the ceremony began. And everyone in town forever held their peace.

'I did *not* ask the caterer to make the angel ice sculpture anatomically correct, that was Cora's idea,' Evelyn Grayson said, as her husband waltzed her around the dance floor.

'Of course not, dear,' he answered.

The Paradise High School orchestra kept everyone swaying and twirling with its lively rhythms. Myrtle settled smartly into Santa's arms and let him lead. 'Jake Jacobsen, you ol' devil, if you kiss me like that again, I'll just have ta—'

'Make me breakfast?' Jake said as he nibbled her ear.

'Grrrr.' Myrtle made a sound like a cat growling. 'Do you like grits?'

The room was lit with a thousand tiny twinkling holiday lights powered by a generator hidden outside somewhere.

This was the same room where Sam had first danced with Kelly. Where she had fallen under the spell of Paradise.

A magnificent Christmas tree stood in the far corner of the room, covered with huge ribbons, red and white roses, lilies, crystal icicles, and angels. Candles graced all the tables, illuminating a feast fit for royalty. The townspeople of Paradise filled their white china plates with delectables and enjoyed themselves up to their small-town elbows.

The French champagne flowed like water, literally, as it cascaded over a huge silver fountain contraption and sparkled into hundreds of fluted crystal glasses. The teenagers stole sips until Reverend Evans placed himself beside the table. Kelly noticed that the reverend was swaying a bit. Fortunately, hardly anyone was driving home, including the reverend.

Sam and Kelly surveyed the wondrous interactions of their wedding feast, as they sat at their royal table, surrounded with family. The towering, artistic creation that was their cake had been cut. Sam still had frosting on his nose from Kelly's traditional cake-feeding moment.

Toasts had been toasted, with tears and thank-yous all around. Kelly sipped her special sparkling cider and watched the dancers. They'd actually done it. They'd gotten married.

'Kelly Grayson, I think it's time to slip away to our honeymoon cottage and leave everyone to the rest of the family,' Sam said to her at last.

'And how are we planning to escape this time?'

'Seems Santa's sleigh is ours for a few hours. Jake and Myrtle hired the Millers' oldest boy to drive us. He's the silent type.'

*

The snow had become tiny flakes that lit on their red velvet lap robe and tickled their noses. A huge December moon could be seen through the haze of snow clouds, just enough to light their way out of town.

As they made the turn out of the church lot, Kelly saw the lights spring back on. All the shop windows glittered from a distance. The only sound was the faint trail of music still coming from the church, and soon even that gave way to the silence that comes on snowy evenings in the country. Just the sound of the horses' bells and the snow drifting down.

After a long while, Kelly snuggled closer to Sam and asked, 'Where are we off to, my husband?' She leaned back and listened to the muffled horse hooves as the Millers' oldest boy kept the sleigh gliding smoothly down a lane of pristine snow.

'It's a surprise.' Sam held her close and kissed her forehead.

'Have we borrowed a cabin to honeymoon in?'

'You might say that.'

They went down a newly paved drive covered with snow that someone had strung with lights along the trees in a glittering line that led them forward. Even the drive looked terribly elegant. Kelly had completely lost her sense of direction and had no idea where they were. Probably the family's extra house.

'Mrs. Grayson, we seem to be home.'

Kelly sat bolt upright in the sleigh as they turned down a short lane of newly planted cherry trees, bare in the winter moonlight, strung with white lights.

'Bloody hell! It can't be. It's the Shipley house. What have you done?'

'Now, honey, don't go getting all upset. It's not all the way done. I left the colors and a million details to you. We do have a bed to sleep in, and a roof to keep out the snow.'

Her head spun. She was going to faint for sure this time. He helped her out of the sleigh and handed the Miller boy a tip, sending him on his way. The jingling of the horses faded into the dark night.

They walked up the porch she and Sam had worked so hard repairing together and approached the double entry doors, which he opened wide for her. She started in, catching a glimpse of a newly shined marble floor and the grand staircase polished and refinished to a mellow glow.

'Hold it, Mrs. G., there's the matter of a tradition.' He picked her up, and a small groan escaped his lips.

'Oh, *now* you're gonna start complaining, now that we're really married!' They laughed together, and it echoed into the house. He set her down as gently as possible, inside the entry. Kelly made tiny exclamation noises and ran from space to space. The rooms were spare, but the original antiques were still in place, completely cleaned and gorgeous in their ornate wood and red velvetness.

Beautiful carpets graced every room she stepped into. The wood floors had been refinished to a dark cherry color.

In the front parlor hung the vivid painting she and

Sam had picked out at the Seattle Art Museum sale.

The house was warm and inviting and beyond her wildest dreams.

She ran to the kitchen, and saw the French country cabinets she had ripped out of a magazine and showed him one time. The painting of the speckled chicken they'd bought together hung on one wall.

Off the kitchen was a large family room, and in the center stood an eight-foot evergreen, completely decked in the same roses and crystal as at their wedding. Obviously Evelyn Grayson had arranged that lovely touch.

In one corner with a big red ribbon on it stood an artist's easel surrounded by brushes and palettes and all kinds of colorful tubes of paint. Her Christmas present, no doubt.

Sam finally caught up with her and put his arms around her.

'Sam, Sam, what are we going to do with you? You're reckless and wild. Look at all this. Did you buy this place?'

'I did buy it. I saw how you loved it. I couldn't help myself. I did promise I'd build a community center downtown in exchange for buying the house from the county, and also I promised we'd have a Halloween open house every year.'

'And how did you accomplish all this in such a short time?'

'I had two months really – I started in right after Halloween. When the Graysons throw their money around it gets things done quickly. And since I'd never done that before, I figured I'd give it a try.'

'Is there anything you didn't think of?'

'I think we're going to have a serious relationship with a plumber for the next few years.'

'Oh, Sam, I just don't know what to say. It's wonderful. How can I ever give you the kind of happiness you've given me?'

'I believe a trip to the master suite would do, for starters.' He took her hand, led her up the staircase, down a hall, and through another set of double doors. It opened on a beautiful bedroom. The huge cherry wood four-poster bed had been draped in gold and beige silks and velvets. He flipped a switch, and a dancing fire sprang up in the fireplace. 'We did some modernizing.'

'Gas fireplaces? Completely redone kitchen with top-of-the-line appliances? I'd say so.'

'Creative subcontractors around here.'

She took in every corner. She found all her clothes hanging in a huge walk-in closet, and saw that her beloved Charles Jourdan shoes had somehow appeared from L.A., now displayed in their own special rack.

'Sam, my shoes! How'd you get them?'

'Your friend from the legal office managed to rescue all your things from . . . somewhere we never have to think of again. After all, a girl's got to have the right shoes for the occasion.'

'Oh, thank you, you are the best husband ever.'

'I'll take that as a compliment.' Sam had peeled off his wool overcoat, most of his tux, and stood there in his black socks, a completely obscene pair of men's thong underwear, and his bow tie. She smiled and came toward him.

He started in on her, losing track of his own strip-tease, she noticed. After a velvet cape and another soft knit wrap, two layers, he was down to her twenty back-buttons. He took his time, gliding his hands around her back and over her full breasts. She could feel herself slip into a dream state as his hands caressed her every hill and valley.

They moved to their bed, and Sam pulled back the down comforter for her. She slipped into the heavenly sheets that must have been a thousand-thread count to feel this good. The room was warm as a summer night by then, and she lay completely uncovered, her arms outstretched to him.

Sam pushed a button on the bedside table, and magically, a haunting Irish melody flowed from some hidden corner of the room. She raised an eyebrow.

'Modernizing?'

'For my green-eyed lassie.'

'Come here, you blue-eyed laddie.'

He came to her.

Months later, he was still coming to her. She was round as a pumpkin nestled up behind him, an early-spring-morning chill bringing her close to him.

Sam lay awake, cherishing the feeling of her next to him. He could feel her waking up, too. He thought about the cherry trees blooming in the driveway. He thought about his new vegetable garden and how he'd better get his peas in pretty soon. He thought about what to name his son.

The baby kicked him in the ribs with a tiny, still-in-there foot.

'I think that was the butterfly stroke, Mrs. Grayson.'

'Well, he *was* conceived in a pool, Mr. Grayson,' she answered sleepily.

He turned over, put his hand on her belly, and felt three more fluttery kicks. 'He's going to be trouble.'

'Nothing we can't handle, husband.' She pulled him into a delicious, never-ending kiss.

little black dress

brings you fantastic new books like these
every month - find out more at
www.littleblackdressbooks.com

Why not link up with other devoted Little Black
Dress fans on our Facebook group? Simply type
Little Black Dress Books into Facebook to join up.

And if you want to be the first
to hear the latest news on all things
Little Black Dress, just send the details below to
littleblackdressmarketing@headline.co.uk
and we'll sign you up to our lovely email
newsletter (and we promise that we won't share
your information with anybody else!).*

Name: ————————————————————

Email Address: —————————————————

Date of Birth: ——————————————————

Region/Country: —————————————————

What's your favourite Little Black Dress book?

————————————————————————————

How many Little Black Dress books have you read?———

*You can be removed from the mailing list at any time

You can buy any of these other
Little Black Dress titles from your
bookshop or *direct from the publisher*.

FREE P&P AND UK DELIVERY
(Overseas and Ireland £3.50 per book)

TO ORDER SIMPLY CALL THIS NUMBER

01235 400 414

or visit our website: www.headline.co.uk

Prices and availability subject to change without notice.